"FUNNY AND MOVING, E  **ENT."**

—

Author o

"A wonderful book, a luminous and . . . lasting work of fiction that tells its story superbly . . . Monica Wood did not begin writing seriously until she was thirty. She's more than making up for it now."

—*Maine Sunday Telegram*

"In Rita, Wood has created a hairdresser who . . . [is] intelligent, quirky, impulsive, and direct. . . . In other words, someone you'd like to have cutting your hair because she would be so much fun to listen to. . . . Wood's strengths are in depicting the small details of intimacy that slowly develop between men and women."

—*Casco Bay Weekly*

"A compelling and unusual tale that combines humor with tragedy, heartbreak with promise."

—*Booklist*

"Recommended . . . At once bittersweet, funny, and moving, this finely written romantic novel is well suited for a summer afternoon's read."

—*Library Journal*

"Engaging . . . Wood skillfully works the competing threads of motivation into a tight, surprising knot of a story. . . . Wood's generous vision is uplifting as well as entertaining. . . . Full of the best human longings."

—*Maine Times*

ENTERTAINING YET TRANSCEND

ANDRE DUBUS III

House of Sand and Fog

My only story

Monica Wood

BALLANTINE BOOKS • NEW YORK

ACKNOWLEDGMENTS

I am indebted to Jay Schaefer, whose intelligence and insight guided the final revision of this book; to Gail Hochman for her loyalty, advice, and encouragement; and to Amy MacDonald, Sheila Bernard, and Monty Leitch, my first readers, for advice and friendship during exasperating early drafts. And thanks always to Dan Abbott, who reads it all and never lies.

A Ballantine Book
Published by The Ballantine Publishing Group

www.randomhouse.com/BB/

Library of Congress Catalog Card Number: 2001116296

First published in hardcover by Chronicle Books, San Francisco, California. Reprinted by arrangement with Chronicle Books.

ISBN 0-345-44293-8

Cover design by Min Choi
Cover illustration by Deborah Chabrian

Manufactured in the United States of America

First Ballantine Books Edition: May 2001

10 9 8 7 6 5 4 3

FOR MY dan

and

IN MEMORY OF MY AUNTS AND UNCLES

We don't see things as they are, we see them as we are.

—ANAÏS NIN

PART 1 families

1

He came to me first in a dream, as a crippled dog angling down a country lane, puzzled by his sudden age, his bum paw, the dry stick clamped between his teeth. I'd been expecting this dream for a very long time, and I woke up moving.

Not a day later I saw him at the back of the church basement of Trinity Congregational, clutching a cardboard coffee cup hard and close to his chest. The way he held that cup was the way he held everything: his thoughts, his passions, all his ordinary wishes, those poor dry sticks.

He was not a handsome man. Flattened atop his broad, pink scalp were thin filaments of hair that glistened like beach sand. I paused near him, catching the clean scent of laundry from his cotton shirt, pressed and buttoned to the top and tucked so tightly into his trousers that a roll of stomach showed all the way around like a second belt. His tie was the sort you see a lot in this part of Massachusetts, the navy-blue emblem of an accountant or middle manager. Up close I could see that despite his translucent hair and soft waist he was not yet out of his thirties, not much older than me. And yet he seemed old, the way all sad people do.

There are two kinds of people in this world. One kind likes the half-empty glass, the I-told-you-so, the nobody-knows-the-troubles-I've-seen. John Reed was the other kind, only he didn't know it yet. He had come for an Alanon meeting, not realizing that the Alton town council had kicked the Alanons out for the evening in the expectation of a bigger-than-usual crowd for a zoning hearing. My next-door neighbor, Danforth Outlet Centers, Incorporated, with whom I had a long and acrimonious history, intended to purchase the old ball field and the Osgood block. On all of East Main, my house and beauty shop was the one holdout from the "before" version of Alton, which was in the process of being transmogrified from an expiring mill town into the outlet-store shopping capital of eastern Massachusetts.

Which is more or iess what I was explaining to John Reed as he stood in the back with his cooling coffee. "In other words," I told him, "your meeting is canceled."

"Oh," he said. "Oh, well. Sorry." He put the coffee down quickly, as if he'd stolen it, and made to leave.

"No," I told him, returning the cup to his hands. "Stay," I said. And he did.

I sat down front, next to a woman from one of the real-estate offices that had popped up on every streetcorner since we'd started selling our town brick by brick. It had seemed like good news at first, those engineer types in good suits eyeballing our peeling shingles, our weedy yards, our boarded-up mill. But that was only step one, as it turned out. I had a pretty good idea whose side the real-estate woman was on, so when the call came for comments from the citizenry I leapt to the podium before she could so much as lift an eyelash.

Although the basement of Trinity Congregational is sizable, one of the largest meeting spaces in Alton, from the podium I had an excellent view of John Reed. I looked him over to make sure he was the right crippled dog, which, as we all know, the world is full of. He looked up at me with a face round as bread, his rose-brown eyes squinted ever so slightly above the ample arcs of his cheeks.

"Hello," I said to those assembled, who knew me well from meetings past. "I'm Rita."

"Hello, Rita," John said from the back, very softly, which of course is what you say at an Alanon meeting, which this wasn't. He blushed to a shade of purple, too mortified even to get up and leave, which was a relief to me.

I tapped my index cards to even them up. "When I was a ninth-grader at Alton High," I began, "I took an aptitude test and topped the chart in a category called 'spatial perception.' Back then I considered it a useless skill, but lately it's been coming in awfully handy." A Danforth rep in the second row rubbed his face, his sweaty fingers spreading peevishly through his hair. John Reed leaned forward, gripping the back of the chair in front of him as if he meant to drive it. "I see two towns when I walk these streets," I went on. "It's been long enough now that people can hardly remember what Alton looked like—before. But I can spatially perceive what used to be. I can go to the Broad Street Starbucks, stand on the new sidewalk, and point to the exact spot where the wooden threshhold of the sewing shop once met the old sidewalk. And I remember the one worn place in the wood where the door opened and shut a hundred times a day."

I believe John Reed was the only one listening.

"Thank you," said the mayor. The other council members stirred at the table, eager to move on.

"I'm not quite finished," I said. "We can pretend nothing died here, that we're all pioneers on some kind of frontier prepared ahead of time by the hired hands, a pleasant town on a river with lots and lots of pleasant places to shop, safe from the howl of the city, a bedroom community where people are hardly ever in their beds what with all the meals out and the jogging on the new river path and all that last-minute rushing for the train. But in the meantime, just downriver behind a screen of trees, there's an empty paper mill abandoned in the weeds like an exhausted elephant left to rot in a field."

For a moment nobody said anything, then the Danforth rep called out, "And your point is?"

"My point is you've taken enough already," I said. "It's wrong to erase things." Before I stepped away from the podium I turned toward the council members and added: "My father made paper here. That was not nothing."

After another pause, I got a smattering of applause. There were still a few of us left.

John Reed was edging toward the door, so instead of resuming my seat I beelined to the back of the room and heaved myself into his path.

"Do you have a name?" I asked quietly. He looked like somebody from the "before" Alton, like somebody I might have gone to high school with.

"John," he murmured. Then he made a sweet kind of bowing motion with his head. "John Reed."

"John Reed." I sidled into the only space between him and the door. The new year had brought in some frigid air that seeped through every door and window, reminding me that January was about the worst time of year to expect people to begin anew, to brim over with resolutions when the earth gave back nothing but naked trees and frozen thermometers. Still, people do. They begin and begin.

I motioned him outside, away from the clabber of voices behind the council table. We stood in the cold street, looking at each other.

"That was, that was a very good speech," he said. "I liked the part about the elephant." He swallowed nervously. "The speeches at Alanon aren't quite as interesting."

"You know, I went to a few Alanon meetings myself right after I left Layton," I told him. "He's my ex-husband."

"Oh," he said. "Well, I'm sorry for your troubles."

"Don't be. Ancient history." I folded my arms against the cold, sizing him up, trying to figure out how exactly he might need my help. "If you're the Anon," I asked him, "who's the Al? Your wife?"

"It's my brother," he said. "I'm not married."

"Does it help?" I asked. "Those meetings didn't help me much with Layton."

"They help some," he said. He paused. "I just listen. I don't talk or anything." He blushed again. "Except for that hello part at the beginning."

"Maybe you should try talking," I suggested. "Might help you get over that shyness."

"I'm not much of a, a sharer," he said, which wasn't true, I could see that right from the start. "You asked me," he said, "you asked me to stay—?"

"I thought I knew you," I said. We both laughed a little. "As long as we're both here," I went on, "how about we go for some coffee?"

He looked at his hands, in which the cardboard cup still rested. "Or tea," I said. "Listen, I'm freezing. Wait here while I get my coat."

He waited again. I believe he considered sprinting away while I was gone, though he denied this later. When I came back he smiled at me, so I took him home.

Because I wasn't expecting to meet him so soon after my dream—my grandmother had told me these things can take years—my house was a mess. Sheldon, my blue-and-white parakeet, flings birdseed out the rungs of his cage when I'm not home. He'd made smithereens of the cage lining, which consisted of missives from my next-door neighbor, who wanted my house and lot for their proposed expansion.

"Do you mind if I open his gate?" I asked. "Poor thing's been cooped up most of the day."

He peered into the cage. "I don't mind. I like birds."

I set Sheldon free. He flew through the rooms just to make sure everything was still there, then lighted on my shoulder.

John cleared his throat. "That's an interesting dress you've got on."

"It's Sheldon's favorite," I said. "He loves bright colors."

For a moment John watched Sheldon, who was pecking at the fringe along my collar. Then: "It was kind of you to invite me here, Rita."

"You misunderstand," I said, remembering my purpose. "You're my obligation." Then I mentioned my dream. "In other words, I'm meant to help you."

He blinked a few times. "Help me what?"

"I have no idea. We'll have to spend some time together and then it'll come to me."

He kept his eyes on me as I moved through my kitchen, setting some water to boil. "Does this happen to you often?" he asked after a while.

"Only one other time so far. Which is why I'm bound to pay attention."

I set down some tea and offered to read his cards.

"You mean fortune-telling?" he asked. "Crystal balls and what-not?"

"No," I said. "They're Tarot cards. My grandmother taught me. They help you think, is all." I took the pack out of its silk purse and showed him.

"Very pretty," he said.

"Pick one. Maybe we can figure out why I dreamed you."

Of course he picked the King of Cups. "That's you," I told him. "Reliable, benevolent, filled with dreams."

He did that funny little bow again, like a minor duke getting ready to throw his cape over a puddle. "That could, that could be me."

"See there, you're already thinking." I dealt out a spread, a Celtic cross. "Queen of Cups," I said, tapping one of the cards. "She's in the position of your fear." I looked up. "Are you afraid of me?"

"A little," he admitted.

"That's all right," I told him. "We don't have to do this now. How about a tour of the mansion? I've got a beauty shop in the basement."

He nodded. "I saw the sign."

"Sorry about the smell," I said, leading him down the stairs. "I gave two perms this afternoon."

"That's no trouble," he said. I liked his way of clearing his throat before speaking, just the tiniest croak, as if he might fear offending someone by the sound of his voice.

I took him through the shop, turned on a couple of the dryers, showed him the facial steamer. "It's all paid for," I said. "One of the conditions of the divorce was that Layton had to help me set myself up. Course, that was a few years back. Things aren't quite brand-new anymore."

There wasn't much else to show. I run a pretty low-rent operation, to be honest. People come to me after the fact, to fix their wrecked permanents, even out a hatchet job, make the streaking disappear. Fix the broken, that's what I do all day long. People come to me because my shop looks like the kind of shop where their mothers used to take them for their grade-school haircuts. They stay with me for a little while, then flock back to Ramon or Bettina over at Shazaam, or Angelique at Hair Tomorrow, a plastic-and-steel joint where they serve cappuccino in porcelain champagne flutes. The stylists wear tight black T-shirts, even the men, and count on the basic tenet of human vanity: We all want to be beautiful in ways that don't suit us. White girls want cornrows, black girls want the kinks ironed out. Chubby ladies like pixies, skinny men like crew cuts, wide-faced women want a wash'n'wear bob that turns their entire head into a pup tent. In all my years in this business I haven't once met a woman who could look into a mirror and actually see herself. Man either. This is a mill town—was, I should say—where beauty can take peculiar shapes, and in my opinion the voodoo artists at Hair Tomorrow should be casting their spells in Boston or Providence. Still, I've got my stable of regulars: Mrs. Rokowski's weekly set'n'style, Rodney's twice-monthly trim and card-reading, little Amy Chang's six-week cut, and so forth. A few dozen in all, people I genuinely like, and not just because they help me meet the mortgage.

All things considered, I've done fine.

John was staring at my fingernails, which I'd painted up in gold stencils. "Occupational hazard," I explained, wiggling my fingers. "The vendors send you something new and you feel compelled to try it out."

"They look nice," he said, then, looking around: "This whole place is very nice."

I admit I was touched, more than you would think over something so small, but it had been a very long time, if ever, since another human being looked that interested in what I do. Not counting card readings. Talk about your full attention.

"Why don't I wash your hair?" I asked him.

"Pardon?"

"Would you like me to wash your hair?"

He looked stricken. "Does it need it?"

"Not technically," I said. "But it would feel good."

What he did then was nothing. Perhaps it passed through his mind that I might have an ill intent he wasn't picking up on, or maybe he was deciding whether or not it was time to put himself, literally, in the hands of another. I like to think he stood there for those few moments just to feel his life change. I took his hand and led him to the sink, where he got into the chair and let me settle his head. His shoulders were stiffer back then, his expression still complicated with the thing his brother had done.

"Just relax," I told him, and squeezed out a quarter-sized dollop of shampoo.

"Smells like, like . . ." he tried.

"Papaya," I said, turning on the water. I ran the sprayer back and forth over his scalp. "It's supposed to relax you."

"Is that right?" He was beginning to murmur, his eyes closing partway like a cat's.

"Believe me," I told him, "I've done the research. Papaya produces an enzyme or some-such that we don't produce naturally unless we're delirious with joy. And you know how often delirious joy turns up in the average day."

"Have you always been a hairdresser?"

"I'm not a hairdresser, John Reed," I said. "I'm a healer." The minute I said it I wanted to take it back, for I have no powers, unless you count the power of observation. But I felt summoned somehow, *called*, and wanted him to know this. His hair, which was thin and filled with light, lay now in pale, damp blades over his tender scalp. I massaged from the neck up, rotating gently so as not to disturb any follicles.

"This feels wonderful," he whispered.

"Well, of course it does. It's the human touch." After a good sudsing I rinsed him off and turbaned his head with a towel pulled out of the warmer. As he sat up, Sheldon hopped onto his shoulder to catch the droplets that tracked down a helpless gully in his neck.

"I used to have a dog," I told him, "but after I left Layton and the dog died I decided to downsize." I opened my hands, trying to show him the whole of my domain.

He was blinking hard. Maybe he was even crying. "Rita," he gasped. "I feel like I've just won something."

I led him to the swivel, where he and Sheldon settled themselves. When the snips from John's hair began to float down, Sheldon flew to the top of the mirror in a huff. John had a spangled, silvery laugh that surprised me in so large a man.

"There you are," I said, and turned him around to see himself.

His mouth opened. I liked his upper lip, which was shaped like two low hills, one rising a little higher than the other. The shape of a question.

"Well, now," he said, leaving his mouth partly open. I submit to you with no false modesty that John Reed was looking at the best haircut he had ever laid those rose-brown eyes on.

"You ought to change your sign," he said. " 'Walk in ugly, walk out handsome.' "

"You're not ugly."

"I used to be slim."

"You're not ugly," I said, turning him once again toward the mirror. "Look."

He looked. And I believe, I do believe, he saw himself. For a long while he said not a word, then: "How did you do this?"

I snapped the scissors a couple of times. "Magic."

For a moment he took me seriously. "Did you train in, in the East or someplace?"

I laughed. "East Main. Jean-Pierre's Beauty Academy. It's closed now, along with everything else useful in this town. My childhood home is a pasta store." I smoothed his forehead. "You're done."

Sheldon followed us upstairs and flapped onto John's shoulder as soon as he sat down. I brought John another cup of tea, and we talked some more. Turns out we both believed the '86 Celtics could beat the bloomers off Jordan's Bulls even on a bad day. We'd voted the same in the last election.

He looked at his hands. "It's like we were supposed to meet."

"We were," I said, but I didn't mean what he meant. He had a nice smile, a white shirt endearingly pressed, but I can't say he was the type a woman expects to fall in love with.

I sized him up a bit, taking in his navy tie, his shirt and pants, his polished black shoes. I said, "I'm guessing you work with numbers."

"Sort of," he said. "Sometimes, yes." Turns out he was district manager for a dental-supply company in Chesley, which was also where he lived, a half-hour drive away.

"I used to be on the road a lot," he said. "Five years ago I asked for a desk job." I heard a quiver, a catch, on the word *five.* But I didn't press him. This man from my dream was a responsibility I was willing to wait out. "Also, I play the piano," he said. "One night a week, sometimes two."

"For people, you mean? You play for people?"

He winced at my surprise, knowing what I was thinking: This man looked about as much like a piano player as my parakeet. I looked at his hands, which were short and blunt, the hands of a gas-station attendant.

"It's not Carnegie Hall," he said quickly. "Just background music at the Holiday Inn." He smiled. "Sometimes they even remember to pay me."

I smiled back. "You can play for me sometime."

He got up and I walked him to the door. He shook my hand politely and left as I stood on my cold steps, watching him as he made his way along a block of East Main that used to house the hardware store where my father bought paint, the grocery where you could keep a line of credit. The buildings that replaced them looked weightless, fleeting, and John Reed's silhouette seemed good and solid beneath them, like something that hadn't yet been altered. He walked calmly, but with a certain gladness I could see in him all the way down the block. I shut the door, feeling like a healer.

After I had fed Sheldon and drawn the curtains and snapped off the porch light, I stole down the basement steps, and I don't mind admitting that I caught the smallest jolt of delirious joy. God's gifts to us are pleasure and purpose, and it seemed I'd been granted both in the time it took for the earth to make one full turn.

The number five fluttered in my head, soft as a moth. I wandered through the shop, where a dim light from the street angled in through the high casement windows. I bent to gather a whisper of John Reed's hair, the equivalent of the fluff of one dandelion, and put it into a glass jar that held snips of hair from as far back as my beauty-academy days, some even farther. The brilliant auburn of my old friend Margaret was in there, and a pearly curl from my grandmother's cancer-gray head, and a single white hair from the kindly judge who did my divorce, and a big black tuft from Layton, roots and all. Into this mix of love and betrayals and partings and death I dropped John Reed's fragile strands and replaced the lid.

2

He arrived with flowers, the way he always did. It was a Thursday, his regular piano night at the Holiday Inn near the highway exit. I had Mrs. Rokowski in the chair, last appointment of the day. The bell jingled over the door, and there he was, picking his way through the white, webby threads of Mrs. Rokowski's hair to hand me the flowers, pink carnations that smelled like the inside of a cooler. They were frilly and sweet, I thought, but Mrs. Rokowski frowned over them.

"Roses were the rage when Albert and I were courting," she said.

"Don't mind her," I said to John. "Mrs. R's never short an opinion." I leaned into her ear. "And we're not courting. I told you."

"Uh-huh," she said. She turned to John. "She's been seeing you once a week for a month because you barked in a dream?"

John nodded. "So she tells me."

"There was no barking," I said. "Anyway, you don't mess with this stuff. These are *messages.*"

"Where are you taking her?"

"To a, to a bar."

"It was my idea," I said. "I thought hearing him play might, I don't know, reveal something."

"There's not much to reveal," John said. He looked at his shoes. "But I don't mind the company of a pretty woman."

"Now, *there,*" Mrs. Rokowski said to me. "Never mind your hocus-pocus and listen to *that.*"

I guess I must have been smiling—I've never been one to shun a compliment—but the fact remained that by this time I'd noticed some things. John Reed moved through this world as if he believed the smallest object could be snatched away in an instant. He had a habit of walking with his hands knuckled into his pockets, clutching the lining lest someone fleet by and make off with his clothes. Other than that, I'd gotten exactly nowhere. On our four outings—a Celtics game, two walks around Walden Pond, and a garage sale—the only mystery I'd uncovered is that I liked his company. We always went in his car, a stolid blue Oldsmobile that made me think of happy families out to see America. He liked to open the passenger door for me, clasping my hand to help me inside. Layton wouldn't have done that on a bet. "How are you doing so far?" he always asked at some point during these times, referring to my dream, and I would realize that I'd forgotten all about my mission and was instead listening to the crunch of our boots on a footpath or watching the white plume of a jet split across the sky. I guess you could say I was falling for his gentle presence, his kind eyes, the light in his face when he looked at me. You might even say I was wondering if maybe a dream like mine could mean more than one thing.

"What do you think of this?" Mrs. Rokowski asked John, pointing to the cards spread out on my workstation. Knight of Swords, Seven of Wands, the Chariot, all the action cards. "Rita says my boring little life needs a lift."

"I didn't say that," I corrected her, beginning to unroll her hair. "I merely suggested you might think about obstacles yet to overcome."

"You and your fancy talk." She slid John a look that could wilt lettuce. "Half the time you need a dictionary."

I tossed the rollers in the sink, *bing, bing, bing.* "I'm merely pointing out that you've had the same hairstyle since 1953. New hair might occasion other sorts of blooming."

"That's just a fancy way of bossing me around," Mrs. Rokowski said, rolling her big watery eyes. Like every other woman in this town over seventy-five—and there aren't many left, believe me—she likes her hair rolled tight and tinted blue. She's one of these cloth-coat grammies who can barely see over the steering wheel. Either people shrink with age, or short people live longer.

"I was thinking maybe a little more width at the temples," I said, "to fill out your face. And we can brush it back some. You'll look sixty-five." I wiggled the brush in the air. "Shall we?"

She frowned toward John. "I wouldn't mind a man's opinion."

"I think you should do whatever Rita says," John said.

So I fanned out the sides, lending fullness to her sweet, withered face, and when she left—happy but not admitting it—she looked like Princess Grace.

"You're a magician," John said, helping me on with my coat. And it struck me then how nice it was to have him there to witness that one moment of my life, which had, I realized, become a lonely thing indeed. It was nice just to have him there to wait while I got my coat, knowing he would. He was a man who didn't mind waiting. When I got back he was sweeping Mrs. Rokowski's hair into the dustpan.

"You don't have to do that," I said, but he kept going as if doing me a favor were the most splendid possible way for a man with an ounce of sense to spend his time. It must have been that evening, when he opened the car door and I slid in, safe from the snowy night, that I first wondered how piano keys might feel under his touch.

"Have you figured this out yet?" he asked.

I shook my head. "Do you mind?"

"Not in the least. I hope it takes you forever."

"John Reed," I said, "I believe you're flirting with me."

He smiled at me. "Trying, anyway. I haven't had much practice." He looked away shyly, then started the car.

When we got to the Holiday Inn, the bar was nearly empty. If there was a convention in the area, the place was lousy with business types in wrinkled suits, but on this night there was no convention, and it was snowing, and the piano bar was empty except for the bartender, a waitress, John Reed, and me. The tables were made up and quiet, the chairs pushed in like people with their hands folded, listening.

I have to admit that when we first met I had no trouble at all imagining him as a man who sold dental supplies. I could see him at his desk in a big cubicle, a stack of color-coded folders at his left elbow, a telephone at his right. In front of him, casting a greenish light over his face, sat his computer terminal, a Grand Central Station of dental supplies, telling him to send Rep A to Office B on

Day C—an entire world, through which he had once moved physically, reduced to dots on a screen. In his peripheral vision, hovering around the edges of the space he cleared for himself, human beings conversed softly, just out of hearing. Technically, John had coworkers—some clerks and secretaries—but he worked alone.

It was the piano-player part I couldn't fathom. I guess I must have had some Liberace images in my head, some kind of ivory-tickling showboat in a loud jacket. My grandmother had been mad for Liberace, partly because my mother considered him vulgar and preferred to listen with her eyes closed. When John walked over to the bar piano on that Thursday night in his beige sweater and brown pants, he looked nothing like a piano player, and yet seemed so at home that the plastic cubicle I'd placed him in melted clear away, along with the computer screen full of dots, and the chirring phone. The piano was big and black and reassuring, absolutely immovable; he stood there a moment just looking at it, clearing a space for himself, so to speak, a space just large enough to hold his shyness, his physical bulk, his private griefs.

"Play something happy," I murmured to myself, feeling sad all of a sudden. He sat down, curling himself over the keys as if he feared they might lift off and scatter like sparrows.

What he played was music from times long gone, "Stardust," "Chattanooga Shoeshine Boy," and like that, music I hadn't heard since my grandmother died. A few people drifted in and out, salesmen on their way someplace else, a few fraidy-cat couples who'd pulled off the highway rather than drive in snow. I got up a few times to push the chairs back in. "I can do that," the waitress kept saying, and then she'd give the chair I'd just straightened a little shove with her fingernail, and I'd have to start all over again. She was the glass-half-empty type, her face drained of color long before its time. My mother was like that, and my father, burdened by the Baptist church, the paper mill rumored to close, a live-in grandmother, the kind of life surprises that tend to chip away at your resolve.

I sat there with my glass of orange juice for four hours listening to John play. Some of the music sounded like falling water, some like trees afire, interrupted every half hour or so by a couple of the fraidy cats who simply could not live another instant without hearing "Muskrat Love." But then they would go off to their room to catch the late show or have sex or whatever people do in their idle hours, and I would place their vacated chairs back at attention. John never took a break the whole time. I understood that what we were doing was having a long conversation, and that John was telling me, finally, about the tender spots that speckled his wounded heart.

I had told him all about the house of straight lines I grew up in, about my sister on the West Coast enthralled by a swami who'd convinced her that God resided in her palms, about my unhappy parents playing canasta in their condo in Florida. And I told him about Layton, who was on wife number three someplace in the state of New York. I described our long and sorrowful parting, and Layton's steamship of a mother, and the floozies he canoodled with at the end, with their tiny little corn-on-the-cob teeth and blond, blond hair. I confided to John Reed that despite Layton's shenanigans I hadn't given up my picket-fence hopes to get married again and have two baby girls. "Of course, I wasted my peak years on Layton," I said, "but I'm still hoping." I told him all this because he was listening, looking interested and respectful.

In turn, when John Reed talked, he talked about the trees or the road, the stillness of Walden Pond, the bracing winter cold. Or he talked about the piano, about the little wing-lift that happened in his chest whenever he pressed his fingers to the keys, or he talked about the dailyness of his job in dental supplies, about whitening agents and synthetic tooth enamel and polishing tools. What he was actually *saying*—what I gathered in the pauses between words, the way he pressed his fingers into his thighs as if playing piano in his head as he spoke—was that he longed to be a piano player who sold dental supplies on the side, rather than a dental-supply salesman who played piano on the side. That he had envisioned a different life for himself. I heard this. If not for *X*, he was saying, my life would have been different. He was stuck inside a story, the way we all are at one time or another, and could not see his way clear.

Midnight, last call, the road to the highway blocked by broad billows of snow. The parking areas had been plowed once, but the snow was coming in so fast that a handful of cars got stranded like cake ornaments in the round central lot. The highway was silent and white, the streetlights misty with weather, the entire world turned into a heap of feathers. I don't believe I'll see anything that beautiful again.

"Damn it straight to hell," the waitress growled, shuffing off her coat. "Nobody's getting outa this hole tonight."

The desk clerk, a boy who looked young enough to like pink ice cream, said, "We got vacancies."

John and I took side-by-side rooms on the fifth floor across from the ice machine. Everything was clean as a spoon, the beds strung so tight they could almost play a note. He followed me into my room to make sure I got settled, but all I had was my purse and coat, so after I stowed them in the closet we had nothing to do but look at each other. "I've got Amy Chang coming in at ten tomorrow," I said. "I'll have to phone her mother in the morning."

He nodded. "I'll have to call in to the office. I've got two guys heading out on rounds."

I sat on the bed and bounced a couple of times, which made him blush, not that it ever took much. "This is like snow days," I said. "Remember listening to the radio, praying for no school?"

He smiled. "I liked school."

I patted the bedspread beside me. "Will you sit?" I asked him. "Just for a minute?"

He sat, but not on the bed. Instead he pulled up a chair so that we were sitting knee to knee. For a few minutes we didn't talk at all, though he was looking at me the way he did whenever he listened to me talk, his head turned just barely, his eyes fixed on my face. The room went all pink and misty, the small space between us closed in so far it felt like a secret. I don't mind admitting that a little *ping* went off in places ladies don't talk about. I had to sit very still for fear I might burst into flame.

"Rita," John said. Without taking his eyes away, he leaned across to kiss me, a sweet, damp, awkward kiss that held more in the way of possibility than all my years with Layton put together. I realized that despite my hopes, my post-Layton years had resigned me to the odd comforts of my house, my shop, my parakeet. I was a woman alone, well into her thirties, and there were no two ways about it.

"I meant to help you," I murmured. "But now, I don't know. I'm the one who feels helpless."

He stood, pulling me up with him, and held me so hard I saw

that crippled dog in Technicolor. I felt him gearing up to speak, a kind of skittering just under his breath.

"Go ahead," I told him.

That's all I said. Then John Reed told me his only story.

"It's my brother," he said.

He fumbled a picture out of his wallet, a color snapshot in a plastic sleeve, of his brother, Roger, and his brother's wife, and their little red-haired daughter up in Portland, Maine.

"He killed Laura. His wife, Laura. That beautiful woman."

She *was* beautiful: sharp, navy-blue eyes, a tangle of black hair falling across her frosty brow. She had a lovely, neighborly face, filled with light. Roger's face was the opposite, shuttered and scared, and though he looked so much like John—a lean, long-fingered version of John—his closed-up expression struck me not as shyness, but suspicion.

John held the picture so hard that his thumbs whitened.

He said, "Five years ago."

"Come here, John Reed," I said, for his mouth was buckling as the words sputtered out. I lay back against the pillows, drawing him down with me, cradling his head on my chest. "Tell me," I whispered, and he did, in fits and starts. It took most of the night.

He begins with her. Laura Doherty Reed.

"She's always glad to see me," he says, as if it's unfolding before him. "She always opens the door before I can knock." She makes John Reed—who has nobody but his brother with the locked-up face—feel like part of a family. She can make anybody feel that way.

"She's the hub," is how John puts it. "The glue." There is the widowed mother in the third-floor walkup on Morning Street. Just across the street, in side-by-side houses, the twin baby sisters live with their husbands, and their handsome little boys, four apiece. Laura and Roger, with their new baby girl, live around the corner in a brick duplex with wind chimes on the porch.

"Roger doesn't like them," John says. He keeps lifting his head to make sure I can hear him. "Roger doesn't want that family." Roger doesn't like the Sunday feasts, all of them pressed around one table. He doesn't like the dropping by and calling up. He doesn't like the pack of sticky children.

"But I would have," John says, his breath moist on my neck. "I love families."

Roger is a pharmacist. He likes things clean. He puts pills in little bottles all day long. He doesn't like the widowed mother, the twin sisters who call and call, the nice husbands who are good with children. He doesn't like the way this family loves his little daughter, the only girl. He resists the Catholic baptism, the high holidays, the clannish parties, the balloons and sparkle paint, the swooping excess that makes him feel like a bystander.

Most of all he doesn't like the way they love Laura, their Laura, the way they never stop needing her.

So Roger makes new rules: You have to check first. You have to ask me. She's mine.

"Imagine how they felt, a family like that," John says. "They felt stolen from."

It happens in the kitchen.

There will be a birthday party tomorrow. Their little girl—her name is Aileen, a winsome, red-haired child—will be three, and the family will have a party. The mother will be there, and the twin sisters, and the husbands. All the boy cousins. All the friends and neighbors, who still refer to the sisters as "the Doherty girls." There are many, many friends and neighbors. This is an occasion—their little girl, their own Aileen, turning three. The husbands, who are brothers, run a bakery, Balzano's Family Bakery, and it is there, the site of all family gatherings, that Aileen will have her party.

Roger does not want the party. "He badgered her about it for weeks," John says. "But she was tired of him. I think she was tired of him. She wouldn't budge." He lifts his head again. "It was probably that. It was probably about the party."

It happens in the kitchen, on the clean white tile.

John wants to know: What induces a man to lift a hand against such a woman? And why would such a woman stand there, watching the shadow of her husband's fist fall over her milky face? You have to believe she trusts him not to hurt her, even as her head snaps back, as her body falls in a quiet arc across the kitchen. You have to think she trusts him even then, in the suspended half-second before she lands against the white Formica countertop, its hard-gleaming corner meeting a soft, bare spot on her temple.

"You have to believe he didn't mean it," John says. "That his intentions went awry."

"Does he try to revive her?" I whisper, stroking the drawn line of his jaw. I am hoping that the next part is about how Roger buckles and falls, going weak with a husband's love.

John doesn't know. No one knows. Roger's body is found sprawled in the bedroom doorway. There is blood. There are spilled pills and a razor near his opened wrists.

The police want to know why. Any problems you know of?

Any prior this, any prior that? *I don't know,* John answers, over and over. *I don't know.*

In the paper John reads about her blue bathrobe, her bare feet, his brother's blood sloping down the floor.

He returns there, to the sickening apartment. The door is ajar, the family inside: the twin sisters and their husbands, mopping up blood. Laura is dead. Roger Reed took her from them once, and now he has taken her again.

Somebody has to pay.

John enters and sees their rage, useless as a smashed glass. The husbands are on their knees, scrubbing. They look bruised, these brothers, these bakers who cannot believe such a thing has happened. They are used to buckets of flour, buckets of yeast and eggs, and here they are bent over a bucket of water and blood. The sisters are going through a closet, lifting out sweaters that Laura once moved inside. They bend their heads together, the same red hair as their orphaned niece.

Hello, John says.

They look at him as one face.

"I was slim then," he tells me. Lanky and hollow-cheeked like his brother. Narrow-hipped, exactly like his brother.

He wants in. He is not his brother. He wants in. He has buried his brother and now he is back. To see his poor orphaned niece. A little three-year-old girl named Aileen. He misses her so much it feels like lightning in his chest. She calls him uncle. When he visits, her smooth face crinkles with glee, that's how happy she is to see him.

I thought I might help her—

No, they tell him.

"They look like a wall," he says, muffling the words in my neck. "Like a wall of family, standing there."

He is ashamed to look like his brother. He tries to show his short, harmless hands, the opposite of Roger's. It's his face they stare at, his shoulders and arms. He looks like a ghost returning from the dead.

But John Reed is not a ghost. He is not a smooth-moving pharmacist who pinched pills from prescription bottles and slammed the door shut on an entire family and killed his wife. He is just a man who plays the piano and sells dental supplies, he is a man who has just buried the last of his family. Except for that little girl. She is all that's left.

They move in to make that wall. Two sisters who married two brothers, side by side.

Please, he asks. *If I could just see her—*

No.

He looks at the stained Formica, the stains on the floor, the bucket of brown water.

Go home, they tell him as he stands flat against the door frame, limp as a coat on a hook. We're changing her name to Doherty. She'll carry her mother's name. We're planning to erase him.

I wanted to say I'm sorry—

You should have known. He's your brother, you should have known.

I think I could help her, if I could see her, I think I could help her—

Nobody can help her. You of all people. Leave us alone. Go.

Just then a stiff breeze blows in through Laura and Roger's open window, cold and full of fingers. Collars flip up, shirttails billow, and for an instant this family appears to be wearing each other's clothes. Their shoes on the linoleum sound like a balloon puffing up. The husbands fold their arms, grim as bouncers at a bar. This is the form their sorrow takes.

Somebody Has to Pay.

I'm not my brother, John Reed says—it sounds like begging—then he backs away, eases the door closed, backs down the front steps. He hears a fist on a wall, a woman's wailing: We were such a happy family!

"That's all," he says, turning deeper toward me. "I never saw them again." Then he rolls away, bringing up his arms to cover his face. This is how he must have turned from them, a slow heaving, blundering down those stairs like a dying animal, missing that child already.

By the time he woke, it was nearly daybreak, and a shimmery snow-light had begun to silk through the windows. We were lying on the bed, side by side, all our clothes on, even our sweaters and our shoes. He startled awake, then I felt his face relax against me as he realized where he was.

"I never knew Roger took drugs," he whispered. "I never knew he was stealing pills." He took a breath, which felt warm on my shoulder.

"Did he leave a note?"

"One word," John said. "*Please.*" He propped himself up a little, letting the word settle. "Aileen was so little, Rita. You should have seen that hair, that angel face. They all wanted a girl—the twins had all those boys—but I didn't care if Laura had a hedgehog,

I was so thrilled just to be an uncle." He sighed. "I'd never been much with women. That baby was the closest I thought I'd get to being a father."

"You never called or anything?"

"I was so ashamed, Rita." He shook his head, very slowly. He had aged overnight.

"It wasn't you who killed her."

"But I loved him," he said. He eased back against the pillows, staring up. Frail tears collected in the crevices under his eyes. "I wanted him back." He lay still for some time. "I've been going to Alanon on and off over the years," he said, "hoping to hear a story like mine."

"Maybe you didn't need to hear it," I said. "Maybe what you needed was to tell it."

He took a breath. "You're not afraid of me, Rita? After what my brother did?"

Afraid of him? Lying there was like bedding down for a long winter with a tame bear. He was soft but substantial; in the presence of John Reed a woman knew beyond a shadow of a doubt that she was not alone. "You're not your brother," I said.

"But there were times," he quavered, "when I was a kid, you know. I wanted to become just like him." He closed his eyes. "I couldn't have known, Rita. Could I?"

I pulled him toward me and laid my hand across his heart. "I'm going to help you, John Reed," I whispered, but it was my life I felt opening up.

3

So there we were: two lonely people, courting. He was shy and slow and old-fashioned, lots of dinners out and kissing on the doorstep. But within a week I couldn't fathom how I had ever done without him.

I sat at his dining table, dealing out some cards as he stood at the stove making a supper omelette that required three burners and the oven. His kitchen was gloomy, with dark linoleum and nothing on the walls, but our presence there seemed to lighten it some.

Next to the cards was a manila folder that held a couple of phone numbers and the street address for Balzano's Family Bakery in Portland, Maine. "I feel like one of those detective teams on public TV," I said.

He sat down, a dish towel draped over one shoulder. "I was thinking I might call up there tonight, tell them who I am, state my intentions. . . ." His voice trailed off as he caught sight of the Five of Pentacles leering from the table, the lonely beggars cast out into the snowstorm. "I hope that's not me."

"Not necessarily," I said. "But I think you might need a little more of a plan. What if whoever answers the phone hangs up?"

He considered this for a minute. "I could, I could write a letter, give them time to think about it."

I glanced around at the little prison he'd constructed for himself, its one pleasure a black piano that cowered in the living room like a circus animal. "They don't want to see you, right?" I said. "Not ever again. They don't want to think about what happened, they don't want to remind that little girl what . . . happened."

"That's about the size of it," he said. His eyes filled. "You can hardly blame them."

"Oh, I think I can," I said, "but that's not the point." I petted his hands, which opened as I touched them. "The point is, you want to see that little girl, your only family. Isn't that the point?"

He nodded.

"Then it behooves you to move carefully, by my thinking. Get the lay of the land, so to speak."

I was doing the best I could. All I had to go on was John's memory of the family in Laura and Roger's apartment, cleaning up the blood. I'd cast the cards a dozen times, and why did I bother? Did I need a Three of Swords to tell me they might not be exactly thrilled to see him? The cards are treacherous sometimes; half the time you're left with just another question. "The way I see it," I went on, "this thing is the yellow brick road with a sweet little girl standing at the end. The trouble is, you've got a few exploding bricks mixed in there with the regular ones. An answering machine. A hang-up. A returned letter. Boom. We have to think this through."

"I could go there," he said. He looked at me. "*We* could go there."

I smiled. "Bingo."

"We'll go there," he said softly, then louder: "We'll go there." He got up and went to the stove. "Rita, you're one hard woman to argue with."

A few moments later he presented an omelette pretty enough to mount in a museum. I took a big bite. "Wow," I said. "You can cook."

"Eat it all," he said, turning my plate. "You're too thin."

We ate for a while, then looked at each other without talking, as we often did. I suppose we were thinking about what lay ahead of us.

"What was he like?" I asked.

John closed his eyes wearily.

"Except for that," I said. "What was he like except for that?"

"I can't remember," he said.

"Tell me three good things."

"I don't—"

"Tell me."

His mouth turned down at the corners. "He paid for my piano lessons when I was eight. I remember that. He was in high school then, working nights. Our mother had nothing, but Roger got scholarships, he studied all the time. He had goals for both of us."

"Two."

He shook his head. "Rita, this isn't—"

"Two. Come on."

"He always acted glad to see me."

"Now three."

This last one took a long time coming. "He was, he was like Laura, in a way. He was a good brother, a good son. Indulgent, you might say. He sent our mother money. He took care." He listed toward me, his voice dropping. "It didn't surprise me, Rita, what they saw in each other. They'd had similar burdens." He bowed his head as if he'd made a terrible confession, comparing a man like him to a woman like her.

"That's three good things," I said quietly. "Whatever else he was, or became, you remember those things you just said."

He cupped my face and kissed me on the lips. Then he kissed my chin, and then the two tiny bones at the base of my throat. One, two, three.

"You love me," I said.

"Yes," he said, with the surprise of a man unaccustomed to fate's sunny side. "Yes, I do."

I stood up. "Then I don't mind admitting I'm sick of waiting." I shepherded him to his own bedroom as if he didn't know where it was. Like the kitchen, it was dark and bare, the construction of a man atoning for somebody else's sins, a tidy little cell suited to a monk or a murderer.

He pulled back the covers of his bed and we snuggled in with our clothes on. I gave him a brief tour of the architecture by placing my hands on his and moving them like a Ouija over the good parts. He rolled on his side, grasping my waist as if I were a bouquet of daisies, but in truth I felt more like a sunflower just then, wanton and bossy and hard to resist.

"Rita," he whispered, blushing. "I'm kind of, kind of clumsy in this respect."

"That's all right," I said. "I wasn't looking for a movie star."

As we fumbled through that first awkward time, I could see he had the makings of a delightful lover who didn't mind taking direction. Never had I met a man so grateful for my favors. It took me quite a while to get out of my clothes, and he was none too practiced in finding the fasteners on my dainties, but I didn't care one whit. I'd spent nearly a decade with an expert who didn't love me and believe me, you can tell the difference.

"I wish I'd met you around the time Layton was knocking at my door," I told him. But of course I wouldn't have looked twice at him then.

"Me, too," he said. He kissed my cheek, smelling of the warm sheets. "I'd give anything to have met you then." Blinking at me in the half-light of his murky bedroom, he said, "I'd have fallen on my knees and made a bargain with God."

I didn't say anything, having made plenty of bargains like that myself.

4

I lost a baby once.

When I met Layton I was nineteen. I went instantly mad for him, that dark-eyed older man, an old, old thirty-four, a Vietnam vet, an engineer with a house and a Harley. He had long eyelashes, a job in Boston, an ex-wife safely moved out west, and a memory he couldn't shake about a small, moon-faced man he shot on a village road one sorrowful, sticky day. The man wore no uniform, just a thin shirt and pants that didn't fit, but those people hid grenades, they pulled weapons out of thin air, you just never knew, you didn't, so he fired. Except it wasn't a man. It was a boy. I had to, is what he told me.

I Had To.

Layton loved noise. The revving of his motorcycle, the clicking of ice in his Scotch glass, the explosion of a crowd at a horse race, the long swipe of his zipper opening and closing, the clenched-teeth growl that passed in Layton for a laugh. Beneath it all you could hear his "I Had To"; it followed him everywhere.

"Please, Rita," he whispered softly. "Be my second chance." His lips were perfectly formed, moving like a butterfly at my ear. "Please, Rita. I've slept my whole life away." I was the type back then to respond to such requests, and so I marched right into his arms and waltzed the wedding waltz with him under a snowfall of confetti at his mother's country club. This was the last time my family would all show up in one place, my mother and father cowed by the good crystal, my sister, Darla (on a weekend pass from her commune in California), parked in one sullen corner all night, my cousins from Salem spilling champagne on the floor.

Layton was chisel-chinned, handsome beyond believing. I moved from my parents' house into his house, which was in the first of the developments that began to spring up after the Danforth people arrived, nice-looking fellows with tape measures clipped to their pleated pants. My father had gone to work for his brother's furniture-moving company after the mill closed—a fifty-two-year-old papermaker moving armoires for minimum wage. Now here were some people who might buy his house, pay his back taxes and plane tickets south.

The first outlet stores constructed along Main and Broad appeared mostly in disguise, lots of rickrack and pickets and hand-carved signs. The paper reported nothing but revenues this and revenues that, and after a few more demolition-reconstruction projects, the schools got good again. Alton became a shopping hot spot where city-weary professionals wanted to raise their kids, a town gussied up to look like a gingerbread town from a children's book, a hello-neighbor kind of place constructed over the bleached bones of the real thing.

Layton moved from Boston to Alton because real estate was affordable in the beginning, and his mother lived one town over, and he liked the commute, roaring his bike back and forth to the city. It was the highlight of his day. The house was on Lilac Drive, in a grove of houses that used to be a patch of woods. Nowadays almost everything in this town used to be something else, but back then the town was steeped in an illusion of forward motion that I fell for hard. I was young. My parents were across town in our old neighborhood, hoping to sell. My grandmother was in Good Shepherd Cemetery beneath a spray of lilies. I felt I'd gotten away with something, stacking my wedding china into brand-new cupboards.

One town over, Layton's mother toiled in her eye-popping frenzy of a flower garden, which afforded her many idle hours to plot ways to make my life miserable. The woman never learned to knock on a door. Nevertheless, I believed there resided within her a reservoir of good will that would come gushing to the surface the instant I made her a grandmother. The doctors told me I'd be fine despite my single ovary; it might take a little while, but I was young, I was healthy, I was bound to be a mother if I so desired. Which I did. I *so* desired! But Layton said wait, we need more money we need a bigger house we need pictures on the walls we need we need we need. Then he said I'm too old I'm too set in my ways I'm not cut out to be a father. By this time I had discovered I did not have the temperament to work in an insurance agency, so I quit my job (over Layton's objections), cashed in my savings bonds, and enrolled in a fifteen-month cosmetology program at Jean-Pierre's Beauty Academy, which turned out to be the saving of my soul.

These people needed me. I got a job at Audrey's, a four-station shop on an untouched block of Broad Street. I couldn't wait to get to work mornings, to run my fingers through all that hair. I couldn't wait to see their faces as they asked for ringlets or flattops or French braids, all the little devices they thought might reveal their true selves. I couldn't wait to fill in the blanks, to fulfill their half-formed intuitions. Sometimes I would whisper things into the helpless fold of an ear: "Think Audrey Hepburn in *Breakfast at Tiffany's,*" and a girl on her way to the prom would burst into blossom right before my eyes. I was newly married, thinking of motherhood; I could take a stranger's hair into my hands and feel connected to the whole beautiful world.

Nights, Layton and I would lie in bed, ticking off the things we needed: a bigger place, another car, etcetera. We needed none of these things, of course; Layton had been working for ten years in a North End office, and before that had been employed by the U.S. Army. But he liked to pretend to be a newlywed in the sense I was: young, bright-eyed, filled with hope. He wasn't drinking too much then, his jaw had not yet hardened against life's unfairness, his I Had To had not yet doomed him. He worked as a civil engineer, making connections to smooth this rickety planet, bridges that moved up and down, off ramps that brought people to the brink of where they didn't even realize they wanted to go. After a couple of years he decided we had enough money, enough pictures on the walls. His job had gone a little stale, his old drinking buddies were home with wives and kids, thriving behind bright front doors and rosebushes.

"What do I need?" he asked me, bewildered.

By this time I was twenty-five years old, he was forty. "Layton," I told him, holding his shiny hair. "You need a son."

First we tried easy, then we tried hard, then his mother whispered "My son married one ovary" to her friend Alma when she thought I wasn't listening. So it was off to this doctor and that doctor, Layton eyeing me like a science experiment, and it turned out that the problem was with Layton, whose beautiful body contained no more than a few sad pockets of dead sperm. I think the other women may have entered the picture then, or at least the idea of them. Poor Layton, spreading his fruitless seed all over creation.

I liked the idea of bringing home a big-eyed child from India or Peru, but the stint in the Army had soured Layton on foreigners. So I took us to a lawyer in Boston who specialized in what he called domestic adoptions, as if we were looking for a baby Rottweiler instead of a baby boy.

The truth was, we couldn't imagine what else might bind us for a lifetime. The lawyer's office was filled with cheap paintings and stick furniture, which I took as a good sign: I'd heard about private adoptions and the spiraling fees, but this guy clearly wasn't making much money. He was morose and bony and heavy-browed, a disappointment more than made up for by the news he had to deliver, namely, that he had lots of pregnant girls looking for perfect parents, namely, us. I can barely stand to remember, even now, that ride home from the lawyer's office, the inside of our car awash with the buttery light of happy endings.

We'd been instructed to take pictures. The two of us doing happy, domestic things together. Your hobbies, Mr. Sutton said. Pets, gardens, hiking, that sort of thing. The birth moms like to get a sense before they choose.

The birth moms. I thought of cozy little tea parties, flaxen-haired girls passing crumpets to one another over their pretty bellies.

So we borrowed his mother's camera on a sunny day and stood in our street, intending to take each other's picture. Instead, we looked at each other.

"I can't think of a blessed thing, Layton," I said. "What do we do?"

He shrugged. "We eat together."

I rattled the camera. "Some *ideas,* please?"

He looked around. My dog, Binky, an arthritic terrier mutt I had dragged out of my childhood and who hated Layton's guts, was lying on the steps, exhausted. "We sit out on the steps sometimes," Layton suggested. "Is that a hobby?"

"Yes, but I don't think it counts." Truly, I was anguished. We worked all day, then we ate supper, then we sat outside while Layton drank Scotch on ice and complained about work, and then, on the nights he didn't go out, we watched a little TV before going to bed. It was a pleasant existence, filled with nice moments, but in pictures it would have looked sterile and odd.

"People-watching is a hobby," Layton insisted. "Some people spend whole afternoons in airports just for the hell of it."

"Dear Birth Mom, my husband and I so enjoy sitting outside watching the neighbors." Which we did enjoy, but again, it looked bad in a photo.

"For God's sake, Rita," Layton said, draining his glass. "We do a hundred different things."

I closed my eyes, ticking off the things I liked to do. Which was just about everything. People tend to think of hairdressers as undereducated, but in my case that was true only in the most technical sense. I wish I could say I'd spent more than a few weeks in college, but the truth is my parents didn't have the money, and I was all broken up about my grandmother, who died my junior year in high school. To compensate, I took adult-ed classes in everything from tap dancing to Middle Ages costuming. I bought the Word-a-Day calendar and the *Information Please Almanac* every Christmas. I learned the chief exports of Central America, the meaning of *noisome, peripatetic,* and *fulminate,* the seven secrets of highly successful people, the court hierarchy of seventeenth-century France.

I'd also developed a taste for lofty reading, thanks to my high-school English teacher, Miss Hyde, who could recite ten-acre tracts of Irish poetry from memory. After I divorced Layton, I spent a week in bed reading *The History of Western Civilization.* In short, it was one war after another, would-be kings snatching crowns from the peachy heads of newborns, villages set afire for a few acres of waterfront, the occasional peasant population rising up and crushing its oppressors, only to begin oppressing one another over the rights to black-faced sheep or the ear of God.

The earth's history can be summed up in three words: I want that.

So I turned to the *Canterbury Tales,* Miss Hyde's favorite, to review a more hopeful lesson: Life is a journey, and you never know who you'll end up walking next to.

I liked walking next to Layton, but my list of hobbies—I could crochet, cook with soy, paint scenes on driftwood—had not the slightest connection to him. He, too, had his hobbies, but some of them—his drinking and the horses, specifically—were a bone of contention already, so I guess he decided not to follow that line of thought.

The truth is, we couldn't think of a blessed thing we did *together* except eat, talk, sit with each other, and make love. Which was no small thing, but still. So we drove over to Layton's mother's and asked her to snap us standing in that angry accident of a flower garden, so woozy with colliding colors we had to wear black so the birth mom could find us in the brush. The following day I asked Audrey to snap a picture of us with Binky, who refused to stand near Layton until I bribed him with a piece of cheese. We even hauled Layton's stationary bike up from the basement and propped that between us, smiling so hard our ears rang. I trotted down to the one-hour-pickup and came back with eight five-by-sevens to tuck into a letter that was supposed to say how happy any baby would be to enter our loving and peaceful household and join us in our many fascinating hobbies.

But the letter, too, was a problem.

"Just tell one reason," I begged Layton. The letter had dragged all through supper and I had exactly one and a half sentences: Dear Birth Mom. We want to adopt a baby because. "Just one, Layton."

"I can't think of anything."

"Layton," I cried, "it's a magical, unexplainable urge. It's a way to make a family. There's two, right there."

"Then use those."

"It's supposed to be from both of us. I want it to be from both of us."

"Okay," he said. "It's like you said. I need a son."

"What if it's a girl?"

He shrugged.

"We don't have to do this," I said. "We can just be two married people with no kids."

"And do what? Sit on these steps watching the neighbors till we're eighty-five?"

I didn't think that sounded so bad; I've never suffered unduly from elevated expectations. But here's the truth: That baby was already mine. I thought she was a girl, my secret wish. She was growing inside some girl's warm wet belly and I was supposed to be her mother and there was no moving the world's design.

"Other people don't have to announce *why,*" Layton muttered. "They just pop out the babies. Pop-pop-pop." I didn't like the way he was sizing me up, a good once-over. He had this truly astonishing habit of forgetting which of us was spermless. You can map whole lives by what people choose to forget.

He was sitting on the stoop, elbows on his knees, his big hands dangling down between his legs. I couldn't imagine those hands caressing a baby. He'll learn, I told myself, because I couldn't muster the heart to believe he would be a bad father. I was too exhausted by now to launch an alternate plan for the next eighteen years. Not that I couldn't think of anything: We could open a store, run a travel company, manage a political campaign. I wasn't short of ideas.

"One reason, Layton," I said. "Give me one reason and I won't bother you again."

He lowered his head. "I'd like to go to my kid's football game."

"But what if it's a girl?"

"You *asked* me for a reason and I gave you one," he snapped, getting up.

I followed him into the house. "You have babies to teach and to learn, Layton," I said. "You teach them to love dogs and sparrows and God. You learn to love the world all over again, the whole emerging world where a spider walking up a phone pole is a great big mystery. You teach them to be kind to others, you teach them to vote, you teach them a little respect for people they don't understand, and then by God's good grace you wind up teaching yourself the same lessons you learned as a kid or didn't learn or forgot, and then the world is just a little bit better for everyone. The world gets better, Layton, because you're willing to scrape out your blackened insides and fill yourself back up with the bright yellowy goodness of a new pair of eyes, a second chance to stumble your way through this vale of tears we call life." I was producing a fair harvest of tears myself by now, trailing him around our kitchen, making him listen. I was begging him, I realized: Layton, please turn into somebody else now that you're going to be a daddy. But people don't turn into anybody but themselves, I've found.

He turned to me, his face melting like glue. "Rita," he whispered. "I want a son. You can put whatever you want in that letter, but here it is. I want a son. That's all I know." He buried his damp face in the furrow of my neck; he was tall and large-boned and had to lean way down to receive my comfort, which I gladly gave.

I led him to bed and tucked him in. He smelled liquory and damp, but I didn't know about Alanon then and hoped I'd married a bad boy who would turn good under the happy load of paternal responsibility. "Never mind," I whispered, kissing his forehead. "I'll do it." I started writing, and as I wrote, that little baby grew a toe, an eyelash formed, a down of hair formed on her big domed head. I tucked the letter into an envelope with the fraudulent photos of our fun-filled life and hoped for a miracle.

• • •

We met her on a windy day in the fall, the city of Boston drenched in red and gold, the brick and cobblestone of the North End ablaze in a rusty sunlight. Oh, it was a day. We found a parking space in about two minutes, which I took for a good omen. That, and the dazzle of the day, and Layton's face, which, despite the frowzy, hung-over crinkling under his eyes, was awash in anticipation.

He looked the way he had the first time I met him when he came into Alton Insurance to buy a policy for the motorcycle he'd bought to go with his new house. I was still living at home, watching my town begin to change while my life stood still. On my lunch hour I took him for the grand tour—the river, mainly, the banks of which back then were brushy and filled with birds. The mill's closing was recent enough so its shadow had not yet passed over our town like a total eclipse of the sun. I still knew most of my fellow citizens, and people believed the mill might open again, or that they might get a better job someplace near, that they wouldn't have to leave home. Just above the dam where the water sounds like a taking-off rocket, he kissed me, this older, handsome stranger; my fingers went numb, my earlobes tingled, and oh my God I thought I'd discovered another planet.

Our walk through the cobblestoned maze of the North End had that same kind of first-date feeling—a first date not with each other, but with *her*: There we were, holding hands, bearing flowers to bring to our lady love. The wind was gusting so bad that petals flew from the tissued bouquet like rice before a bride.

"I'm nervous," said Layton, who—during the week between Mr. Sutton's call and this day—had undergone a conversion. I'd filled the spare room with baby stuff: a layette and a month's supply of diapers and some bottles, a pacifier, all those tiny T-shirts and booties. Layton got to wandering in there evenings, taking inventory. He marveled at the size of a baby's things. Then he came home one night with a heartbreaking pair of plastic rain boots, as if he expected our baby to be born walking, brave enough to ford a river.

"Do you think she's there already? We're early."

He squeezed my shoulder. "I hope so." I tripped a little bit then, over a cobblestone that had come out of its nest, and he held me from falling by cradling my elbow in one of his big smooth hands. We'd been married nearly six years then, but I believe his helping me up was the first time I felt like a wife. Since the call from Mr. Sutton we'd become married. We went to bed at night all a-tangle, we got up smiling, he brought me pea-sized hats that said I LOVE DADDY and LIL' SLUGGER, we'd found a fascinating hobby at long last. This baby who was waiting. Or, we were waiting. We'd been waiting all our lives in one way or another—we were alike in that one respect—but on the day I answered the ad from Mr. Sutton, God put down walls and a roof around our waiting, so it felt less like floating in space and more like setting up camp before nightfall.

She was the prettiest girl I had ever seen. A long, rippling washboard of chestnut hair, deep green eyes. Except for where her dress plumped in the middle, she was hard and lean as a mop handle.

"This is Mary," Mr. Sutton said, and she looked like a Mary, a present-day Madonna, and I filled myself to the brim with her, struck dumb with the knowledge of what this lovely girl was willing to give me.

"It's a girl," Mary said, touching her belly.

Layton presented the flowers, which lighted her face in such a way that I could imagine my grown daughter in her. I could see us having lunch in a fast-food place near her college, the clatter swirling around us as she confided an intimate problem with the boyfriend Layton didn't approve of and I did. Oh, your father, I'm telling her. Pay no attention, he loves you anyway.

"She's kicking," Mary said. She had shiny teeth and good skin and I found myself staring at her, grateful for her genetic predispositions. It never occurred to me, not once, to sneak a peek into her heart. I laid my hand on her belly. I felt nothing there, but made a sound as if I had. We all laughed a little. Suddenly I was overwhelmed with what I assumed must be her path here: an empty checkbook, some boy who didn't want her.

We gave her a thousand dollars to start with, an oil bill she couldn't pay, we gave it without a thought; it was partially refundable, said Mr. Sutton, but we didn't think about that either. We talked about her family, who were far away and lost to her but had left her with a love of sports and a knack for math. She told us a little about the boy, who was blond and selfish and good at science, and while Layton stared at her sweet belly I recited our hopes for the baby girl who at that very moment I imagined turning in her watery darkness toward the light-filled sound of my voice.

"You're sure it's a girl?" I asked.

Mary looked at me, those green clear eyes taking in the exact size of my want. "Yes," she said, and smiled.

I looked at Layton, who to my relief was smiling, too.

We had three months before delivery, and we would not see her again. All financial correspondence was to go through Mr. Sutton. Anything personal, too. (I did write Mary a couple of little notes, things I'd forgotten to tell her, about how much I had loved my grandmother, and the fact that I'd won the Styling Shootout at the previous year's trade show in Springfield.) After the baby was born, we were to come to the hospital to get our child in swaddling clothes and thereafter send pictures and letters, again through Mr. Sutton's office. It was all very civilized and kind, I thought, set up in such a way as to cause no one undue suffering. No one would be stranded with a lost ending.

By this time it was cold enough that we could no longer sit outside, so we sat in the baby's room—I in the rocker, Layton on the matching hassock—and read children's books to each other. Layton would be a little drunk, but only a tiny bit, enough to be loose and charming, and he'd make squeaky noises for the little lost duck, small groans for the bad baby bear, and I think I can look back on those moments with him—the two of us sheltering together under the silken roof of our waiting—as the happiest of my life.

"Mother's here," he said, and I could hear the belated click of the door I'd forgotten to lock.

When we came downstairs, she was going through the cupboards.

"Anything to drink?" she said, which was what she always said, rummaging.

"May I help you?" I asked, which was what I always asked.

"No," she said. And so forth. Though I had gathered not a shred of evidence, I held to my original plan that she would turn out to be a good grandmother.

Layton offered her tea, which was a code for a couple of fingers of Scotch prettied into a cup. She began to lower herself into a chair, her restless eyes scanning the fingerprints on my dinette. I had a bowl of dropped leaves set down as a centerpiece, a little slice of the season. She jellied herself into the chair one tier at a time, first her thighs and rear, then the great mezzanine of her belly and bosom, then the full measure of her head and shoulders.

"We were practicing," I said cheerfully, holding up a copy of *Little Beaver and the Echo,* a tale about a poor little beaver looking for a friend.

"Practicing what?" she asked.

When Layton didn't answer, I realized he didn't know. "Practicing for being happy," I answered for him. For us both.

She stuck her pinky out and lifted her teacup. "When my Layton was born I thought I'd died and gone to hell," she said. "Course, Mr. Rosario was nowhere to be found." Mr. Rosario was her husband, now among the grateful dead, whose first name, Stephan, she never uttered. As for his last name, it corresponded to exactly nothing, since Layton's lineage was a long crooked line of mutts, but I can see why she liked it. It had a certain ring, which is why I kept it after we divorced.

"Layton will be here to help me," I said.

She snapped her eyes over. "Somebody'd better be." She picked at her dress, which was thick and grim and patterned with man-eating daisies.

"I'm taking a leave from work, Vicky," I said. "I told you that."

She set down her teacup. "You told me lots of things." She leveled her gaze on Layton. "You said you'd give me a grandchild."

"She *is* your grandchild," I said. Layton's jaw was moving funny, but he'd never once defied his mother and wasn't about to now.

"If you say so," she sniffed, brushing imaginary dust off the menacing sleeve of her dress.

"Vicky," I said, "go home."

Her mouth flopped open.

"Rita—" Layton said.

I stood up and pointed to the door, as protective of my baby as if she were floating in my own belly, which at this moment felt warm and fertile, suffused with blood. "Go," I repeated. "You can stuff yourself back into that cruise ship of a car you're driving and sow your sour oats elsewhere. You think my baby can't hear your hateful talk?" I turned to Layton. "Why aren't you defending our baby?"

Vicky lifted her crinkled eyelids. "Your so-called baby is sitting in a trailer park ingesting secondhand marijuana."

She was wrong. My baby was nestled inside me, telling me what to say.

"Get out, Vicky," I said. "And don't come back till you're ready to do something about that dried-up pea you call a heart."

Softly, surprised, she said, "Why, you little bitch," and I may even have detected a quarter-note of admiration. She got up. "I'll see you later, sweetheart," she said to Layton, and then to me: "Don't expect to see me in this house again."

"I'm counting on it," I said.

I listened to her slog her hateful self into her car and screech away from the curb.

"She's an old woman," Layton said. "You shouldn't talk to her like that."

I looked at him. "You have to stop drinking."

He stood there, deciding, holding the book with the innocent little beaver shouting into a pond.

"It's not good for a baby, Layton. It makes for an unhealthy environment."

"I know that," he said. "The second that baby crosses this threshold, I've taken my last drink."

I looked out our window into the long street, just catching Vicky's taillights rounding the corner, which was noisily under construction. Suddenly I knew that Layton did not expect a baby to cross our threshold. He had filled that room with rattles and books, but it was a hollow, theatrical gesture, a tipsy impulse, like buying the house a double.

"Stop now," I said. "If you're going to stop later, then stop now."

"You think I can't," he said. He opened the cupboard and took down some bottles—I was surprised how many there were. He uncapped them, held them high over the sink, and let them drain.

"Well, thank you," I said.

"I mean it, Rita." He stashed the empty bottles under the sink. I thought about asking him to quit the track, but didn't want to press my luck. "I love you," he said. "I want a life. I slept my life away and now I'm awake."

I believed him, for our baby's sake. I believed in the transforming powers of parenthood, and had a picture in my head of Layton's first look at our baby as Mary, that blessed, blessed girl, gave her over. It was a picture with lots of fuzzy light, all dreamy and Hallmarky, a jewel of a setting for all my best-laid plans.

5

Layton's transformation lasted only a week, but Vicky had a lot more resolve, sticking to her promise. I suppose she was waiting for us to notice her sorrowful absence, which I certainly did. Nobody inspecting the fuzzy back of my refrigerator. No more once-overs, my clothes shriveling under her cool judgment. Layton went over there, though; at least that's where he said he went. It could be he was out testing the waters already, but I believed he was at his mother's, drinking stinky tea in her moldy parlor webbed with hand-stitched doilies. But in the days just before Mary's due date, he changed. He really did stop drinking. I chalked it up to the tidal force of my deepest desires corralling him back.

It was during this same period that I first began to read cards. One of my customers at Audrey's was Rodney, an oil-burner man with about forty cowlicks, a hairstylist's despair. My first regular. One day as I tried to fashion a silk purse out of a sow's ear, he spotted my grandmother's Tarot deck, which I had propped on my workstation the way the other girls kept pictures of their kids or boyfriends. "Are those gypsy cards?" he asked.

I looked at them fondly, having kept the cards with me through the humiliations of senior year, my half-semester attempt at college, my engagement and marriage, my unhappy tenure at Alton Insurance, my training at Jean-Pierre's. They were my good-luck charm, a reminder that Gram had predicted happiness for me, that as long as I was happy she wasn't really gone. "They were my grandmother's," I told him. "My inheritance."

Just before my grandmother came to live with us, I dreamed of a spotted pony prancing in a tiny, tiny paddock. When she walked into our kitchen with her big black bags, the dream popped back into my head. "I'll be darned," she said, showing me her spotted hands. "That pony was me."

I gawked at her—she was wearing a chartreuse muumuu and purple earrings, which seemed vaguely sinful in my mother's immaculate house. Plucked from her yellowy Kansas fields and delivered into the smoky heart of New England, she had managed to arrive smiling. "Dreams like that mean something," she whispered, cupping my chin. "You've been summoned to help me." She glanced around at my mother's things, then looked at me with relief.

The cards were the only thing I asked for after she died. By the time I moved back into the room I'd given up for her, it seemed big as a church, all her furniture gone except for the bed. Nobody wanted a bed somebody had died in. I was a teenager then, had been spooning Hi-Cal into her poor puckered mouth at the last, hoping for miracles. She died anyway, no matter what I did, and her talc- and medicine-smelling bed was a true comfort.

"Will you tell my fortune?" Rodney asked, looking at me through the mirror. His expression was desperate, pleading. His wife was running around, maybe, or one of the kids was sick. Something.

"Whoa, Rodney," Carla called from her station. "You sure you wanna know the outcome of your evil ways?"

He took the cards off my workstation and handed them to me. "Your grandmother didn't hex these or anything, did she?"

"Of course not," I told him. "She was the first optimist I ever met."

"Don't do it, Rodney," Louise yelled over the running water at her sink. "Ignorance is bliss, especially in your case."

They were teasing him, treating him like the wild man, which we all did with guys who came to us to flirt the way they wish they'd had the nerve to back in high school. In truth, Rodney looked like the helpful neighbor in a wholesome television program. But the seams were beginning to show in his sewn-up life; he'd adopted a sad, read-between-the-lines kind of swagger to make up for the buttons that kept dropping off his shirts. It wasn't a money thing; because he fixed oil burners, the mill closing left him mostly unaffected, not counting that his best friend had gone to work at a mill in Georgia. Rodney's problem was something else altogether, sparking out of his eyes even as he pretended to be yukking it up with the girls.

"I'll read you, Rodney," I said, though at the time the cards were merely a keepsake. I was about to become a mother; surely I had more earthly things on my mind. But I liked being reminded of Gram right then, who would have been thrilled about the baby.

"You won't hurt me now, Rita," he said, rolling his eyes at the girls, aw-shucksing to beat the band. It took him a long time, an excessive amount of time, really, to finally put out that oil-stained hand and reach for a card.

First I tried to concentrate, conjuring my childhood days watching Gram read cards on our screen porch for our Catholic-lady neighbors. At nine years old I had my first job, booking Gram's appointments, while my scandalized mother wrung her hands and my father, in one of his weary acts of solidarity with my mother, shook a Bible in our faces. But Gram was crippled with arthritis and through with rules by the time she moved in with us, and she single-handedly saved me from turning into the kind of person who wouldn't understand a person like her. It was too late for my sister, Darla, who was two years older than me, old enough to hate Gram's claw hands and swollen eyelids, her lurid getups and rolled-down support hose. I was just the right age to think her a creature sent in from God, though in fact she flew in from Kansas, followed by a van full of huge, hopeful furniture designed to make people slow down. You couldn't whisk angrily from a room without banging your elbow on an iron drawer-pull or tripping over a hassock the size of a hippopotamus.

It took Gram about a day and a half to realize she would be given nothing to do in our house but die politely, so she broke out her pack of cards and set up shop. Though she owned a guidebook that matched the cards to their meanings, she freelanced quite a bit with the prescribed interpretations. If you turned up a robed figure with ten swords plunged into his back, the creases in her face would lift heavenward as she crowed, "Unexpected news!"

In the end my parents suffered her ravings, perhaps chalking them up to senility, which was about the only thing in my mother's form of the Baptist faith that didn't count as a sin. My own feeling is that my father felt indebted to his mother, who had raised him and his brothers with nothing but sweetness and an all-purpose God and no husband to speak of. Or perhaps he took a small comfort from Gram's clientele—my father held no truck with Catholics, whose rituals appalled him. He took Gram's card money, which was considerable, to buy steaks on Friday nights, which we ate with the windows open while our Catholic neighbors pushed fish sticks around on their plates.

Gram's lessons came winging back as I watched Rodney pick a card. He handed it to me solemnly.

"Unexpected news," I said. "You lucky duck."

He looked at the card, at that poor flattened fellow with swords sticking into his back. "What kind of news?"

"Just what I said, the unexpected kind. A surprise. You just wait."

He tucked the card back into the pack. "If you say so."

"Actually," I said, "that card can mean all kinds of things." I began to ad-lib, imparting all the lessons I thought a good person should learn. I yearned to do what I could to improve the world in advance of my child's birth. Take better care of yourself, I told him. Get a checkup, an eye exam, a teeth cleaning. Forgive some person who needs forgiving. Pick up flowers on the way home. Tell your kids you missed them all day. I figured I'd covered all the bases of things that go wrong in a life.

I looked at him, this nice man, this man who got his hands dirty every day in the service of the oil-burning public. I liked him. He needed me.

He got out of the chair and rubbed his head. "I guess that's enough," he said. Audrey was eyeing me from the register. Rodney paid her and went out, shooting me a nervous backward glance.

"He *asked*," I said.

"He didn't ask for some guy getting stabbed to death, Rita," Audrey answered irritably. "Look, why don't you knock off early. I'll take your four o'clock."

I walked home, through a town whose death was being disguised by elaborate stagings and the sound of jackhammers. I looked across the river, half expecting to see steam from the mill rising in prayerful wisps from the heart of the valley. But there was nothing but a creepy vacancy. When I got home, Binky hobbled after his own tail for a few minutes, overjoyed to see me out of schedule. I bent to pet him, then picked up the scent of a fresh drink. I wandered through the kitchen, spotting Layton's jacket on a chair. I found him in the living room staring at a soap opera on TV with the sound off. The morning paper was strewn in sections over the couch like a shroud.

"Why aren't you at work?" I asked.

"Where did you find these people, Rita?"

"What people?"

His face was quivering a little, his eyes creased as he stared at me. I realized at that moment that I had been chosen by a man far too old for me. "Sutton," he said. "Sutton and the Virgin Mary. Where did you dig them up?"

"There was an ad," I said, searching his face for signs of something soft—anything—though I had already gathered that he had nothing but bad news. I had Gram's cards in my pocket, so I put my hand there.

"An ad," he said. "You answered an ad for a baby."

"The agencies take too long. We agreed on this. What are you talking about?"

"You never told me it was an ad."

"Yes I did. I think I did. What does it matter how I found her?"

He tipped his head back, rubbing his hands, hard, down his face. "Your girl's not pregnant, Rita," he said. "Your little madonna, little angel-face herself. She isn't pregnant. Her name isn't even Mary. It's Tonya Kurgan. Nice touch, though—Mary. That was a nice touch."

"Who told you this? What are you saying? Who told you such a thing?"

He scooped up the paper and threw it into the air, and the story came raining down over my head: HARVESTING HEARTACHE, was the headline, about a crooked lawyer, a cold-hearted girl, the prosecutor's sting. The couple set to testify—a pilot and his wife, who thought Mary was carrying twins—was out their life savings.

"The D.A.'s office just called here," he said.

I folded up the paper and laid it on top of the TV, which was still going, soundless people in color-coordinated clothes mouthing their soundless sorrows. "There's no baby?" I said.

"We were lucky," Layton said. "He only bagged us for seven grand."

"There was never any baby?"

"It's a con, Rita," Layton said. "A scam. Read it."

I guess I was weeping, because he softened, struggling off the couch to hold me. Poor Binky, who was fifteen at the time, dragged himself under the TV table and hid.

"See what happens?" Layton said, trying, I suppose, to be husbandly. "See what happens when you put your trust in people?" And then, as if the thought had some direct connection to the meanness in Mr. Sutton's heart, he added: "I told you I was too old to be a father."

I went to the phone, not believing Layton, or the paper, or the certain knowledge flapping in my chest like a trapped bat. I let the "disconnect" message buzz in my ear, then I dialed again. Listened again. "Oh, God," I said. "This isn't possible." I sat down right where I was, which happened to be the small hallway between the kitchen and the living room, an empty tunnel echoing with my cries and the quieter, more mysterious reverberations of Layton's grief.

Of course I knew we would never survive this. The difference in our ages split like a fault, shaking everything in the house. When Kennedy was shot, I was in a bassinet and Layton was a teenager, a young man who believed in his country, headed to Vietnam, and found a moon-faced boy standing on the road to a village.

Layton had an entire life behind him, an ex-wife and the darkness of his soldiering and all those bottles and horses and bad bets. I had what I dearly hoped was an entire life ahead of me.

That night he went to the track and I went to bed, my small dog nested into the curve of my body. In the morning Layton came home, cleaned himself up, and readied for work reeking of aftershave, his hair wet-combed and his skin rubbed pink with a washcloth. He looked like my father. He belonged in a condo in St. Pete, stiffening into a tweed recliner, its seat softened to the shape of his butt. "Good-bye," he said, kissing me. "I'm sorry about yesterday." It struck me that he would be going to work the same as any day, for he had not told anyone about our baby, about the rattles and kids' books and month's supply of diapers waiting in our sunniest room. I, on the other hand, had told Audrey and the girls at the shop, all of my customers, our next-door neighbors, the clerks at the grocery store, my parents, and even my sister, in a long letter that may or may not have reached her, since in the place she was living they opened each other's mail.

"You take care," Layton said. His voice heaved with sympathy, as if this entire thing had been my fault and therefore was mine to suffer—the natural consequences of hope. It sounded a whole lot like I-told-you-so. I told you. In Layton's world you were either the soldier or the boy on the road.

Somebody from the prosecutor's office called the next day, and the day after that, but I refused to give them anything. I wouldn't even admit we had ever set eyes on Mr. Sutton and Mary.

"Then we won't get our money back," Layton said. "Not a dime."

"I don't care," I said, peering out at him from under the covers. Binky was under there with me. I wondered how close to a baby's sleep a small dog's panting might sound.

"It's a lot of money, Rita," Layton pleaded, sitting on the bed next to me, petting the top of my head the way as a child I'd wished for my father to do.

"It wouldn't be any big deal," Layton said. "We go down there, give a deposition or whatever, and that's the end of it." He gave me a long song and dance—how that man could talk—about the ins and outs of the law, which he didn't know spit about. "Besides," he said, "it'll never even get to trial."

"I don't care. It's humiliating."

He took his hand away. "Rita, I worked hard for that money."

"That money would've gone to the horses and you know it."

He got up. "That son of a bitch stole our money, Rita. He and his little slut strung us along like rubes at a casino. Maybe it's their turn to be humiliated. A little prison justice would be all right with me."

"There's that other couple. Let them do it."

"The D.A. needs more."

"There must be dozens of couples like us. Let somebody else admit their baby wasn't real." I peeled back the covers, staring up at the ceiling. "I'd rather believe our baby died than that she never existed at all."

He stared at me, his face soft and pulpy around the mouth, not understanding.

"We lost a baby, Layton," I told him. "That's the truth of it. If I go signing papers and talking into tape recorders, what am I supposed to tell myself I lost? An idea? That I lost an idea?"

He shook his head slowly. I had married a man who could not understand how much I needed for that baby to have been real.

"Rita—" he began, then thought better of it. He petted the bedcovers and got up heavily. I heard his step outside, then the Harley grinding to life.

I think I slept most of that day, and the day after, then I packed up the baby things and put them in my car. I had gotten almost everything at one place, Great Expectations at the Walker Creek Mall, in a fit of joy one afternoon on my way home from work. Now I was taking it all back. I found a deserted shopping cart in the parking lot and dragged it over to the trunk, where I unloaded diaper packages the size of hay bales, baby undershirts and inch-long socks, two four-packs of bottles, a case of formula, a Snugli. . . .

People watched me as I pushed that cart through the lot, one wheel going *zippity zippity zippity.* And me with my slippers on, pushing all this hopeful bounty. Maybe I looked homeless, or crazy, my hair undone, my lips cracked to bleeding, a coat thrown over my nightshirt.

I was raised, heaven knows, with the idea of God on my side, but that day, with my bedroom slippers and cold hands, His presence was a mean and distant thing. God has one deaf ear, is what I was thinking. I wheeled that cart into the big scrubbed automatic-door foyer of Great Expectations and felt He had invited me to a party, then made me wait on the doorstep for my number—a high, high number, the least likely to be called.

"Welcome to Great Expectations," said a smiling girl in a polyester blazer. "Can I help you find something?"

"I'm making some returns," I said.

She looked at the cart, then at me, then snapped her eyes away. Her pity was more than I could manage, so I took the whole caboodle outside again just to draw a decent breath. I wheeled the cart back and forth, looking for my car, which was missing, it wasn't anywhere, so I headed up and down, looking at numbers on the poles that didn't ring any bells, and finally I wound up at the back of the lot where the asphalt borders Walker Creek. One by one I took the things out of the cart and pitched them into the water. First I opened everything, tearing the plastic with my teeth. The first things—a diaper, a shirt, a bonnet with eyelet lace—seemed to float a long time before sinking. I was halfway through the cart when the police got there.

"Miss, please don't do that. Don't, Miss."

One of them, a lovely-looking fellow, barely of age, with black,

black eyes and a uniform so clean I guessed his mother washed it, took my hands away, gently. *Miss, please don't do that. Don't, Miss.* I keep a list of people I must not forget, and that baby-faced officer in his impeccable uniform is right at the tippy top. He kept out a little T-shirt, a pink one with rosettes stitched into the hem, and gave it to me to hold as they brought me to the station and called Layton to bring me home.

I think I slept some more, and then one afternoon, a Tuesday or a Wednesday, I woke filled with dread. My bedroom was sun-buttered except for a thick shadow that turned out to be Vicky, hunkered just inside the door. She had on her gardening clothes, a black sweatshirt the size of a parachute, cotton slacks, a pair of worn-out Keds. They looked like clown feet, so I laughed.

"Layton told me you were sad," she said.

Her words were so simple—each one a perfect, painful pin-prick of truth. I opened my mouth and wailed, banging my fist on the mattress. Binky startled awake and scrabbled away.

"Are you finished?" Vicky asked.

"I lost a baby," I told her, rolling over so I wouldn't have to look at her pale, pressed-together lips.

"You did no such thing," she said, yanking the covers back. "You lost your self-respect, is what you lost. You put your famous faith-in-people into a cheap hustler and got what you deserved." She lifted me by the shoulders and sat me up. For an old woman she had the power of a heavyweight champ. When I first learned that Layton had a mother, I hoped I was going to get my grand-mother back, but Gram had been a flyweight with size-two feet. "Now, you can stay in bed for the rest of your life, having yourself a great big pity party, or you can get on the phone. You want tea and sympathy, you call up some girlfriends, like a normal person."

I blotted my eyes with the sheet. "I don't have that many girlfriends."

"Miss People Lover herself? I find that hard to believe." She lifted the bedside phone and jiggled it at me.

"It's humanity in general I love," I said. "People in specific I can't ever seem to connect with." There were a few people I could have called—Audrey would have been sympathetic, and Carla, the middle-aged mother hen who worked two stations down from me. But how could I ask them to sorrow over an empty space, a lost idea? In truth I thought it was more than the average person would be able to rise to.

Vicky looked disappointed—worried, even. Layton had called her from work, asking her to please come up here and straighten me out so he wouldn't have to come home to another conversation he had not been trained to comprehend. Apparently she thought she could storm in, get the troops in order, and storm out, like yanking a few weeds from the daylilies. Now she had a real problem, me in my nightshirt at three in the afternoon, my hair matted from neglect.

"Get up," she said. She ran me a bath, arranged my beauty products in an imposing line along the side of the tub. "Get in," she said. In front of her I stripped off my nightshirt and stepped into the water, which was too hot. I sank into it anyway, my skin burning, my punishment for being born hopeful.

I wept some more as she rattled around in the kitchen, getting tea. It goes without saying that she knew where to find everything.

When I came out, there were two steaming cups on the table. I gave hers a sniff and smelled nothing but tea. I found her in the baby's room, holding the pink shirt I'd brought home from the police station.

"Put that down," I said.

"I can pack these things up if you want," she said. "Maybe you don't feel like looking at them."

Although most of the stuff was now in the muck at the bottom of Walker Creek, there remained a few things I couldn't take back, mostly the things Layton had bought in what I now recognized less as enthusiasm for fatherhood as an awkward try at loving me.

"All right," I said.

Everything went into one box. Vicky kept her hand on her wheezy chest the whole time, but was surprisingly efficient, and quiet. We worked side by side as our tea cooled in the kitchen.

"I lost a baby, a year after Layton," she said, tucking the LIL' SLUGGER hat into the box.

I looked up. "Miscarriage?"

She took a long time jamming a book down behind some receiving blankets. "Stillbirth. Another boy." She passed a hand over the great soft accordion of her belly. "They didn't know up from down about women back then, so they took out the whole works while I was knocked out."

For a moment I thought she might be lying, until I saw the watery eyes behind those bulky glasses. "That must have been awful," I said.

"Mr. Rosario was no help, of course. I bore all that alone."

She had me again. Who was I to be blubbering over my phantom, when she had a flesh-and-blood baby to mourn the rest of her days? I trudged out to the kitchen and curled my hands around the cold teacup, hating her.

"What I wanted to tell you," she said, sitting down, "is that he was a real baby. They let me see him, just for a second. Little squinted-shut eyes, toes all in a line. I only got a glimpse, and that's what I saw." She slid her fingers up under her glasses, took a sip of tea. "My boy had a full head of black hair. He was as real as you can imagine. But listen. He *became* an idea. With time, I mean. In time. My baby became an idea of how my life might have gone. Grandchildren, family vacations with two boys in the back, a son who could carry on a conversation without my having to ply him with Scotch. But I still hold to my idea of Layton, too, don't I? All that love and devotion I insist on believing in." She leaned heavily on one cheek, the skin on her face rising like bread dough over her fingertips. "His other wife was just like you. Bubbly little thing. A silly little optimist." She sighed. "Layton didn't deserve her, either."

"You always gave me to believe it was the other way around, Vicky."

"Wishful thinking on my part," she said. "There isn't a mother alive whose children aren't more idea than reality."

That's all she said, meaning to give comfort, and in a way she did. This was the best she could do, and I felt better, I actually did, thinking that my baby had already become what she would have become eventually, given enough time and other sorrows. I could mourn her all I wanted, and I did.

6

A month later, I returned to work. I wasn't back an hour when Rodney, my oil-burner man, arrived. At the time I was setting a perm for Mrs. Rokowski, so I couldn't fit him in, but it turned out he didn't want a haircut, he wanted to tell me something.

"You saved my life," he said. "I went to the doctor. Like you said in that card? They found a spot on my X ray, but it's early, it's nothing, I'm getting the treatments, I'll be fine." He kept trying to grab my hands, which were gloved and dripping with neutralizer. "She saved my life," Rodney announced to everybody. Audrey looked worried, sitting up at the cash register with her new red hair, a mistake I wasn't about to point out since she'd read about the incident with the police and was watching me like a hawk.

"Unexpected news," he said. "Just like you predicted. A cure is the last thing I expected. They find a spot on your X ray, you think you're a dead man. I didn't expect a cure."

"That's wonderful, Rodney," I said. I was stunned, to be honest.

I'd given him my grandmother's all-purpose predictions, was all, but he was staring at me as if I possessed special powers. Of course, there was that look of desperation he'd given me. There was that. There was a certain power, maybe, in seeing that.

Mrs. Rokowski twisted her head around—she was still pretty spry back then—and grimaced up at me, one eye open. "You some kinda gypsy?"

Heads swiveled over. A couple of women lifted the dryers so they could hear better. "She's sensitive," Carla called over. "No harm in that." Her voice was round and filled with sympathy; she was the only one who had sent me a condolence note. *So sorry your baby did not come to you,* she wrote, which I thought was about the most delicate, loving thing I'd ever heard.

Mrs. Rokowski was still eyeing me. "Sensitive?"

"Not with everybody," I said quickly. "It only works on some people." I smiled at Rodney, who smiled back. I wished I'd married him instead of Layton just then, though the first woman—the first I found out about, anyway—was still a few days off.

"What kind of people?" Mrs. Rokowski asked.

"Ordinary people with a big fat life wish," I said. "You can't read people unless they believe in life." This had been my grandmother's mantra, and I have found it to be true. Mrs. Rokowski nodded, looking pleased, obviously counting herself among the life-wish crowd. When I left Audrey's the next year, she followed me to my basement salon, and she likes being read because the cards improve her memory. The Six of Cups, a pretty card depicting children sniffing flowers, once occasioned a long tale about her rosy-cheeked little brother skating on a Milford frog pond back in 1923.

"You watch yourself with the other kind," Gram used to tell me, shuffling the cards in her stiff old hands, all those knights and peasants learning their life lessons. Temperance. Judgment. Strength. "People with no life wish'll just use your words against you. There's no point giving advice or counsel. These people can I-told-you-so straight into the middle of next week." She was referring to my parents, but I took most of what she said on general principles.

I suppose you could call the incident with Rodney's X ray a turning point for both of us. Rodney was a decent man, but somewhere along the line he'd gotten the idea that nothing worked out, and now that it seemed something *was* going to work out, namely his continuing to be alive, he changed. I saw him change. Even his clothes, nothing you'd notice if you weren't looking—but there was a new belt, a button replaced, his wedding band returned to his finger, as if all of a sudden his life was a sort of ceremony he had to come dressed for.

I got home that day filled with Rodney's news and my part in it. Recent circumstances had primed me for caring, and I was surprised how much comfort another person's happy ending brought to me. I gave Binky a hug, filled his bowl before I even got my coat off. I laid out some cards on the kitchen table, hoping the room might fill with the light of my grandmother's life wish. Instead I found the moon card, which according to Gram's softened, dog-eared guidebook was a sign of treachery. The moon leered up at me, commanding the entire spread. I thought: That's the deceivers, Mary and Mr. Sutton, who according to the paper were in big trouble with or without my testimony.

But it wasn't Mary and Mr. Sutton; it was Layton that terrible moon was pointing to, Layton and some underpaid waitress he picked up at the Stargazer. Probably he begged her, Be my second chance, I've been asleep my whole life and now I'm awake.

When he arrived home, I was studying Gram's book. "What now?" he asked.

"I'm filled with the light of my grandmother," I informed him. "I saved a man's life."

He looked worried—and guilty, too, only I didn't realize that part except in retrospect. "How?"

"He looked at me in a certain way," I told him, "and I turned into Gram."

Layton pursed his lips, the expression he used whenever he thought he was getting into a conversation he had no hope of making heads or tails of. "Maybe you went back to work too soon, Rita. It's only been a few weeks."

"I need to be back in the world, Layton."

"What if you saw a doctor before plunging back in? Mother thinks you're having a breakdown." He said it gently—he sounded like a husband, I'll give him that.

"That's what I thought, too, for a while there," I admitted. "And I'm sorry about putting you through the little episode with the police."

"It wasn't a little episode."

"I meant in the grand scheme of things."

"In the grand scheme of things, it wasn't a little episode."

I folded up my cards and kept them in my hands just for something to hold. "Our baby died, Layton," I said, "and Rodney will live. The Lord giveth and the Lord taketh away." My father used to pull that one out every time my sister or I wanted something, but I got its meaning now, its beautiful balance.

"Seems to me there's a helluva lot more taketh than giveth,"

Layton said. "Life's one big fat taketh, seems to me." He was talking about Mr. Sutton and our seven thousand dollars, not about our baby. "You keep your rose-colored glasses on, Rita, if it makes you so happy."

I felt so sorry for him, I really did.

"Layton?" I said. "I have to ask you. I never asked because I knew I wasn't supposed to."

Layton looked at me, his lips pressed together now. He looked like his mother, and he knew exactly where I was going.

"What I want to know, Layton, is did that boy have a grenade in his pocket?"

He ran his hand through his hair, which was dark and full, graying only slightly. He had the carriage of an ex-soldier, prideful, squared at the shoulders, eyes sharpened by things he wished he hadn't seen. "He *could* have," is what he said. He slid his arm over the table, knocking away my cards, then took my hand with a weird, held-breath gentleness. The gentleness of a fugitive fresh out of options who agrees to be taken in quietly. "He could have, Rita," Layton said. "He could have. That was the whole point."

This moment—his hand on mine, the two of us locked into the plain, sad truth—was the precise end of our marriage, though it was another six months before he brought that floozy home and another four months still before we faced each other down before a judge. In the end I forgave him; and I forgave those women. One of them had a twelve-year-old son with asthma so bad she had to carry a beeper to track him. Another had a little old sickly father withering under his sheets.

I would spend most of those final months studying Gram's cards, trying to recover her meanings, working from my own memory and the notes she crabbed between the single-spaced lines of her book. Under the Moon she had inked out "treachery" and scrawled *PAY ATTENTION.* Which is good advice no matter what your problem. I followed Mr. Sutton and Mary's progress through page-three articles in the paper (they were both fined; he got an eye-blink of jail time), but in truth they didn't interest me anymore. I'd read a line or two and then suddenly be thinking of my parents' sunporch, where Gram and I placed a table covered in paisley cloth over which she might improve people's prospects. She wore long skirts for these sessions, and the afternoon sun cast a reddish light over her tufted hair and her age-rumpled face. I believed she told fortunes, I believed she had gifts sent from God.

What I saw later, poring over those books stained with ink from Gram's ballpoint, was a woman recovering from the terrible shock of old age. My father was her youngest, and she had already outlived two of her children. All of her friends were dead, or wished they were. She had two choices and took the one that required a paisley cloth, a granddaughter at her elbow. I waited through a few seasons, sitting nearby with my lined notebook, taking in the perfumes the Catholic ladies dabbed behind their small spongy ears. I waited for summers on end, watching the living fire of Gram's eyes as her body collapsed around her; I waited at her elbow while my friends discovered boys with cars and parties where people moved mysteriously in shadowed corners. I waited.

It was my mother who finally said it. "You're just like her," she said one day in disgust. I had brought home a stray dog (who would become the venerable Binky) on the strength of Jesus' admonition to do unto others. "Two peas in a pod," my mother said. And my grandmother, who never looked up as she let the new dog walk into the folds of her fortune-telling skirt, said, "She could do worse than be like me."

Gram would have asked Layton about the boy. Gram would have let Rodney believe she had powers. Gram would have forgiven Layton and those women, believing that unforgiveness was an illness that attacked the vital organs, beginning with the heart.

Layton let go of my hand and picked himself up from the chair. "I never expected any of this," he said. "I pictured something so different when I married you."

"So did I," I told him. We were not accusing each other; in fact we were comforting each other. Clearly I had not turned out to be the second chance he had in mind; then again, as first chances went, I hadn't done so hot either. Even though our marriage was ending at that moment—I could almost hear a lock clicking shut behind us—we were capable of understanding each other's disappointment.

"We could make a fresh start," Layton said, not specifying how.

"People can put a lot behind them, Layton. I really believe that."

And there it was, the sum total of our Big Try. I began to gather the cards up from the floor, and Layton helped me. For this tiny moment at the end of our marriage we knelt together in our kitchen touching hands, as if life's inevitable outcomes might simply decide to pass us by.

"Pick one," Layton said, handing me a fistful of cards.

I turned one over. "A journey uncompleted," I said softly.

A vague dread shimmered through me just then, the softest dread, the gentlest fear. I must have sensed that I would go on looking, in one way or another, for our lost child. But I had no way of knowing that I would find her.

PART 2 the queen of cups

7

The Queen of Cups turned up again and again. A benevolent woman. Me, I figured, flattering myself. It wasn't until we got there, on the last Friday in March, that I discovered the other sister.

It was my idea to case the joint, so to speak. We left Alton in the dark, drove two hours north, and installed ourselves in the parking lot of Balzano's Family Bakery on Morning Street in Portland, Maine. It was five-thirty, and still winter—ice patches on the sidewalks, snowbanks piled against foundations—but the day was shaping up to be strangely balmy. You could hear whole snowbanks melting. John and I slipped out of our coats and hung them loosely over our shoulders, like capes.

The King of Cups and his queen, that's what I was thinking.

We had a good view of the storefront from where we parked. The lot was wide and opened onto the street, revealing a lot of the houses and cars. Their world was small enough that we could see it all.

John reached into the backseat, poured a cup of coffee from the thermos, and handed it to me. "I feel like a criminal," he said.

"You have every right to be here."

"My rights don't count for much if they don't want me."

"There's a way into that family, John," I said. "All we have to do is find the right door. Maybe one of the husbands, the bakers. They might understand an uncle wanting to know his little niece."

"They might."

"All right, then. That's a possible." I set my coffee on the dash. "What about the sisters? There's always a soft-hearted one. Which do you think?"

"Callie or Susanna," he murmured, shaking his head. "I don't know, I barely knew them. They didn't come around much when Roger was home. I visited every five weeks like clockwork—Portland was part of my territory. But I don't think I ran into either one of them more than two or three times." He pressed his fingers into his thighs, playing some melody I was glad I couldn't hear. "They were always wanting Laura to listen to their problems or watch the kids or take their mother to the doctor," he went on. "That's how Roger saw it, anyway. The mother had all kinds of heart trouble and whatnot. One time Laura got up in the middle of dinner to run up there and turn on a faucet."

"Layton's mother was like that. She couldn't sort her mail without calling us to complain about her bifocals."

"I think Roger was afraid of them," John said. "He'd rant and rave about her smothering family, but I think he was afraid they'd steal her back." His fingers stopped moving. "Rita, I don't know what happened. I don't know why people do what they do."

We looked at the street for some time. Daylight began to

spread, appearing over the pitched roofs and pooling at all the front doors. A light burned at the back of the bakery, and the lights of kitchens and bedrooms blinked on all down the street.

"That's where the sisters grew up," John said of the building next to us, a white triple-decker with neat green trim. "Top floor. The mother still lived there." Then he pointed directly across the street. "The twins were over there—I forget which houses."

Every time he looked at me, I felt two spots of warmth from those big, rose-brown eyes. At this hour the front seat felt small and shadowed, but there was enough light from him to fill a football stadium.

The next thing that happened, this woman in nurses' whites comes out of the triple-decker, holding the hand of a little girl. The little girl had on a school uniform, a starchy white blouse and green jumper, thick green tights, boring black shoes. I turned to John, whose eyelashes were quivering. His mouth made a spooky downward turn, the sign of a man not crying.

"That's her," he said. "Aileen." And didn't her name melt sweetly on his tongue! He slid his hand across the back of the seat and cupped my shoulder. We might have been new parents gazing through the nursery window—absolutely bowled over, a new way of being in the world unrolling before our eyes. "I knew she'd turn out beautiful," he said.

Well, she wasn't. She had the wild red hair of her twin aunts, the kind of wiry ringlets that are famously hard to cut, and a faceful of freckles. Little bird legs and apple knees. Not beautiful, no, but a pleasure to look at. This one's a pistol, I told John, she's not as docile as she looks.

The nurse and the child walked side by side in identical white sweaters, matching strides. One was tall and one was short, but they walked in sync; I couldn't figure out which one was altering her stride to suit the other. "Why is she with a nurse?" I asked.

John's mouth parted. "I'll be damned. That would be Beth." He leaned over the dash, squinting. "I forgot all about her," he said. "There was another sister. The youngest."

She had a kind face from a distance. You do a makeover on this type of face, gilded lipstick and the whole works, and what you end up with is a face that looks unnecessary, like frosting on a pound cake. They can't rise to the props, or don't care to. It's actually a lovely quality in a person.

"She was the quiet one," John said. "The only one Roger didn't complain about. Mostly she was away at nursing school. In Boston, I believe." His face flooded with color; it was all coming back. "Beth was home visiting when Laura died. She had just gotten her first job, as I recall. Mass General, I think it was."

Beth stopped to adjust Aileen's collar, her nurse shoes holding her fast to the ground. "Doesn't look like she ever went back to Boston," I said.

John looked at me. "She's the one who found the bodies. How could I have forgotten her?"

By this time the shade had been pulled up on the day. The street came alive with people on their way to work or to each other's houses or to school. It was a busy neighborhood, full of stray cats and storm windows and teenagers packed into small, secret herds. Although Portland was a city, this part of the city, called the Hill, felt like a town. I could picture the place all through the seasons, the ticking of garden tools or snow shovels, the wailing of the fire station, the delirious shrieks of babies and children chasing loose dogs, or each other, or a ball with not enough air in it. It reminded me a little bit of Alton, before.

As Beth and Aileen made their way toward the bakery, two side-by-side houses across the street opened up, spilling look-alike boys in assorted sizes. Two redheaded mothers scurried down the stairs, herding kids—some of them too big to be herded—across the street. The family converged on the bakery side of the street, their voices rising genially, heads bobbing and shoulders bumping and hands darting, hello, hello.

"Now we're cooking," I said to John.

I thought they were beautiful. Strong arms, rising and falling voices, big smiles; my eyes felt too small to take it all in. Aileen stood in their midst, and they bent to her, all of them, even the smallest boys. There were eight boys in all, the bigger ones in jeans and letter jackets, some of the smaller ones still carrying grade-school backpacks. The younger ones wore the boy version of Aileen's uniform—white shirts and green pants, snappy green bow ties. Their jackets flapped open to the crazy warmth of the morning.

"Four boys apiece," John said. "All growing up."

I took a sip of coffee. "Somebody should've given those girls a talking-to."

"She looks like Laura," John said. "She always had Laura's eyes."

Of course he couldn't see Aileen's eyes from where we were sitting, stowed at the side of the suddenly busy lot like a couple of fugitives. He was erasing his brother already, clearing a path to the one decent thing his brother left behind.

It was six-thirty. The family stood together for some time, conferring about something, then Aileen plowed from their midst, pushed open the bakery doors, and the motion broke a hole in the day.

We let go our breath, which we didn't realize we'd been holding.

"Boy," I said. "Oh, boy."

"She's got Laura's way of holding herself," John said. "Did you see that, how she stood so still?"

I was thinking she was built the way John was once built—bony and long-waisted, and her left foot turned in just barely, the way Roger's did in the other pictures John had shown me, digging them out of his piano bench like a stash of secret codes.

Two of the medium-sized boys were cleaning the bakery windows from the inside. Another one pushed a mop back and forth. After a few minutes, one of the husbands, a hearty-looking guy with a baker's apron draped around his middle, dragged a yellow sandwich board out to the sidewalk. Aileen trotted out behind him, holding a box. He chucked her under the chin and left her on the sidewalk to mull over the box, which turned out to contain plastic letters twice the length of her hand. She put up three and a half words—TRY OUR YUMMY RAS—snapping the letters into place on horizontal tiers, then took them down, frowning once again into the box.

"Look at her," John murmured. "Oh, Rita, look." His eyes didn't move, not once. She put up some other letters—TRY OUR FABUL—then down they came.

"Do you think kids that young should be working?" I asked. Then I remembered the thrill of working for my grandmother.

"They're not working," he pointed out. "They're dressed for school. These are chores."

"I'm just saying, maybe they don't know everything about raising that child. Maybe you have your own special wisdom to impart." As for me, I could think of a thousand things I wanted to tell her.

He smiled slightly, his eyes still fixed on Aileen. "I'd say they've made a pretty good job of it."

Already he was defending them, this family who had cast him into the cold. Who had not regretted their coldness, had not once tried to call him or write him or tell him it wasn't his fault. But it was hard to feel anything but tenderness, watching this big, blowsy quilt of a family spread itself over a new day.

The bakery was filling up with customers now, many of them pausing on their way in to pet Aileen's shoulder or say hello. She was tiny for eight, with little elf hands, the mascot of Morning Street.

"Look," John said. Up went the letters, bing, bing, bing: DAZZLE HER EYE WITH OUR RAZZLEBERRY PIE!!! "Will you look at that," he murmured. "I knew she'd turn out smart."

"She's a poet," I said, then my eyes stung. I was reduced to a bucket of slush over this redheaded child who was no relation to me.

"I used to have this picture in my head back when she was a baby," John was saying. "The two of us sitting at my piano bench, her little shoes ticking against the cross rail." He shifted to see her better. "Probably her feet would touch the ground by now. I've already missed so much."

I started to put my coat back on. "I'm going in."

"But we're not ready, Rita. We were going to find the right door." He looked frightened; now that he was here, he understood how much he had at stake.

"I won't blow our cover," I assured him. "I just want to see."

As I walked past her, she didn't look up, so intent was she on her sign. But I fancied I could feel something from her, maybe the blazing heat of her life wish. I glanced back at John, who was out of the car, leaning against the door, his fists opening and closing impatiently. I pushed open the bakery doors, looking for her handprints and placing my own hands there.

I don't know what I wanted to find. The first thing I noticed was a raised shelf on the counter that held an enlarged photograph of the four sisters, the Doherty girls, arms linked, beneath a banner that read BALZANO'S BAKERY GRAND RE-OPENING. Four laughing girls with light streaming in on their dresses. Laura was the one with her head thrown back, her throat exposed, her dress brighter than the others. The frame was expensive, etched with flowers. I could imagine the party exploding outside of the frame—little boys running around, neighbors and friends waltzing in and out, trays of pastry set out on the brand-new coppertop tables. The two brothers strut across the brand-new floor tile, sunlight pinging off the chrome napkin dispensers, the tabletops, the shined glass of the pastry cases. Somebody rounds up the sisters for a picture. Laura tips her head as if catching a drink from a waterfall—that lovely throat, those parted lips. Perhaps she has already met him, she is giddy with him, filled with possibility. Perhaps she knows how she looks this day—immense and mighty, powerfully separate, possessed of a secret.

I was not the only one in line; business was booming. The two brothers—Aileen's other uncles, is how I thought of them—darted back and forth from the kitchen, chatting up the customers. Behind the counter bustled the redheaded twins, their work so practiced and elegant it resembled a dance. I bought a muffin from Susanna, the short-haired one, while Callie plucked a sourdough from the bread display for the man standing in line behind me. Susanna dropped some change in my hand, glancing at me only briefly. Her amber-colored eyes had a dry, practical, but not unfriendly look. She was pretty—they both were, with soft lines signaling the onset of middle age—but Susanna's bones were sharper, her eyes darted more quickly, her spine had straightened hard against sorrow. Callie was more the shape of a mother, her hair long and wavy, her chin soft, her wrists sweet and doughy. But the way she kept her eye on those kids, even the big ones, gave me to believe she was a woman who felt she had much to lose.

Wrong door number one and wrong door number two, that's what I was looking at.

I took my muffin and sat at a table, out of the way of traffic. Through the storefront window I could see Aileen taking down letters and repositioning them, apparently discontented with her spacing.

Beth sat at a table near the back, helping one of the older boys work out a chemistry problem. Up close she was plain as a broom, a colorless version of her dark-haired, vividly beautiful, dead sister. But the calm that surrounded her like a scent worked as a form of beauty.

As the customers came and went with the first morning rush, I tried to match up the family: mothers to sons, wives to husbands, sons to fathers. I had a terrible time of it, for there were no natural cues. I had to wait for a boy to say "aunt" or "uncle" or "Mom" or "Dad" to make the matches; the sisters called their husbands "honey," but sometimes called their brother-in-law the same thing.

Even Beth, who, judging from her naked fingers, had no husband to sweet-talk, sometimes called her brothers-in-law "dear."

It was all a-jumble, the pack of customers, the boys running through their chores, the husbands darting back and forth with flour flapping off the front of their aprons, the twin sisters working behind the counter, one brewing coffee, one twining cake boxes with one of the boys.

Then there was a lull.

"Did Aileen's geography notebook ever turn up?" Callie asked suddenly, easing a cake box into a bag her son or nephew was holding.

"No," Beth said. "We looked everywhere."

Callie frowned. "When did she have it last?"

Beth made another mark on her nephew's homework. "Tuesday night," she said. "That's you, Susanna."

Tick, went an item on my mental list. Tuesday nights with Aunt Susanna. A traveling niece.

Everybody looked at Susanna, who handed a bag of doughnuts to a customer, then put up her hands. "PJ," she said, "weren't you helping her?"

A big, handsome boy looked up from the pastry counter, where he was arranging a tray of biscuits. He looked like his father and uncle. They all did. "Don't ask me."

"Well," Beth said. "It's gone now."

"Aileen lost a book?" said one of the youngest boys. He was moving from table to table, filling napkin dispensers.

Another boy laughed. "The Great Organizer lost a book?"

Just then Aileen walked in, jangling the bells over the door. Her cheeks blazed with accomplishment, the sign completed.

"Razzleberry's not a word," the smallest boy grumbled. I guessed him to be ten and making a futile run for family pet.

Aileen sailed past him, holding her box of letters. "It's called poetic license, Owen," she informed him.

I laughed. She did have her mother's eyes, as it turned out, and as she looked at me, those navy-blue irises left a delicious streak of warmth across my face. The others smiled over, their faces soft as cake batter, as if to say *Isn't she something? Our little girl?*

"Aileen," Callie said. "Think. Where did you have your notebook last?"

"I already did it over," Aileen said, settling herself at Beth's table. "I like writing about explorers."

Now everyone was shaking their heads, all love and puzzlement, a burbling murmur that surrounded this child like smoke. *She did it over! Imagine the perseverance!* The children put away their mops and Windex bottles, picked out a bagel or a muffin and a carton of milk each, and parked themselves at various tables to eat. One of the husbands came around from behind the counter, pausing to touch a son or nephew on the shoulder—they were always touching one another, I noticed, as if counting heads—then continued toward Aileen with the aplomb of a fancy waiter. "And the lady's having?"

"Half a cup of cocoa, please, Uncle Kevin."

He wrote it on a pretend pad. "Would that be the top half or the bottom half?"

Aileen giggled indulgently, and her uncle smiled down at her. This routine of his was stale as old bread—no one else so much as raised an eyebrow—and yet there she sat, giggling. I could see she was a kind child. One of my uncles used to call me "cuckoo-girl," which sent me into spasms when I was four, but I kept laughing all the way into my teens, infused with pity.

After a moment the other uncle—Pat, his name was—came out with a mug of hot chocolate and a delicate froth of a pastry, an exquisite-looking strawberry something-or-other that looked like a bouquet of roses. How such a creation sprang from the thick, homely hands of those brothers was a mystery to me. Did those men ever envy Roger Reed, I wondered, with his long, slender fingers sorting pills into bottles?

"Try this," Pat said. "My latest."

"Pat," Beth said. "It's too much sugar this early."

"But she's my official taster," Pat said. "That's why we pay her the big bucks."

Beth looked to her sisters, who merely shrugged or smiled. Aileen munched awhile in silence. "Good," she said. "Really, I like it."

"It needs a name," he prodded her.

"Something with no *b*'s," Aileen said. "I'm almost out of *b*'s."

"You know who would've loved those?" Callie called over.

Aileen's eyes snapped to the photo on the counter. "Who?"

"Your mother."

The words *your mother* hovered hotly. An odd silence descended, and it was then I truly saw her for the first time, this little child holding up everything in the world. When the hub of your family dies, you have two choices. Either you drop and roll like a bunch of broken spokes, or you find a new hub. It struck me as a tall order for an eight-year-old girl.

"How about Strawberry Dream?" Aileen said. "Only one *b*."

Pat nodded indulgently. "That's possible. That's got legs."

The children took this as their cue to leave. One of the oldest boys picked up Aileen's sweater and handed it to her. "If you're riding with me, you'd better come on." A second wave of customers flurried in, and the place once again took on a sound I found inexplicably moving: the rattle of doughnuts being packed into bags, the snap of coffee lids, the metallic clicking of the cash register, the clunk of car doors opening and closing, the mechanical heartiness of good-mornings and how-are-yous.

Wasn't that the sound of a family getting on with life? The sound of forgiveness?

At this point I was grinning crazily, finished with my muffin, watching the way of this family—this was a family with a *way* about them, not the hilter-kilter of my family scattered all over, our common memories splintered like a run-over bottle. I watched these people give to one another: hugs and kisses, sweet looks, long strands of laughter, endearments, bread and coffee.

Aileen went outside surrounded by boys—their swaggery voices and Godzilla feet and many agitations. Some got into cars, some started down the hill walking. She was a button in their midst, small and dainty compared even to the youngest boys with backpacks hoisted onto their shoulders. I got up then, following them out. I watched them disappear, all those kids who made one family. As I walked across the lot back to the car, I eyed the houses—the two side-by-sides and the triple-decker. In all of them the windows were cheerfully curtained, the same kid-made lawn ornament—a goose with a bow tie—stuck into the melting snow. Three houses that made one house.

"Tell me," John said, rushing from the car, hands opened.

I put my arms around him and he held me fast. "She's like

you," I told him. "Sweet and willing. Filled with dreams." Through his coat I could feel his shuddering; I felt the same way, giddy, alive, fearful, as if we'd been lost in the woods and found the gingerbread house in the clearing.

"What else?" he asked.

"Well, they adore her," I said.

We settled back into the car and I made my report: "We can forget the uncles. There are man families and woman families, and what we've got here is a woman family." I counted off my findings: "Callie's the long-haired one, she's married to Kevin. His brother Pat is married to Susanna, the one with the bad haircut. I couldn't quite match up the boys. If the mother's still around she's in a home or something. Nobody mentioned her."

"He wasn't Catholic, he wasn't from the neighborhood, he wasn't even from Maine," John said quietly. "Roger must have seemed so alien to them."

Hot from sleuthing, I took my coat off; the weather was truly a trick from heaven. We huddled together for a while longer, then Beth stepped into the street, her car keys jangling in her hand as she walked back toward her building.

"There's your door, by the way," I said. "Right there. The one you forgot."

"You missed your calling, Rita," he said. "You should've joined the FBI." He was so happy. He loved me so much right then.

You would think we'd have seized the day, interrupted Beth as she was starting her car, called her that evening, knocked on her door. But John said wait, and I felt what he felt: fascination, awe, maybe even a titch of fear. The next day found us back in that lot, watching the Saturday version of the family dance, the kids loaded down with hockey sticks and ice skates as they herded into the bakery for chores. Aileen introduced Strawberry Dream to the world on her sign, Beth took Aileen and three of the boys someplace in her car, the other boys went somewhere with Callie, Susanna stayed to work in the bakery. On Sunday the bakery was closed, but out they came, spilling down the steps, dressed for church. Again they came out of the three houses that made one house, flocked like finches. "I don't know how they breathe," I said to John.

On Friday morning Aileen came out of Beth's house. On Saturday morning Aileen came out of Callie's house. On Sunday morning Aileen came out of Susanna's house.

They were a family of fierce devotions. I could see what Roger Reed might have been afraid of. But here's the thing: I wanted them. This family whose world was small enough that we could see it all. They blurred the lines between son and nephew, niece and daughter, sister and wife, brother and husband. A close family, tight. Tight as a fist, no way in or out.

But I wanted them. I wanted to go to that family with the man of my dreams and make them love me.

8

On Sunday evening, winter came back. John parked the car on Morning Street and we got out. We looked up at Beth's house, three floors with three porches open to the starless night. Cold air funneled down our necks.

"I hope this isn't a bad sign," John said, closing the top of his coat.

"There's no such thing as a bad sign," I said. "Only bad interpretations."

"Are you sure?" he said, peering up at a night so cold it looked breakable.

"Positive. Come on."

I waited for him to move, to take that first step into the rest of his life.

Instead, he remained where he was, standing at the foot of Beth's stairs. "Six people came to Roger's funeral," he murmured. "Me, the funeral-home folks, and my landlady. She was a nice woman." His face looked like a stopped clock, blank and round. "No one wanted anything to do with it. Not that I blame them, I don't. But I kept hoping somebody—anybody—could find it in themselves to say I'm sorry for your loss. Isn't that what you say? I'm sorry for your loss? My brother, dead. My sister-in-law, dead. I couldn't stand it. But, see, neither could anybody else."

I was listening hard as the sky filtered down, big and black and merciless.

"I had some friends back then," he went on. "They were shocked at what Roger did. But it was me they couldn't look at." He made a brief, bristly shudder, then began to inch up the stairs, holding tight to my hand. "There was this one woman in Accounting who came to me on my first day back," he said quietly, his feet bearing down gently on each tread. "She had these sharp little heels that clicked across the floor. She kept saying how horrible it all was—horrible, horrible, horrible, she kept saying—which is kind of like saying I'm sorry for your loss, but at the same time she's looking at me like I'm the one who did it." He stopped on the first landing. "Rita, I tried with all my might to hate his guts. I never even put a headstone on his grave."

He hunched toward me, the weight of the past five years perched like a crow on his shoulder. "Come on," I whispered, then led him up the remaining flights.

At first I thought he might not do it. But then he cleared his throat, removed one glove, and knocked. She opened the door, a plain wooden door with a curtained window—no chain, no screen, nothing but a sheet of cold to divide us. She stood in the open doorway, the creamy light of her kitchen burning behind her.

"Hello, Beth," John said.

She flinched, as if a ghost, trailing blood and tatters, had spirited itself through her door. In this light she seemed almost pretty, with long, lovely arms and smooth hands that she brought to her face. "Oh," she said, covering her mouth. "Oh."

"It's John Reed," John said. He looked mortified. "It's me, John."

"Your . . . voice," she said. She spread her arms across the doorway.

His voice. Is that how Roger had sounded, like clouds, like warm water, like lavender yarn?

"What do you want?" she asked, not unkindly. Alone, she looked different. Within the flock of family, she had seemed like a smaller-boned woman. Here she was bigger, her shoulders more square, the kind of person whose secrets took up room. I guessed her to be thirty-three or so, a little younger than me, but she seemed years older, lifetimes older.

"Might we come in?" I said.

"This is Rita," John said, taking my hand. "She brought me here."

Beth looked at me. "I saw you in the bakery." She eyed us both warily. "Have you been *watching* us?"

"Not in the way you mean," John said quickly. "It took a couple of days to work up some courage."

She stood there, taking this in. "I don't understand what you want."

"It's freezing out here," I said.

After another moment she dropped her arms from the doorway and stood aside.

The kitchen looked a lot like the kitchen I grew up in. Commemorative plates hanging on the wall, rooster wallpaper, the whole shebang. Not only had she kept the family homestead, she had enshrined it. John cleared his throat again, smiling nervously. Could she see, now, how silly was her mistake? Could she see his generous belly, his soft, rounded jaw, his whole body a testament to how far from his brother he had fled? They stood there, their dear departed ones settling like mist between them.

"Might we sit down?" I said finally, breaking an awkward silence. I slipped off my jacket and made myself a place at her table.

John sat next to me, Beth across from us. In the center of the table sat a jelly jar full of tulips, the kind of thing a woman buys for herself. I liked her already. There was something sweet and spinstery about the place, the kind of place that always has an extra lightbulb handy, a place where the person, who sincerely believes God cares about her life, does nice things for herself anyway in case He has no current plans to do likewise.

Next to the tulips was a sketchbook with *Aileen Doherty* scrawled on the front in pink sparkle paint. I put my finger on her signature: It felt warm.

"Aileen isn't here," Beth said. Across the street the twin houses were fully lighted, both kitchens filled with a mother and a father, boys revolving around them like satellites. In one of the kitchens Aileen was helping Callie tip a pot of spaghetti, or maybe it was rice, into a big green bowl. This was how close the view.

John glanced around. "Your mother—?"

"She died," Beth said. She placed a hand on her chest. "Her heart. It was about a year after Laura."

"I'm sorry for your loss," John said.

"Thank you," she said. She waited. "I don't like it that you watched us."

"It was my idea," I said. "Blame me."

She glanced at me, then back at John. She was at least listening.

"I was so afraid to be turned away again," John said softly. "I was looking for the right, the right door." Oh, the sound of his voice!

I could see her softening; the delicate skin around her eyes gave way. After a long wait, she said, "We played cards once."

John nodded vigorously, remembering. "You were home on vacation, I believe."

"You were visiting," she said. "On a business trip?"

"Yes," he said. "We played Crazy Eights. You and Laura and me and, and my brother."

She looked kind, though she was not smiling. But I sensed the surprise of a good memory letting air into the room: four ordinary people playing cards, sunlight carpeting through the windows, four ordinary lives not yet touched by the terrible turns of fate.

"Aileen was just a newborn," Beth said to me. She paused, then looked straight at John. "That was a nice visit," she said. "I thought you were a nice person."

"He *is* a nice person," I said. "He's a wonderful person."

She looked down. "I didn't mean to imply—"

"That's all right," John said.

I asked myself, How could he have forgotten her? But of course he had not forgotten her. He had *removed* her, taken her out of his memory because he did not want this kind woman to become part of that wall of family standing near the bucket of water, saying *no.* She had a strong face. She had found the bodies. She had suffered the most.

We had decided to move slowly, sniff the air, so to speak,

show Beth all of John's good intentions. Don't ask for much. Take baby steps. But I'll admit I was already imagining the long haul, vacations to the White Mountains, the three of us—John, Aileen, and me—perched on a log and singing camp songs as birds and birches flared in the setting sun. I braid Aileen's hair, let her try on my wedding ring. Eventually we have two girl cousins for her to dote on, two little girls with bow-shaped mouths, a shower of grace from her father's side of the family. But for now we were to make one simple request.

"I'd like to see her," John said. "I've missed her so terribly. She was such a sweet baby. Wasn't she a sweet baby?"

Beth smiled faintly. I found myself wishing I knew what she knew: the *before* version of John Reed, the sunny visitor to her sister's house, the besotted uncle stopping by on his rounds. The man whose silence was just shyness, not shame; a man who could make that little bow without a trace of apology.

"I wrote her some letters," he was saying. "Little bits of news, where I'm playing this week or how the neighbor cat is coming along after having the kittens. Things I thought a kid might get a kick out of." He had to stop here to catch his breath. "Would you have given them to her? I mean, if I'd sent them?"

"I don't know," she said. "We would have had to explain so much."

"I've been so sorry," John murmured.

"Yes," she said. "It's been very hard."

"Don't think I haven't thought of her."

"I didn't."

He shifted inside his coat but still did not take it off. "Does she remember back then?" he asked.

"She knows what happened to Laura, if that's what you're asking." She squeezed her hands together. "I found Aileen in her bed after I found—everything else. There's no way to know what she heard or saw." She looked down again. "She doesn't remember it, of course. She was barely three. They'd left a radio on, maybe to block out their voices. But there's no way to know what she heard or saw."

He kept looking at her.

"We don't talk about it," she said. "If she remembers you, she hasn't said."

There was a long, terrible pause.

John cleared his throat. "She's eight now? A third-grader?"

"Fourth. They put her ahead."

Then I asked a question, just to see her turn those kind eyes upon me: "Where does she live?"

"Here," Beth said. "I'm her legal guardian. But that was just a formality. Somebody's name had to go on the paper. We're all raising her together. That's what we decided."

She said this in the most normal-sounding tone imaginable, but just then a tick of intuition went off in my head, and I began to detect just the smallest discontent, a little bitty something that felt like a belt cinched too tight.

John glanced around. "Well, this is a nice place for a little girl. Very nice."

"Actually, she stays one night a week with each of my sisters," Beth said. "Sometimes more. It depends. They each have a room for her." Color began to burn faintly in her cheeks, the red-orange of yearning. Her body began to move a little; her fingers tapped against her sides ever so slightly. Tap. Tappity. Tap.

"I didn't forget her, Beth," John said. "Not for a day."

"I believe you," is what she said.

John still had his coat on, looking terribly like a stranger, but I could see our unfolding future in the strong, forgiving planes of Beth Doherty's face.

"I'm her uncle," John said then, in that warm-water tone. What else was there to say? I could see how it pained her a little to hear the lovely roundness of his voice, and also how she was beginning to hear it not as his brother's voice, but his alone.

"Yes," she said. "You are."

And there it was. We had chosen the right door.

"May I?" John asked, sliding the sketchbook toward him. He began to leaf through it. "Oh, Rita," he whispered. "Here she is, look at her." She did seem to be there, in the sparkle-paint pictures of snowmen and horses and birds, everything bright and oversized, rolling right off the pages. This child had the life wish of a stunt pilot; her pink and purple lines looped and spun.

At the end of the book she'd squeezed in some family portraits, all the aunts and uncles and cousins arranged on a horizontal line. There was something prim and orderly about them, especially after the runaway horses and flapping birds. Eight boy cousins, three aunts, two uncles. Her own red-haired self floated somewhere above them, her feet dangling down like Christmas ornaments. In some of the drawings she sketched in props to identify them: a tin of muffins, a hockey stick, a baker's apron. She gave nothing to herself except air.

The phone rang. Beth jangled out of her seat and grabbed it on the second ring. It was an old-time dial phone mounted to the wall. She spoke with her back to us, in low tones. Across the street in one of the kitchens, Susanna stood at the window, squinting over, a portable phone pressed to her ear. I leaned toward the window for a better look. It was then I saw the lost notebook, dropped down behind the baseboard. *Aileen Doherty,* it read on the front. *GEORGRAPHY NOTES! IMPORTANT!!!* I slipped it into my purse as Beth hung up the phone. John started to say something but I shook my head, hard.

Beth came back to the table. "Aileen's quite the little Picasso," I said. "Maybe she inherited some creativity from her uncle here."

Beth lifted her arm and in one soft, liquid motion closed the blinds. They made a little click and the family in the windows disappeared. We were alone. Beth looked at John. "You still play the piano?"

He nodded, his jaw relaxed, he was thinking I'm home free, we've done it, I'm an uncle again. He began to take off his coat, then didn't. "You were in nursing school back then," he said. He made it sound like a very long time. "And after that it was, it was Mass General, right?"

She nodded. "Pediatrics. I'm a school nurse now," she said. "It was the only thing I could find with regular hours."

On the stove was a covered pot, and next to it one bowl. I was beginning to get a glimpse of all she had forsaken. A job in Boston, a sunny apartment, maybe, with a view of the Charles; perhaps there had been a man ready to marry her, a man who didn't want a child tottering room to room, calling for her dead parents. So Beth came back home, put on some regular hours like a dowdy sweater, and let her brand-new skills dry up in a numbing parade of ear infections and head lice. All this for the pleasure of a child she was condemned to raise by committee.

"Wait here," she said, then got up to rummage in a cupboard, high up. "I saved these for you," she said to John, handing him a few wallet-sized photos of Aileen, one for each school year.

I leaned over his shoulder as he looked at them, Aileen's babyish face becoming sharper, wiser, fierce with questions. I could see what it might mean to this family to bring Roger—the idea of Roger—back to her life. Beth's face had softened, but I could still recall her expression as she opened the door to us: *Oh no, not this, not now, not ever.*

"Thank you for these," John said, sliding the pictures into his breast pocket. Those pictures pained me, those piled-up years, those fleeting glimpses, a different haircut for every year.

"Why didn't you mail them?" I said.

John looked at me.

"I didn't know the address," Beth said.

"You could've found it. It would've made all the difference in the world."

John covered my hand. "Rita, I've moved ten, fifteen times since then." He turned to Beth. "I've moved a lot."

"Running," I said. "Running, running, running. From what his brother did."

"I'm sorry," Beth said. "I *could* have mailed it."

Now he did, he took off his coat. In his shirtsleeves he looked more like one of them, and suddenly I could imagine the two of us as part of this family of blurred lines, stepping into one of Aileen's family drawings and taking our place in line. The plain fact is, I was inside out with longing.

"I'm not running now," John said, squeezing my hand. "I'm right here."

Beth's eyes were closed. Probably she was seeing her dead sister, the bare feet bleached and still on the kitchen tile.

"I always wanted to think it was a sudden thing," John murmured. "That it was the drugs, not him. That he didn't mean it."

Her eyes opened, looking straight at John. "I blamed you." He was nodding, agreeing with her. "No," she said to him. "I'm apologizing."

"No need."

"Yes," she insisted. "There *is* need. There is need to apologize." Her color deepened, and she turned to me. "We loved her so dearly. She was more than just our sister. It's hard to explain." Her eyes were very blue and clear. "We've tried so hard to keep Laura alive for Aileen, but of course it's Aileen who keeps Laura alive for us."

I kept her gaze as their names floated and faded. It's no small thing to be pierced by another person's sorrow. She took a long breath, wiping her forehead with the heel of her hand. "I want to do what's best for Aileen. To do right by her."

John looked bewildered. "Are you saying I can see her?"

Tap. Tappity. Tap-tap-tap. "I want to know exactly what you're asking," she said.

He looked at me, confused, for where did he begin? With those little shoes ticking against his piano bench?

"He wants to meet her," I said.

John nodded. "If she likes us"—he said *us,* I remember how nice that sounded—"then maybe we could start a regular visiting schedule. We could make any number of arrangements."

"We've made so many arrangements already," Beth said. So very softly, she said this. The Queen of Cups, I realized then. Here she was, that benevolent woman. She had lost so much—her sister, her mother and father, a parallel life in Boston that surely haunted her at the times she had to look at that single soup bowl on the stove. Unlike ninety-nine percent of the human population, this good woman—this queen—possessed the capacity to think of somebody besides herself.

"She hasn't heard so much as Roger's name in five years," Beth said. "I'll need time to prepare her."

"How much time?" I asked.

"A week? Is that all right? Can you come back in a week?"

"Oh, Beth, thank you," John said, getting up. "I'm so grateful."

"My sisters will have to agree," she said. "This is—this isn't going to be easy."

"Isn't anybody in charge here?" I asked, suddenly choked with impatience.

She looked at me. Waited. "Yes," she said. "I am." And I saw her lips move over the word *I*.

"It's not my intention to cause anybody pain," John said. "It's just that"—here is where he looked at me—"not until recently did I recognize how, how silent my life had become."

I nearly swooned to hear this, that I had brought a sort of music into a silent life. Not many people can say that. I believed I had shepherded my King of Cups to his happy ending, and it looked exactly like the happy ending I would have designed for myself.

"Will you tell them," he said to Beth, "will you remind them that Laura liked me?"

"I will, yes."

"My brother was not a bad man," he murmured. "Maybe a little girl should know that about her father." The words seemed to cost him, for his shoulders dropped in surrender, and his mouth opened, and his tongue moved inside there, pink and panting. I had never seen the contortions of grief so evident on a man's face. I covered his hand with mine, feeling the sediment of five years, a bumpy coolness, like scar tissue, a welt for every time he had denied his brother.

Beth saw it, too, that hard-won forgiveness. She didn't say anything—what she thought of John's brother she kept to herself—but I could see she was able to separate what he meant to her from what he might mean to a little girl who had been denied the very mention of her father's name.

"I knew you'd come back," she said, standing in front of those closed blinds. Tappity-tappity-tappity. This woman was ready, she was ready to step out of this still-life and start taking charge.

We shook hands, exchanged phone numbers, and then John and I were back out in the cold. In one of the side-by-side houses the family was just gathering around the table. In the other their heads were bowed for grace, Aileen's red hair glowing beneath a hanging light.

"Do you think it would've been different," John asked, "if they had gotten to know me back then?"

"No question," I told him. "They'd have loved you like a brother."

He snugged his arms around me. We watched them for a few minutes before getting into the car.

"Rita," John crooned as he guided the car down the ramshackle of streets toward the highway. "Rita, Rita, Rita." He was smiling, clutching my hand across the seat, laughing a little bit now and then. "It wasn't all awful," he said. "I kept remembering nice things." Before we got to the entrance ramp, he pulled the car over.

"Marry me, Rita," he said. "Please, Rita. Marry me," begged this man who had never followed an impulse in his entire life. "You saved me," he said, his face lifting with wonder. "I was dead and now I'm alive."

I'll admit the phrasing gave me a turn. But the fact is, I could have said the same thing back to him. And I did so love the sound of his voice on my name.

And there was that child. An idea that had turned real, instead of the other way around. She existed. I had seen her.

Generally speaking, I don't make the same mistake twice. Not that I hadn't entertained thoughts of our future wedding, our two pink-cheeked babies, our twilight years playing golf in Arizona and buying toys for the grandkids. Oh, I wanted to say yes, to shout yes, to climb onto the roof of the car and holler yes at that stunning black sky. I'm a great believer in impulse myself. But I kept remembering that crippled dog. Despite his infirmity, and the heaviness of the stick he carried, that dog was headed someplace, following a scent he did not yet understand. I suppose my instinct was to wait a bit, to see how everything turned out. I had tried to save one man from a long sleep, after all, and wound up alone in my cold sheets.

He was waiting, his soft eyes damp with expectation, and I felt like the object of his desire. In the end, I suppose I decided to bide awhile just to savor the romance of it all.

So I did not say yes, exactly. "I believe in long engagements," is what I said.

"Then I'll wait forever," is what he said, and for a man long used to waiting, this was no idle promise. Imagine being wanted this much. I held him, hard, as the nighttime traffic zinged past.

Not until we crossed the Maine border did I remember the notebook hidden in my purse. "Look," I said to John, switching on the map light. She was a good student, everything spelled mostly right, periods at the end of all the sentences. She wrote about the early explorers, those stouthearted voyagers looped on life and setting sail for the edge of the earth. As we headed back to Massachusetts, the night darkening around us, our own journey just begun, I began to read aloud. John smiled, his hand resting on the seat beside me. I balanced the book on my lap, reading Aileen's dramatic accounts of Da Gama rounding the Cape, Magellan forging ahead to the Pacific, Ponce de Leon longing for the fountain, their eyes fixed to the horizon, looking for someplace to land.

9

I was a woman freshly proposed to, but after I got home I felt strange in my skin, less than my usual self. It was the way I felt sometimes when the cards didn't fall just right. None of what I remembered of Beth quite went together: that single bowl, her air of calm, her tapping fingers. She'd behaved graciously, clearly she was kind, but her eyes were deep and noisy, filled with all the things that make life worth living, namely, a struggle between what she wanted and what she got. As grateful as I was, as much as I liked her, I fought the notion of our fate being in her hands, her restless hands. To calm myself I kept indulging in a vision of that little girl walking down a beach between John and me, the setting sun sparking off her hair.

"You and your notions," said Mrs. Rokowski. "Those people won't let you have that little girl." She was squirming in the swivel, trying to get comfortable. She'd come in for her weekly set'n'style only to discover that the chair no longer fit. Shrinking is what she was doing, her poor blue ankles whittled down to sticks. I'd slipped a chair pad under her bottom so she could see herself in the mirror, and now she didn't like the feel of the foam. Her face looked like a dropped apple beneath the swirl of towel on her head.

"I didn't say anything about wanting to *have* her," I said. "John wants some regular visits, is all. I'll admit I'm the one who set things in motion, but this is his own private matter to work out. I'm just the helpmate."

"Allow me a doubt," she said, rolling her eyes, which were round and doll-like, an intense, marble blue.

"Fine, then. Who wouldn't want her? Smart and kind. How many people you know fit that description?"

"Not a one," she agreed. This was the sort of mood we were both in. Her arthritis was acting up, and I had a head full of plans.

"All right, Mrs. I-Know-Everything," I said, drubbing her head with the towel. "So I'd like to see her once in a while. What's the crime?"

"She's no relation to you."

"She will be."

"After a long engagement," she said, tsking all over the place. "A girl your age snags a man, she should speed him to the altar on the express train."

"My first engagement lasted a week," I told her. "Look where that ended up."

"That time you were too young."

Mrs. Rokowski had an answer for everything, which is why I liked her. She claimed to believe only half of anything I ever said, but I noticed she turned up her hearing aid whenever she stepped into the shop. She lived with her husband, Albert, in one of the few original Alton neighborhoods, on River Street near the mill. I confided in her because she didn't carry tales. Most of her friends were dead anyway.

"I want what you did last time," she said, waving one crinkled hand at her damp hair. "Only not so fouffy on the top."

"That's what gave height to your head. The fouff was the whole secret." Mrs. Rokowski has a head shape that can be most kindly compared to a squashed squash—no forehead, no chin.

She eyed me in the mirror, up and down. When I worked on her I didn't wear my smock, which reminded her too much of hospitals. "When you went up there on your goose chase, I hope you didn't wear something like that."

I looked at myself. "Like what?"

"That dress. What's that little ruffly thing, looks like a lion's mane."

I smoothed the flounces at my chest. "It's supposed to make me look like I've got a bustline. I thought it looked nice."

"On a lion."

"This isn't what I wore, anyway."

"And that nail polish," she went on. She picked up my hand, not without affection. "This shade of orange is fit for a hunting trip."

"They keep sending me this stuff, I can't just toss it."

"All I'm saying is you might've scared them off, dressed like you escaped from the circus. Some helpmate."

"Well, excuse me all over the place."

"Don't get huffy," she said. "It doesn't matter what-all you wore, I'm sure your sweetness shined right through."

Which was like something Gram might have said. Mrs. Rokowski was one of the few people I knew who remembered her. They used to frequent the sewing shop that the Rancourts ran over on Spring, back when this town still had a comprehensible purpose. When I was growing up here, people stood together on street corners for long, indulgent chats about their sick babies or new wallpaper. They really did. An eyeblink later, I was living in a house with an Italian restaurant on my west side, and on the east side a raft of outlet stores that had recently expanded its hours to midnight to accommodate all those emergency purchases of Birkenstocks and cappuccino machines.

I kissed my fingers and pressed them to the top of Mrs. Rokowski's head, grateful that she used to see my grandmother, and me, and other people I used to know, back when Alton was still a real town.

"What was the name of that sewing shop over on Spring?" I asked. "I can picture it clear as a bell but can't recall the name."

She tapped her head. "If you hadn't asked me, I could tell you." We were conversing through the mirror as I stood behind her, rolling her hair.

"Something cutesy, I think," I said.

She cocked her head, then shook it. "I had it, but it's gone. Now I'll be up all night."

By the time I got Mrs. Rokowski settled under the dryer—her knees were cold and I had to tuck a warmed towel around her legs—the phone rang. It was John.

"She said no," he quavered. "Maybe when she's a little older, she said. But not now." He cleared his throat. "Rita, she said no."

I glanced up the length of my shop. I had two walk-ins waiting and a jittery realtor fuming in the chair. "Didn't she say she'd tell them?" I whispered, cupping the receiver. "She *said* she'd tell them

Laura liked you. She said she was thinking of Aileen, what's best for Aileen."

"It wasn't her," he said. "It was them." His breath was quick and shallow. "Was I just dreaming?"

"We'll get a lawyer," I said. "You have rights. You're the uncle, same as them."

"I need you, Rita. Can I come over tonight?" he asked.

"Every night. All my life. I love you, I love you, I love you." How I wanted to weep, that he was all I had.

"Can you hurry *up?*" said the woman in the chair, Edie, her name was; we went to high school together and now she worked for Dryden Real Estate, which had sold most of East Main to Danforth Outlet Centers, Incorporated. She was one big bramble of split ends, which is what a couple of years at Shazaam will do to a person; she cowered beneath her wrecked hair as if she couldn't bear to belong to her own body one more second.

"I can fix that," I told her. "You're gonna look like you never had one troubled day."

"Fix *what?*" she said. "I'm in a hurry." Being in a hurry was part of her outfit. She had on a smart little suit, a pair of matching heels, and thought of herself as one of the people who moved here *after,* though in truth she'd grown up in a peeling three-story on Gleason Street. This is what the town had become, befores and afters. She barked little orders at me—clearly she liked to think of me as a "before," as if I'd never been anywhere past the LEAVING ALTON sign, never read a book or held an interesting conversation. The whole time she was putting on her act, I was thinking of our tenth-grade class picture with her slip hanging four inches below her hemline.

After I closed up for the day, I took a walk by the river, which I had to admit was a little more picturesque without the noise and the smell, the mill's belching stacks. I didn't miss the yellowish foam that used to settle on the banks, the peels of bark that used to float down the water like thrown-out hamburger wrappers. They say you can fish in this river now, though I wouldn't test that theory myself. Looked at in a certain light, it's not so bad, what's happened here. Business is brisk; I'm not complaining about that. And I'll be the first one to admit that the mill was not the most pleasant place to spend your working life, especially if you were my father with his delicate need for solitude. He was not a happy man, is not a happy man, but I believe he felt something when he brought home those stiff white packs of paper on which Darla and I drew pictures of our house and street, on which my mother wrote lists like *beets, milk, shampoo.* He would set it down before us like a prize, that bleached, razor-edged paper, as if to say *I made this.* Or perhaps he merely wanted to show where our money came from. I don't know. It's just that when I was a child there was more of a connection between what you thought your life was and what it actually was. That I miss.

When I got back to the house, I let Sheldon out and started supper. I dearly wanted some sound in the place, but it takes some effort to get Sheldon going sometimes. I made a bunch of kissy noises and sang a few bars of "She'll Be Comin' 'Round the Mountain," but he just sat there with all the get-up of a grape. So I got out a tape of a basketball game and popped it into the VCR I keep for him in the kitchen. Sheldon loves the sound of sneakers on hardwood, and within minutes the room filled with not only the voice-over of Bob Cousy and Tommy Heinsohn announcing a game from the Celtics' glory days but the hoarse burbling of Sheldon, who, though he didn't know any words, created a sort of bird static that made me feel less alone. Thus serenaded, I set the table, which gave me a great pleasure: two plates, two sets of utensils, two glasses. I almost set out three, just to see how it might look. Already I was missing the possibility of that little girl in my house. Her place at the table took on an absence that had presence, an emptiness that filled with something close to a color.

All day long I'd been thinking of my childhood friend Margaret Thibodeau. Her house was a big green thing filled to the rafters with her Franco-American family—a boatload of brothers and sisters, a mother and father, four bouffanted aunts who flitted in and out with their bald-headed babies. In Margaret's house they sat on the screen porch summer nights singing in French, terrible sad songs about dead soldiers and lovers flinging themselves over cliffs. On certain lucky days, when Margaret chose me over the other girls on our street, I sat at their dinner table, eating their sinful, greasy food and hanging on their shrieky talk and laughter. Then Gram moved in with us, and my house became interesting enough that I no longer had to wait for a summons from Margaret.

I peered out the window, hoping for John's car. Sheldon sat on my shoulder, nibbling at my ear. "Oh, baby," I said to him, "I'm lonesome." So I found an old, old number in my address book and dialed my sister.

"This is the House of Peace," said the ghost-voice that answered the phone.

"Darla Cooper, please."

"You want to speak with Patience," said the voice. They picked one name where Darla lived, like rock stars.

"Fine, then," I said. Patience was something Darla never had one detectable shred of, but I wasn't about to get into that with him. "Tell her it's her sister."

He put me on hold with a sitar for about fifteen minutes. Apparently old Patience was busy hoeing cabbages or making incense. My sister, the smart one in the family. The artistic one. The rebel.

There was a click, and another hesitation.

"Did somebody die?" Darla asked.

I hadn't talked to her since her birthday eight months previous, which was no longer her birthday, as it turned out—there was some other calendar they used that put her spiritual birthday on roving months in alternating years. "Everything's fine," I told her. "I didn't mean to scare you."

"What do you want?"

"Darla," I said, "please, please don't use that voice."

"What voice?"

"It sounds like you're talking to me from a lake on the moon."

"I can't imagine what you mean," she said. "Why did you call me?"

Now, that was a good question. I had no idea. "Do you remember Margaret Thibodeau?" I asked her.

"No."

Which was a lie, since she used to hang around with Margaret's older brother, Frank. They had sex in the sumac grove by the railroad track one summer night, which she confessed to me after sliding back in through our bedroom window, drunk. It was one of our few intimate conversations, though I had to keep holding her head over a bucket and praying our parents wouldn't hear.

"They were Catholics. The house next to ours."

"Maybe," Darla said. "I guess I vaguely remember. Did she die or something?"

"Honestly, Darla, that place has you obsessed with death." I tried to picture her in a sari, or a black shift, or whatever uniform they wore in winter. In high school Darla ran around in fishnet stockings, and the second she graduated rattled off to Worcester to live with her boyfriend, who dumped her in less than a week. The House of Peace swooped in shortly thereafter, recognizing an easy mark: She was aching to get out of Alton and couldn't find a boy willing to marry her just then. Plus Gram had taken a long time to die and she didn't like the smell in our house. One of their envoys met her in a Burger King and that was that.

"What do you look like?" I asked her.

"What's that supposed to mean?"

"I mean, would I know you anymore?"

"I hope not," she said. The last I'd seen her was at my wedding, her last normal act before officially "renouncing" us.

"You'd know me," I told her. "I change my hair color every few weeks, but it's the same old me." She didn't answer, so I kept going. "I met a family that reminds me of the Thibodeaus. All chummy like that. There's a little girl who lives with them. Her parents are dead, and they're all raising her together. She goes from house to house. Do you think that's good or bad?"

"Is this why you called?"

"They all love her," I went on. "Everybody Loves Me, that's her. But I wonder if belonging to everybody is a lot like belonging to nobody."

"What are you talking about?"

"Nothing."

"How's Layton?"

"We've been divorced for three million years, Darla. Don't you listen?"

"I forgot."

"I'm engaged," I said. "I met him in a dream." Nothing. "What about you, any wedding bells?"

"I've given myself to someone. We don't have weddings. It's better than a wedding. It's a sacred trust."

"The swami won't let you have a wedding? It's not enough he took your money and your clothes?"

"I *shed* those things. And Kenneth isn't a swami. He's a prophet. A prophet who has God's ear."

Of course, she had told me this before—along with the blow-by-blow on the Seven Stages of Peace. My sister believed she was quite literally disappearing, becoming ever-increasingly peaceful until the day she and her new "family" would become nothing but air, which is to say, one with the breath of God. The way I perceived it—and I didn't like to ask too many questions—the devotees of Kenneth Boyd, Ph.D., were planning some sort of mass exit, not a Jonestown-type thing, but a resurrection of some kind, bypassing something as mundane as death and instead ascending to heaven on a puff of air, their earthly bodies dissolving like sugar and leaving nary a trace. Apparently the rest of us were doomed to get there the old-fashioned way, by living a decent life and then dying of cancer and meeting St. Peter at the gates.

"God's ear?" I asked. "Says who?"

She didn't answer questions like this. Questions like, Ph.D. from where? But she didn't hang up. Probably she was racking up points for every minute she stayed on the phone describing the route to heaven to one of her misguided relatives.

"What's the name of your betrothed?" I asked.

"Dance."

"Dance? That's his name?"

"Yes."

"That's his actual name?"

"Is there anything else you wanted?" She was testing the outer limits of her new name now, her words hard and measured.

"Are you going to have kids?"

"When Kenneth confirms our union."

"When will that be?"

"When we've both reached the fifth stage."

Conversations like this exhausted me. "Don't wait too long, Darla," I said. "You're not getting any younger."

"Actually," she said, "I am."

"I just remembered why I called," I said.

She waited a moment. "My time's almost up."

"Do you remember the name of that sewing shop Gram used to like over on Spring?"

"No."

"It's a Starbucks now. You don't remember what it was called?"

I could hear something in the background, a peaceful tolling. Sometimes—not often—I could almost understand why my sister had gone there.

"No," she said.

"Well, thanks for trying. Do you want to know how Mom and Dad are? Besides being not dead?"

She didn't answer. Instead she tuned me out, breathing loudly.

Inhale, hold, exhale. Inhale, hold, exhale. It was very annoying.

"They're fine," I went on. "I call them once a month. They get on both extensions and start hissing at each other."

"There was no love in our home, Rita," Darla said.

"There was plenty of love in our home, Darla Cooper," I told her, striking hard on her old name. "You had to be willing to look for it."

Inhale, hold. "Ten minutes are up, Rita."

"They are? It feels more like five."

Exhale. "They called it the Bob-In," she said. "That sewing shop. It was supposed to be a play on the word *bobbin*."

For a moment we fell silent, steeped in what I hoped was a communal nostalgia for the landmarks of our childhood that had disappeared into light.

"Darla," I said, "I love you," which is what I always said at the end of these conversations.

"Thank you," she said, and was gone.

The fact is, sometimes you did have to look kind of hard for love in our home. After Darla renounced us, my parents contacted a cult deprogrammer who told us to go out there and get her. One of the keys was to say over and over to the cult victim: "I love you." But my parents couldn't do this; their vocal chords would not take those three words in one gulp. We flew to San Diego and headed to the House of Peace straight from the airport. A guy in a white choir robe showed us into a tree-filled waiting room, a courtyard that opened to the sky and stank of compost. The floor was hard and tiled, stained from rain. There were no chairs. The walls contained seven framed photographs of the swami, encased in glass to protect him from the elements. We stood there in our wrinkled traveling clothes, our suitcases lying like spiritual baggage at our feet. After about ten minutes my sister came in, draped in an orange tunic reminiscent of a prison uniform. Without a word she sat on the floor, cross-legged, looking straight ahead. I scrambled down to get her at eye level, but my parents remained standing, looking useless as a couple of bowling pins left after the second try.

My sister was thin from eating too much seaweed and brewer's yeast. But she was bright-eyed, with pink in her cheeks. She looked happier than her usual, which still wasn't saying much. Our eyes caught, and I thought I got a glimpse of the old Darla—arrogant, demanding, competitive, my one and only sister.

"You'd never make it here," she said, as if in my wildest dreams I would entertain such a notion. "You've got too many ideas about your importance in the world."

If I hadn't been so horrified I might have laughed—leave it to Darla to find an arrogant way to express her own humility. "Oh, Darla," I said, flinging out my arms. She did hug me back, briefly—she at least did that—but then she caught herself, looked at my parents, and asked why they had come.

"What in Sam Hill is the meaning of this letter?" my father demanded, pulling out the letter Darla had sent each of us, about renouncing us in favor of her new family, and then two pages inviting us to join her "path," to "go toward peace," to give ourselves over to the "ruling spirit," and like that. Then a three-page blurb on Dr. Kenneth Boyd, who, according to the letter, had Ph.D.s in everything from agronomy to zoology, all part of the path that led him to a "day of revelation" when God chose him to cultivate peace in the world. This is actually how these people talked.

"We scrimped and saved to have our daughter fall for this

shyster?" my mother shrieked. She stamped her tiny feet on the rainy tiles.

I watched the words float through my sister's bright eyes. I envied her that much. "Go toward peace," she kept saying. That, and "Look inside yourselves," and "There was no love in our home." She had all the lines, which I found out later they memorize for just such occasions. My father blew up, my mother cried and hollered, I repeated "I love you" like a trained parrot. After ten minutes the choir-robe guy appeared in the doorway behind her.

I don't know how she even knew he was there, but she rose, giving us this eerie little salute: her hand lifted, her palm turned toward us, the idea being that she was dousing us with some sort of God-air that they channeled through their palms. They all did this. Really. She was bestowing God's cleansing breath on our smothered souls. Then she left. I stayed on the floor for a few minutes longer, then went out with my parents, foiled utterly.

"You could have said it," I told my parents. I followed them out the long brick path we'd just come through, a path burgeoning with overwrought rosebushes and some kind of oddball blue grass. "Why couldn't you just *say* it?"

"She knows we love her," my parents said, nearly choking on the magic word. "She's our daughter, for heaven's sake."

"You have to say it," I said. Oh, those three little words. In six months I would be married to Layton Rosario because of those three little words. "Why couldn't you just *say* it?"

Well, they couldn't. Instead they went to the attorney general's office, and to one of the city councilors, and to the better business bureau, all of whom told us these people were harmless, operating entirely within the law so far as they knew. They reminded us that Darla was a grown-up woman with a mind of her own.

So my parents gave up. We got on a plane for home. This is how unwilling they were to say that one-two-three.

After I hung up with Darla, I kept my hand on the phone, thinking maybe she was doing the same. Hoping. A few minutes later John arrived, puffy-eyed, bewildered. He blundered through my door like a lost hunter crashing through the woods.

"I was so sure," he kept saying through our dinner, our walk by the river, our aching slide into bed.

"We'll look for a good lawyer," I said. "You can force them to give you visiting rights."

"And make enemies of them all?"

"She's afraid of those sisters of hers. Give her some courage. Tell her to stand up for herself and that child."

"They convinced her it's for Aileen's own good." His eyes reddened. "Maybe it is. How do I know what effect I might have on that child's innocence?"

"You think that little girl never wonders about her father?" I asked him. I sat up in bed and looked down at him. "You think she doesn't have a picture of her father in her head, his eyes bulging, his fist raised, intent on evil?"

"Rita, don't," he said. "It hurts."

"But listen. Along comes this other man, a man with soft eyes, a beautiful smile, pressed and sweet-smelling clothes. His voice sounds like a rain of pebbles. He can make a piano sound like a choir of angels. He's an ordinary man who can do no bad thing. How terrible can her father be, to have a brother such as this?"

He rested his hands on my bare hips, gazing into my eyes. "I'm willing to wait."

"That's no way to live, John," I said, welling up. "It's marking time, that's all it is. That child has a broken place that only you can heal."

"Rita," he whispered. "Let it go." It was then I heard it—a high, almost inaudible, silvery note of blame. It had been my plan, my urgings, my hand he took and followed. Maybe he didn't even hear it himself. He gentled me down into the bed again and held me hard, kissed my earlobes, cupped my face. I was used to his look of love and gratitude, but that night I saw something else. He reminded me of one of my customers, Kenny Batchelder, who won a living-room suite on a game show. He talked of nothing else for weeks, waiting for delivery, and then when the stuff finally came, the delivery guys couldn't fit it through Kenny's front door. That's how John looked, like a man who'd won a prize he couldn't fit into his cramped spaces.

"Maybe in a couple of years I can try again. She'll be older. She'll be able to understand. A couple of years, that's not so long."

"But it is, John, it *is.*"

"Rita," he whispered. "Listen to me. We get married, we have our two children, and someday, God willing, I'll get my chance to sit down with that child and tell her three good things." He ran his hand over my back as if petting a skittish cat. "The fact is, Rita, I've got no choice in the matter."

I said nothing for a while, wondering how to teach this tender man the difference between surrender and politeness. No choice. The words had a weird kind of weight, a certain snowy presence. I shook it off, remembering Layton's *I Had To* leaking out his body and marking itself on his face, in the downward-turning lines, the broken capillaries, in his joyless, pinned-back smile.

"There's no such thing as no choice, John. You can go back there."

"We'll make our own family, Rita."

I rested my hand over my stomach. "We don't know that, John. My plumbing's incomplete."

He smiled. "Some things you just know."

"Even so. Think of your poor little children, growing up with the burden of replacing a lost loved one."

"That's not how I'd feel."

"I won't do that to a child of mine, John. No, thank you. You have to—you have to *rectify* things—before you can move on."

"What things?"

"What Roger did. What he deprived you of. The affection of a lovely little child. Your only family. He took that from you, John. You have to go back there and take back what you lost."

He closed his eyes. "I'm just trying to see this from Beth's point of view. Isn't that what you do all the time? Try on the other person's shoes?"

"I suppose." He had me there. "Sort of."

"That's what I'm doing. She's got a whole lot more to think of than what would make me happy. I'm trying on her shoes. It helps some."

So there we were, lying side by side, that little girl dissolving, our desires suddenly appearing brazen, maybe even foolish, in retrospect. I felt grateful for his weight just then, for the physical certainty of him, the way he filled my bed. I didn't feel much like a helpmate, but I turned to him anyway, smoothing my hands over his eyes, his mouth, around the broad back of his neck, rocking him gently, gently. It was nothing, maybe it was even worse than nothing, but I was out of plans and this was all I had.

healing. Then she gathers the child, shields the small, startled face, and spirits her past the bodies and out the door and down the stairs. As she struggles over the two blocks home, she feels the small heart beating against hers, the hot breath wetting her neck, and as she reaches the corner, turning toward the twin houses, freighted with news, the child grows heavy and, miraculously, falls asleep.

Then what? She will have to tell them. She will have to bear their grief, and also their desires, and in the end she will have to share the child whose heart she feels thumping against her skin.

But now, in this moment, in this bubble of time between before and after, she feels suspended. There is nothing in the world but Laura's beautiful girl. She already knows what she will give up for the love of this little girl who inherited Laura's eyes. Her apartment in Boston, the sun, the River Charles, the man with flowers—they dissolve like smoke after fire. These things are gone. Just like that, these things are gone. There is nothing but this child.

PART 3 round and round

11

So I went back there. I rescheduled Amy Chang, Kenny Batchelder, the Dornan sisters, and Rodney, and on the following Friday—so early it was still dark—I headed north alone.

As I sped down the River Road, I thought of Beth in her kitchen bent over a cup of tea, thinking of her lost sister. I hoped that already she was regretting her decision. I hoped she could close the blinds on those twin sisters watching from their windows. Beth had bent to their wishes, hoping for the best. She had taken the path of least resistance, which is almost never the right path.

That's what we decided, Beth said, but how do you get five adults to land on one desire? I had seen firsthand how they kept their peace, how they bumped shoulders and smiled at one another, their life together one big please and thank you. That child grew among them like a prize dahlia. But who picked out her clothes? Who signed her report cards? How many times in a day did somebody want to shout *I,* when the word *we* was what they'd agreed upon, the word that kept them tethered to the earth?

I gunned the engine. The night was a big, black, bloomy thing, a surprise. The River Road unrolled before me, a long, bewitching curve, then the straight shot northward, that smooth, black, shimmering path. Above me the trees broke open, and the moon bore down, drenching everything with a strange, cool light: the road, the river, the part in the trees. I cracked open the window, calling *Hello, hello, hello,* and the trees whipping by answered *Yesss.*

My grandmother had weak eyes. She wore a pair of blue-frame glasses with wavy lenses that gave her the look of a seer. I liked to imagine a world the way she saw it: nothing too precise, just wave after wave of possibility. Often she took off her glasses when certain people spoke to her—my mother, my father, Darla, one or two of her Catholic ladies. Without glasses her eyes went dim in a way that made her seem deaf, and this kept people talking.

"Margaret Thibodeau has a lazy eye," I told her one morning as we were setting up the card table on the sunporch. Gram shook out the paisley tablecloth and let it drift down on the table. "She's getting a patch," I said. "Not a pirate patch or anything. It's blue with teeny flowers."

"Don't you go wishing for a lazy eye," said Gram, who could read my mind. "Those hawk eyes of yours are the best thing God gave you." She shuffled the cards, again and again, getting a feel before the Catholic ladies began to line up. "When I was your age I was terrified of losing my glasses. I used to hold them to my face with one hand when I walked home from school. I spent all my time scared." She peered down at me, her eyes floating behind her lenses. “Don’t you spend one minute scared if you can help it.”

“I won’t,” I said.

“You better not. Why do you think the good Lord gave you two feet?”

“I don’t know.”

“For jumping in with, Rita. Aren’t you listening?”

“I am.”

“Of course you are, you special thing,” she said, kissing me noisily, dropping her upper plate against her tongue, a sound of childhood I can still conjure when I need to. “Now, dear one, where’s my bandanna?”

I trotted back through the living room and kitchen and my mother’s telephone nook, squeezing myself between the high heavy sides of furniture, until I reached Gram’s dresser, where the bandanna lay folded into quarters. On my way back to the sunporch, my mother stepped out from between the sideboard and the hutch. “Where do you think you’re going with that?” she demanded.

“I’m helping Gram.”

She put her hands on her hips, but the way her fingers flickered, I realized she actually wanted to have her hands on me; to touch me, reminding herself that she had once done something right. Gram had taught me this, long before you saw all these boatloads of books on body language. I watched my mother’s fingers: I was her favorite, the easy one. Darla had been brought home the night before, late, by my red-faced father. We thought she was drowned, murdered, left in a ditch to die. But she’d been sitting on the riverbank, smoking cigarettes with those kids from River Street. My mother was exhausted, her face streaked and ashy, so I put my arms around her to quiet those poor fluttery fingers. She sighed, long and hard. "Rita, you're my one good girl. Don't listen to that nonsense from your grandmother. She isn't right in the head, and your father has no spine when it comes to that woman, so I have to turn my house into a carnival act and say nothing of it, but I see no reason on God's green earth why I have to let my one good girl turn into a gypsy."

"It's not gypsies," I said. "Gram helps people think. You look at a card that tells a little story about strength, and so that reminds you to be strong and not go off your diet." I tried smiling at her. "Most people don't think."

My mother heaved another deep rattle of a sigh. I looked at her small, round eyes, colored a precise shade of brown. This is how she saw the world: small and round, not especially vivid. I tucked my arms a little tighter around her, gave her a squeeze, then left her stranded amongst another woman's furniture. Already I was forming my rules of life, the first of which was that when given a choice you listened more to the people who called you "dear one."

Gram was cutting the cards into different configurations, humming a little something to herself. Mrs. Langevin, who was considering remarriage to the head of her parish council, waited outside the screen door, her arms softly folded, a black purse dangling from one fist.

Gram paid no attention. She was "gathering herself," as she liked to put it. Her glasses were off.

"What does it look like, without them?" I asked her.

Gram stopped what she was doing, which she always did with me. "Everything gets bigger," she said. "People, animals." She chucked me under the chin. "Sometimes I can see the insides of things."

"Like X-ray vision?" I asked, impressed.

"Not exactly. But everything looks kind of inside out. Every snowflake explodes, every flower opens into a palm. Trees turn into these wild, fleecy things, not trees but the souls of trees."

I had a pretty good idea this was the sort of thing my mother had warned me not to listen to. My grandmother was given to flights of poetry that I lapped up like water. She smiled. "After I stopped being scared, I began to think of my eyesight as a sixth sense." She leaned forward, another secret. "Without my glasses I hear not what people are saying, but what they *mean* to be saying."

What would people mean to be saying? I love you? I'm afraid? Don't hurt me? I wondered if she could hear what I meant to be saying to her, all the time: Don't leave.

So when I got to Portland and saw that everyone was there at the bakery, just as I expected, I wished for my grandmother's eyes. Aileen was outside, finishing up her sign for the day: OUR ICE CREAM CAKES ARE HOT STUFF!!!

"My name is Rita," I said.

"I saw you last week," she said, clicking an exclamation point into place. "You sat at the back table and ate a muffin."

I pointed at the sign. "Nice work."

"I'm almost out of *b*'s," she said. "Everything starts with *b*. Bagels, baguettes, buns, bombes." She tsked, then continued: "Banana creme, Bavarian torte. My uncles keep forgetting to re-order." Her shoulders drooped; she might have been the sheriff of the world having trouble keeping the deputies in line.

Do I need to say I felt poured into my shoes? She was smiling at me, a good, steady gaze, but in my half-melted state I could gather her only in pieces: a spark of red hair, a quick blue cast of the eye, a scuff of sun glancing off her small, pearly teeth. John was far, far away. I forgot that I loved him, that I was here on his behalf. It was just me and this sweet child, chatting on the sidewalk.

"May I help you?"

There was Susanna, her hard chin jutting forward as she scampered between us. Now I remembered, and I took a deep breath, resuming my mission. Her face looked less than friendly, but I held out hope that I was reading her wrong, that in truth she was afflicted with a heart so dangerously tender that she couldn't afford to show it to just anybody.

"Go on in, honey," she said to Aileen. "The boys want to get to school."

Aileen picked up her box of letters, gave me a last glance, and pushed open the bakery doors.

"Is your husband here, too?" Susanna asked me, looking around.

"Of course not," I said. For the briefest, weirdest second, I thought she meant Layton. She was looking at me, chin to chin, married woman to married woman. I decided not to correct her, and wondered whether a husband might have made a difference for Beth, given her an authority she couldn't muster as the single sister, the youngest, the one with no babies. I guessed Susanna to be four, five years older than Beth. Darla once cowed me daily by virtue of her two measly years.

"I was just coming in to buy one of your delicious muffins," I said. "I thought we might all say hello, face-to-face, like normal people with a little something in common."

Her jaw worked and worked. "We don't want you here,"

she said. "You can't expect us to go through this again." Then she went inside.

The day was cold but confusing, with spring-scented air wafting in from the ocean. I settled myself on the wooden bench in front of the bakery window and tried to adjust my body to resemble a force of nature—a mountain or volcano, something heartless and immovable, something no mortal could match. I had on a big coat, which helped some. After a moment Beth appeared beside me, her face filled with worry.

"John didn't tell you?" she asked.

"He told me. Here I am anyway."

"Where is he?"

"He doesn't know I'm here," I told her. "Beth, you broke his heart."

She sat down. "You don't understand the position I'm in. I have to think of everybody."

"You said you'd do right by her. That's what you said." From behind me I could feel the heat of the family's collective stare.

"I thought enough time had passed," she said. "But I was wrong."

"It's been five years. How much time do you people need to do the decent thing?"

She looked at me. "We're decent people. Something indecent happened to us." Her hand drifted to her chest. "We've already lost so much."

I reached into my purse and pulled out the Queen of Cups. "See this card? This is you. Kind, honorable, maternal as all get-out."

She looked at the card, studied the draping robes, the gold chalice, the open sky.

"John doesn't want to take anything away from you," I said. "He wants to give something back." I touched her arm, briefly, and she did not draw away. "Aileen needs him, Beth. I know you can see it."

Just then the children surged through the doors, wrestling with book bags and jackets and yelling at each other to hurry up. The oldest boys, practicing to be fathers, corralled the younger boys, directing who would get the front seat of which cars. They glanced at me curiously, but the surge of activity had a momentum of its own and carried them past us. Aileen turned her lighted face to Beth, showing her teeth, waving one hand.

Beth blew her a kiss. *I want to be your mother,* is what she was thinking. *That's what I want.* I didn't need my grandmother's eyes to know this.

When the children roared away, Beth stood up. "You can come in."

It smelled so good in there. I thought, Someday we'll all look back on this and laugh. Truly, I thought this. I imagined us at Aileen's sweet-sixteen party, dancing to the Rolling Stones, wearing pretty dresses. I tried to smile very hard.

Nobody smiled back. Instead, they bent to their work, making their way back and forth over the clean, checkered tiles, rubbing down the tables, bagging doughnuts, ringing change into the cash register.

A group of customers straggled in and out, and then it was just us. They crowded behind the counter, all except Beth. She stood somewhere in the middle, in neither one camp nor the other. I'd memorized a dozen speeches on the way up, but couldn't think of a word now.

Callie said, "He can't come up here after all this time and drag everything up."

Tight. Tight as a fist. Tightened over the thing that would not be dragged up. Their faces seemed small and slapped-looking. The room felt short of air.

"What's everybody so afraid of?" I asked. "Your little girl should know she came from two good places."

Susanna banged the cash register shut. "Don't you tell us what our little girl should know." She glared accusingly at Beth: *You never should have opened the door.*

Callie said, "Just hearing Roger's name makes me sick," then burrowed beneath her husband's hefty arm.

Another flurry of customers, another exchange of money and doughnuts, then we were alone again.

Beth's fingers began to tap, a little trill of fingernails against the sensible cotton of her school-nurse skirt. "Laura liked him," she said to them. "John, I mean."

"What?" Susanna said.

"We played cards together once. He was a nice person. He doesn't even look like Roger anymore."

Instead of answering her, the twins turned their reddening faces to me. The husbands looked away. "We're not blaming your husband," Susanna said. "We feel sorry for him, in fact. But whatever else he is, his brother killed our sister. Whatever else he is, he will always be that."

"I—" Beth said, looking at them with great tenderness. Maybe she was measuring the chances of losing them as well, calculating the amount of loss one life could handle. The word *I* weighs so much.

"I—" she began again, and again she could not say what she meant. She couldn't say that she wanted this fist of a family to open into a hand.

"Go ahead," Callie said. "For heaven's sake."

Beth spread her hand on her chest. "You think I don't feel this?"

Those twin faces buckled. I could hardly bear to look at them. I thought of them as two craggy boulders blocking my way out of a tunnel, but still. I could see how sad they were.

"He's her uncle," Beth said quietly. "That's a fact. They deserve to meet." She was still standing in that same spot, neither with them nor against them. In her own spot. She was tired of that tightened fist, anybody could see that. She was tired of loving them, tired of sharing the child she wanted so dearly. Tired of pretending the dead were still alive. As I watched her she seemed to get bigger. Her shoulders straightened ever so slightly, her color deepened, her feet met the floor in a firm, defiant *no.*

They saw this. Callie came around the counter first, then Susanna, and there they were, three sisters in the same breathing space, close enough to kiss. Three sisters who had once gathered in Laura's stricken house, going through her things. Maybe a locket with their names in it; a program from somebody's graduation; a blouse she'd lent out, fragrant with talc.

"I don't want to feel this again," Susanna faltered.

Beth touched her sister's shoulder, very tenderly. "I know," she said. "But it's not us I'm thinking of." She turned to me. "We can arrange a visiting schedule." Looking back at her sisters, she added: "I can do this now, with all of us here, or I can do this later."

Her sisters' pretty mouths parted at the word *I.*

"But we discussed this," Susanna said. "We decided."

"I changed my mind."

"You have no right," Callie said.

Beth's body seemed to wave like a distant heat, inflamed with yearning. "I'm the guardian," she said. "I have all the rights."

Susanna raised her amber eyes. "Don't."

Beth held her ground. "John Reed did nothing to us." She gave them a sweeping look. "I owe him."

Everybody held their breath. The sisters slid little rabbity glances my way. For a long moment no one moved, or spoke. They stood as if in a tableau, this family of women, the two husbands tucked behind the counter, the well-loved bakery shining all around them. *We were such a happy family!* They did seem a family that had once been happy—wholesome and good, excused from the whims of God. How exhausted they must have been! I could almost see them buckling under their story's feverish weight.

"Please," one of the husbands said to me. He followed me to the door—it was Pat, the taller one—and hung a sign that said BACK IN 10 MIN. Then he closed the door behind me.

So I waited in the pearly sun. It was still early, the light cold and bright, the air still. The neighborhood began to stir. People got in and out of cars, cats sidled between fence posts, phones rang from behind shut windows. A small group of customers gathered on the sidewalk, looking puzzled at the sign on the bakery door. The houses along the street looked undisturbed, the pavement solid, the trees big and old and tired. I could hear the sound of ocean, even older and more tired. It must have looked and sounded like this when the Doherty girls first discovered it, tumbling down the steps of that triple-decker with their first tricycles, a red wagon. Here were the same streets and trees, the same ocean rumbling from the same distance. Here was that same family—a few more apples on the family tree now—traipsing in and out of one another's kitchen doors, holding up their notion of how the world worked.

I imagined myself walking a long line, a continuum with a light at either end. One of those lights was the past; that's the end I walked toward, looking to recover my losses—my town, my family, my marriage, my child. Beth was walking this continuum, too, in the opposite direction, arms stretched toward that other light. We were just about to meet on that line, and I saw no earthly way for us to cross paths without embracing.

Finally the three sisters emerged, bunched at the bakery door. Susanna and Callie had their coats on. Callie was crying, her lips white with rage. "Don't," Beth said, "wait," but they tore past me, the sweat-and-perfume scent of their hair gusting back. They charged across the street and banged up their stairs. Beth looked after them, her hands fluttering at her sides; their leaving looked like something being ripped from her body. But she was still whole.

I looked up.

"Let's walk," she said.

We walked side by side to the end of Morning Street, two souls with something in common, two unmarried women who had not given birth. Of course, she had a child—but only sort of. And I had a husband—or an almost-husband. We turned east at the corner, toward the ocean. After a block the peninsula ended at the Eastern Promenade, a wide, grassy space overlooking the sun-bleached waters of Casco Bay.

"Laura used to call this view the meek inheriting the earth," Beth said.

We sat on a bench, looking down at the wide water, the bluish islands, the trawlers easing over the water's silvery skin. Below us was a public boat dock, a scrabble of city beach. In the water near shore, boat moorings the size of beachballs bobbed along the riffled surface.

"Nothing meek about those sisters of yours, if you don't mind my saying," I said. "My sister and I used to fight all the time, but I never saw anything like this."

"It's pain," Beth said. "It still hurts."

We sat awhile, looking at the water. "I bet this view hasn't changed a whit since you first saw it," I said.

She pointed. "We used to play tag down there on that field."

"The place I grew up's all erased," I told her. "Sometimes I feel like invisible ink; every step I take erases behind me."

"Really? Every step *I* take erases in front of me." She watched the water, the brightening sky, her eyes set high on the horizon.

"I don't understand why you didn't adopt her," I said. "Back then."

"We all wanted her."

"You were the one with no kids."

"She was all we had left of Laura."

"In my opinion? They should have let you have her."

"You don't understand how much we loved our sister."

"You've got me there," I said. I could hardly count my feelings for Darla as one of the world's great love stories.

"At the time, we were nearly blind with grief," Beth went on. "We wanted Aileen to always know who her mother was. Is." She squinted out at the horizon, shaking her head. "We tried to do everything right. I hope you and John can see that. At the time, none of us could bear to take Laura's place."

"And now you can?"

"Maybe," she said softly. "Maybe that's what's happening." She paused a moment. "So much of that time is a blur now. Unbearable grief, is how everybody put it. I must have heard those words a thousand times. But I learned something. Grief is bearable. You bear it." She looked at me. "You just do."

"I've always thought of grief as like living underground," I said. "All spongy and muffled like that. You're not yourself." She was nodding solemnly, her eyes bright. "Maybe you even do things you don't know you're doing," I went on, "like throwing things away that shouldn't be thrown, or talking to people who don't want to listen. But then a day comes when the unbearable thing isn't the first thing you think of. It's the second. And then comes another day, when a muffin on a plate makes your mouth water, and you notice that food tastes like food again. And then another day, when you're all the way through breakfast and finished with two customers before the unbearable thing pops into your head, and you realize you've been waiting and waiting, for a month, maybe, or a year, or two years, or five, you've been asking yourself, When will life begin again? And all of a sudden you see that it already has. It began when you weren't paying any attention."

She looked at me for a few moments. "Yes," she murmured. "It's like that."

I studied her blue eyes, that ordinary hair, those strong fingers. She had a habit of clasping her hands, as if she'd captured something in the hollow between her palms, something small as a ruby, an acorn, a wish.

"How long have you and John been married?" she asked suddenly. "I never thought to ask."

"Oh," I said. "We're not married. Yet."

She glanced at my bare hand. "I just presumed," she said.

"We're extremely engaged."

"You must love him a lot. Sticking your neck out like this."

"Prick him, I bleed," I said, and I meant it. I knew exactly how it felt to be John Reed, the idea of a child lodged in his heart like an ungranted wish. "He's a good man," I told her. "He deserves your kindness."

"Yes," she said. She gazed out to sea again. "He does."

The echo of *I owe him* hung between us.

"I'm glad you came back," she said.

Her mouth barely moved. *There is need,* she had said to him that night in her kitchen. *There is need to apologize.*

All at once, I knew. I settled myself on the bench, looking where she was looking, so in this way we could be together. "Beth," I said. "He was still alive, right?"

She didn't flinch. After a long, long wait, she said, "That's none of your business." Then she looked at her folded hands.

I imagined her back in that kitchen, Roger's body slumped in the doorway. Maybe a finger flutters. Or he makes a sound. Or they lock eyes.

"I don't think anybody could blame you," I said, "considering the circumstances. John certainly wouldn't. He's the forgiving sort."

"I'm a nurse," she said tightly. "I'm a Catholic. It would have been my duty."

"But your sister was dead."

"The second I saw him, I knew what had happened. I'd never seen her with a bruise, there was never a whisper of violence in that house, but when I saw him, I knew."

"So you left him there."

"Don't you think I would have remembered he was somebody's brother?" Her eyes were brimming. "He looked so small, I remember. Sort of crumpled-looking. We've turned him into such a monster over the years, but really, at that moment he looked so—small." She stood up abruptly, the sea breeze ruffling the soft hair at her forehead. "I hated him for so long, but then I got tired. For Aileen's sake I have to hope he didn't know what he was doing."

She got up and began walking along the green, so I followed her. "We used to have friends," she told me. "We used to have parties and barbecues. Now it's just us, and our kids, and this thing that happened." She sucked in a breath. "I never intended to turn into this kind of person."

At the next bench she stopped and sat, exhausted. I felt the way I had back in the days when Gram would confide to me how she missed her old house in Kansas and those yellow waving fields. Her eyes would pink, her wrinkled hanky of a mouth would quiver, she would put her thickened fingers on my shoulders as if I might help shore up the freight of her memories.

Beth looked at me. "Don't say anything to John. Please."

Was this a confession? Her eyes blazed. "If there's anything to tell," she said, "I'll tell him myself."

I nodded, feeling entrusted. I couldn't begin to imagine what she dreamed at night. "I have a sister," I said. "I understand what you must be going through."

Beth folded her arms, hugging herself. "Sometimes we can see Roger in her," she said. "A certain way she moves when she's in a hurry, and there's something across the brow. We don't mention it, but it's there. And I'm thinking it might be nice to start connecting those things to John instead of Roger." She checked her watch. "I have to get to work."

We walked slowly back to Morning Street, side by side.

"Maybe we should have a party, a celebration," I said. "Kind of like a homecoming."

She stopped. "Please don't make too much of this," she said. "I'm doing what my sister would have done. That's all I'm doing."

"All right," I said. "Fair enough." But I continued to walk beside her, discussing the nuts and bolts of a visiting schedule. I wanted once a week—in truth I wanted every day, every minute—but we settled for twice a month. I kept adjusting my step to her long strides, enjoying the nearness of this sisterly woman. As a child I'd wanted to walk this way with Darla, and waited first for her to notice me, then for her to like me, then for her to like me enough to walk like this, shoulder to shoulder, making plans.

When we stopped at my car, she shook my hand. "Tell John to call me."

"I'm so grateful," I told her. "You have no idea."

"Don't be."

I got into the car, started the engine, then smiled up at her.

"Who am I again?" she asked.

"The Queen of Cups."

"I'll try to remember that."

She stood on the street watching me go. As she receded into the distance, I thought of Darla again, my only sister, as good as dead to me. Maybe she was in her garden, her pointy elbows moving back and forth as she hoed a patch of ground. I knew so little. I hoped she was happy.

12

The drive home flew, and you'd think my head would have sparkled with bright thoughts, namely, a dear, solid man and a pixie-faced girl. But it was Layton I was daydreaming about, and the children I used to imagine early in our marriage, those chubby faces peeking over the banister of a house we did not yet have, eyes aglow at the eight-foot Christmas tree we never got. I did buy the ornaments—fifty porcelain snowballs that cost me a week's pay—but the biggest tree we ever managed, the year Layton finished the bridge project over on 128, could take only twenty-nine of those snowballs before tipping over on the dog.

I suppose he was on my mind because at the time I was thinking of him, he was thinking of me, roaring his bike up the interstate from New York—wondering if I still had my dog, whether I used the divorce money to set up my own shop or skip town and move to the tropics. He always assumed the worst in people, which is why, even if he'd gone stone-cold sober and figured out all the little ways to say "I love you," we wouldn't have made it in the long run.

The last time I'd seen Layton, he was swinging a leg up over his Harley outside the courthouse.

"I wish you wouldn't drive that thing in winter," I said, feeling more wifely now that we were officially divorced.

"Rita," he said. "You know I'm sorry."

"That's all right," I told him, and I almost meant it, for I could still see that moon-faced boy he shot, and maybe even his dead little brother, that stillborn baby his mother could not get over. And I saw how he thought he wanted me once, how he believed he had been asleep and that I was the one to wake him. We believe these things at first. We do.

I had lifted my hand to wave good-bye, but instead my fingers froze in a sign for "Stop." He got off the bike, his hair whipping across his forehead, the brown leather of his jacket making little groaning apologies of sound as he reached for me. We stood there, entwined, on the snowy sidewalk. I don't know how long; a long time, I think, though eventually, obviously, he did leave.

That's how I was thinking of him—that tangle of hair, the sound of leather, the bigness of his arms crossed over my back—when I got back to Alton. It was near suppertime. My house looked more stranded than usual after the old-timey ambiance of Morning Street. There was my deep-pitched roof, my thawing flower boxes, my shutters, my frozen yard—stranded along a row of stores and restaurants. My house was the only structure left on the block that looked as if a human heart beat behind the doors. On the way in I picked up my mail, which included a letter from my next-door neighbor, another offer to buy my house just to tear it down. I threw the letter away and stowed everything else on the mail table. Then I let Sheldon out and turned on the basketball tape.

After the emotional disorder of the Doherty girls, I was seized with a desire for neatness. I wiped down the counter and cupboards, vacuumed the living-room rug, put in a load of laundry, cleaned Sheldon's cage. When I shook out a section of newspaper to line the bottom, I saw Vicky's obituary.

John came in as I was reading about her lung cancer, her prizewinning zinnias, her civic largesse. Survived by one son, Layton Rosario of Poughkeepsie, New York. Predeceased by her husband, Stephan Rosario, and an infant son, Lloyd Rosario. That lost baby, still alive in the smudged newsprint of an obituary over fifty years later. Vicky's story, going on without her.

"Who's that?" John asked, kissing the top of my head.

"My mother-in-law," I said. "Former, I should say. It says cancer. I hope she didn't suffer."

He took the newspaper, read the obit, gave Vicky her moment of silence. "I tried calling you earlier," he said, laying the paper down, gently. "You weren't here."

"I went out to get you a present."

"Where is it?"

"In Portland, Maine."

He waited, his hands loose at his sides.

"I wish I could wrap this with a big red bow," I said. "I wish I could sprinkle it with fairy dust."

He sat down, eyeing me steadily, his face lifting in small, unbelieving increments as I told him what I had done. How stunned he looked, how fearful to receive this brimming cup of news.

"How—?" he asked. "Why—?"

I put up my hands in a shrug. *Go figure. Women change their minds.* That's what my hands said, though Beth's *I owe him* circled our heads like a moth.

"I can't believe it." He stumbled out of his chair and lifted me clear off the floor. "Thank you. Oh. My Rita."

I laughed, tightened my arms around his neck. "You deserve to meet, she said. That's what she said. You *deserve* it. Oh, John!" I said, thumping her place at the table. "She'll sit right here."

For the next hour we moved slowly around my kitchen, quiet and careful. It was almost as if we were afraid to voice our thoughts for fear they might pop like bubbles under the weight of words. Every few minutes one of us would laugh, then the other, but still we said nothing. He made a chowder. I polished some water glasses. We came apart, circled in, laying linens and stirring pots, as if readying not for a weeknight supper but a banquet at which we would be giving or receiving an award. When we finally sat in to eat, he kissed me, and our voices came back in a gust. We would take her to the beach and walk in the shallows. We would waltz her through Disneyland. We would loll in this very kitchen, or in John's, watching a basketball game or listening to piano music or teaching Sheldon to say words she loves. We would. Dizzy with our dreams, we volleyed hushed words back and forth, a lovely minuet that I took for love.

"You did this for me," he said.

"It's a wedding gift. If you still want to marry me."

"Let's get a ring," he said, getting up, pulling me with him. "Let's go now."

I didn't make him ask me twice. Just like that, I was done with waiting. I didn't want to wait for another thing as long as I lived. I coaxed Sheldon back into his cage, put on my coat, and had my fingers tangled in the top button when I heard Layton's Harley in my driveway.

Needless to say, the introductions were awkward. John stood with his arms rigid, trying to slim himself. Layton looked older—he was nearly fifty—but he was still lean, thick-haired, moving his body through space in that certain deliberate way, aware of his charms. He stood outside my door, glancing up and down the street.

"This is John Reed," I said. "My betrothed."

The men shook hands, eye to eye, then Layton stepped into my house with a package tucked under one arm, a medium-sized box wrapped in wrinkled packing paper. My hall light caught the spider veins along his nose and cheeks, the sign of a middle-aged drinker. But his eyes were sober. Blue, bright.

He was still eyeing the street, his gaze flicking out one window, then another. "This place has sure changed," he said.

"It sold its soul, Layton," I told him. "You sell your soul, it tells."

"My mother died," he said.

John nodded. "We saw it in the paper just now. I'm sorry for your loss."

"I hope she didn't suffer, Layton," I said, and my voice caught. She had done me an almost-kindness once, in my hour of grief. It was not a kindness such that I'd put her on my list of don't-forgets, but she had done the best she could.

"What can we do for you?" John asked. We were all standing in my narrow hall, breathing one another's hair-care products. Layton still used a mousse that smelled of limes, and I'd lately convinced

John to take care of his flyaway problem with just a titch of pomade.

"My mother wanted you to have this," Layton said, handing the package to me. I took it, which meant we all had to go further into the house so I could look at it. I set it on the kitchen table. "What is it?"

"Open it."

So I did, and the sight of Vicky's stemmed, Waterford-crystal cake platter—an inheritance that, not surprisingly, I could see no earthly use for—brought her house back to me in an instant. It had been full of breakable things; it glared with crystal and china and blown-glass figurines. She and her one living son would sit amongst the flash and cut of all that glass, drinking from their fragile, flowered teacups.

"Well, thank you," I said. "She said that? That she wanted me to have this?"

Layton shrugged. "It was the prettiest thing in the house, Rita. I thought you should have it."

We all stared at the cake platter, or rather at the space where a cake might have gone.

"Well," I said to Layton, "we were just about to go buy an engagement ring."

"And I was just about to ask you for a haircut." Layton unzipped his jacket but didn't take it off. "My mother's wake is tomorrow, over at Hammond's in Leavitt, and I'm kind of a mess."

What could I say? I felt a little weepy, in fact, as if my marriage to Layton had been some kind of Norman Rockwell portrait instead of one of those billboard-sized canvases splattered with different colors of paint. I was remembering my first good times with

Layton, maybe even I was remembering his big slouchy bed. I was not what you would call experienced back then, and with Layton I thought I'd won the love lottery. There were some sweet times.

"It's all right," John said. He cupped my cheek, briefly, then nodded at Layton—granting permission, man to man. He picked up the cake platter, carefully, as if it held a cake, and took it into the dining room. He didn't come back out.

"It's downstairs," I said to Layton. "My own shop. I've come a ways since the days I used to cut for Audrey. Her place went under and now she's cutting at Shazaam."

"What's Shazaam?"

"Don't get me started," I said, and led him downstairs.

So there we were, Layton and I, like old friends. He took his jacket all the way off and laid it on the counter next to the cash register. He walked around for a minute, asking how much things cost, and I had to laugh, since he had paid for mostly everything, and then he laughed. "Boy, that judge had it in for me," he said.

"You deserved it."

"I did." I sat him in the swivel and spritzed his hair. "I figured you'd be married long before this," he said.

I combed his hair back. "You still parting it on the right?"

"Yeah. Same old me."

"I hope not. For Wife Number Three's sweet sake."

He smiled. "Ex–Number Three, if you want to get technical."

I sighed. "One of these days you'll have to quit looking elsewhere for your soul, Layton. Bend your head." Snip-snip went my scissors, and down floated his hair, like old times.

"You still building bridges?" I asked.

"Sewer systems. It's more interesting than you might think.

And lucrative. There's no shortage of shit in the world, Rita, I can guarantee you that."

I laughed, and for just a moment rested my hands on his shoulders. We caught each other's eyes in the mirror.

"I didn't know enough about you back then," he said. "That was my mistake."

"Your mistake was putting your hands up ladies' skirts, Layton. That was your mistake."

He swiveled the chair around to look at me in the flesh. "I didn't know enough about you. How you keep on. How you don't forget anything. That judge was right. You deserved better."

"You still drinking?" I asked.

"I've been on the wagon for two years. Scouts' honor."

Now, this impressed me. "And you haven't fallen off? Not once?"

He shrugged. "I might've asked the driver to slow down a couple of times."

I turned him around again so he couldn't see my disappointment. What did I think, that he could have turned out to be the man I always hoped he was?

"So," Layton said. "How long has your new man been in the picture?"

"Three months. It was a beautiful winter night."

"You're engaged to a guy you've known for three months?"

"You're a fine one to talk, Layton. Besides, we met under what you might call extraordinary circumstances."

"What's the big attraction?" he asked, hiking up one sleeve, the better for me to admire the knot of his forearm.

I laid down my scissors. "He doesn't look at me like I'm a piece of fruit waiting to be peeled."

"I never did that."

I started on the sides, trimming along his ears. "He wants the same things I want—a little, ordinary life. Some kids. Evenings on a porch where your neighbors walk by and say hi."

Layton glanced up through the windows, into the street still dusty from some construction across the way. "Huh. I'd say you've picked just about exactly the wrong spot, then."

"My old house is a pasta store."

He smiled. "We used to call it spaghetti."

"John's got a niece, a little eight-year-old girl. Prettiest red hair you ever saw." I told him a little bit of John's story, not too much.

"You helped him because you dreamed about a dog?"

"That's right. And it was my great good fortune that he turned out to be a man who can cherish one woman till the world ends."

He was smiling: *Ol' Rita, good ol' Rita.*

My scissors stopped. I lowered my voice. "Did you come here looking for forgiveness?"

"Yes," he whispered, and a tuft of hair landed just right and pricked me on the hand. "I'm sorry for all my betrayals."

"There was only one that mattered to me, Layton." If he heard me—and he may not have, my voice was so low—he gave no sign. "Remember our baby?" I asked him, loud this time.

He nodded, not looking at me.

"I told everybody she was coming. Coming soon, I said. Coming soon. I told the neighbors, that crew-cut guy at the grocery, the girls at work, I even wrote to Darla at that godawful commune."

"I remember."

"You never told one friend, one person at the office, nobody. You had no faith."

Instead of saying "Of course I had no faith, and I was right," he said, "No, I didn't. I wish I had." Softly, he said this, with regret.

"All those women, the horses, the late nights when I waited and waited. That was nothing, Layton. It was not telling about our baby—that was your betrayal."

He didn't say much for a while after that. I gave him a nice haircut—he'd always had such easy hair—and took out the clippers to shave his neck. I was thinking about our divorce judge, how stately he'd looked in that pressed robe, the lovely polish of his mahogany chambers. Layton was badly hung over. We both had lawyers but the judge wouldn't let them say anything. He kept leaning forward, his pretty white hair combed dryly back from his forehead, his left hand graced by a wide gold band. I loved that robe, realized right then the purpose of any uniform, to instill fear or reassurance, depending on whether or not you'd done wrong. Layton slumped low in his chair while I sat up like a schoolgirl.

When I saw the judge afterward, in the street behind the courthouse, he had left his robe behind and was wearing a lovely houndstooth jacket, very Mr. Chipsy, kind of fussy-looking and dignified, not enough clothing against the cold. I had been standing there for quite some time, waiting for the rumble of Layton's disappearing Harley to finally fade from the middle of my head. "Mrs. Rosario," he said, and I turned around, walked straight to him, and placed a tiny kiss on his sweet, wobbly lips.

"Thank you, Your Honor," I said.

He never even blinked. "You're a nice young woman," he said. "Now, do me a favor and don't waste what remains of your youth looking for a carbon copy of that creep you just got rid of."

I thought he might be violating a tenet or two of jurisprudence with his word choice, which was not what you'd call impartial, but we were standing in a light snow, and the Christmas lights strung from the phone poles blinked on and off, and it was really like a scene from some grainy old movie, and for that reason as much as any I did what he said and remained single. I smiled up at him, making a mental note to put him on my list of don't-forgets. Then I plucked a stray white hair from his lapel jacket, put it in my pocket, and said good-bye.

Layton's voice startled me. "Are you done?" He was still looking at me through the mirror.

"Sure." I gave him the hand mirror and swiveled him around. "That short enough?"

He studied the back of his head and nodded, then his eye strayed toward my jar of hair, Gram's cards, the old talismans. "Some things don't change," he said, picking up the jar and shaking it. "Who've you got in here now?"

"You're in there."

He winced, touching a spot on his head. I was glad to see he had a physical memory of my leaving.

"And some others," I said.

He put down the jar. "I don't suppose you'd consider coming to Vicky's service with me. It'll be filled with old ladies I don't know. Her gardening friends. Some cousins I met once or twice."

I started to sweep up. "That's a lot to ask, considering."

"I guess I never had trouble asking you for a lot."

"Did she suffer long?"

"I don't know. I wasn't there."

"She died alone?"

"I live in goddamned Poughkeepsie, Rita. What was I supposed to do?"

I could have named ten things without trying, but I said nothing.

"Will you come?" he asked.

"I can't, Layton. I'd like to be through with you. Really."

He nodded. "You've moved on, is that it?"

"That's it."

"Well, that's good. I'm glad for you, Rita." He got up to get his jacket. "I hope you know what you're doing. Remarriage isn't all it's cracked up to be."

"Don't worry about me, Layton. I know a second chance when I see one."

"The little girl sounds charming, Rita, but—"

"The second chance I referred to was my fiancé," My cheeks were burning, so I kept on talking. "I'm planning to have two children with John. But first I'd like to see my obligation through to the end."

"It was a *dream*, Rita."

"I'd like a man with a finished story, Layton," I said, dumping his hair in the trash can. "Is that so much to ask? I'd like a whole man the second time around."

He looked at me, then lowered his eyes. "I won't argue with you there." He put his jacket on, shrugging into both sleeves at once. The smell of leather reminded me again of that last day, standing in the snow in front of the courthouse.

"Did you write the obituary?" I asked.

He nodded.

"You put your baby brother in there."

"Why wouldn't I?"

"I'm glad you remembered him, is all. For your mother's sake." I touched his sleeve. "It was a nice write-up, Layton. Vicky would've loved it."

He didn't say anything, and for a moment I thought he might kiss me. I wanted him to; I wanted to compare his kiss to John's and find it wanting. But he didn't kiss me, he just glanced around once again at the shop, and I hope he was seeing what a nice thing had come of his mistakes.

He picked up my grandmother's cards. "Read me?"

I shook my head. "There's nothing to read. You're still going round and round."

"That's the truth," he said, then put the cards softly down. "I'm glad I was your husband once."

"That's lovely, Layton," I said. "As a girl my one dream was to become the type of woman a man could say that to."

He laughed quietly, drew one finger briefly down my cheek, then slipped up the stairs and went out.

"How'd it go?" John asked me. It was too late to go ring shopping. He had water boiling, some teabags set out. Sheldon was sleeping on his shoulder.

"About what you'd expect. He's sad about his mother, feeling sentimental."

John put his arms around me. "Where were we?"

"Getting married."

He rocked me a little. "We'll get a ring tomorrow."

"Promise me something, John."

"Anything."

"We won't walk in circles."

He didn't understand what I meant, but agreed anyway, smoothing his piano-playing fingers over my back, acting like a husband.

13

People come through my shop sometimes and never return. Maybe they didn't like the haircut, maybe they were passing through town on their way to a board meeting or class reunion. Or maybe they were experimenting, stepping out on their regular cutter, hoping to find the haircut that will finally alter the God-given limitations of their face. Breaking up with your hairdresser is a social snafu nobody talks about. In any case, whether they've come through here once or a hundred times, I remember their names. I follow them.

They turn up in the morning paper, on the evening news, on the letterhead of an outlet-mall conglomerate asking you to turn your house into a heap of rubble. I recognize them, and sometimes they have done things I don't believe they could have done. One killed his best friend in a barroom brawl, another saved an old woman from a third-story fire. Two died, one of lupus and another of a brain tumor. They turn up in odd places, is what I'm saying, and when this happens, I try to remember a lock of hair silking between my fingers, the sound of scissors, a fragment of conversation. Some connection between A, a person sitting in my chair hoping to become more beautiful, and B, a news story about one guy stabbing another guy in the neck.

If it's a bad thing that happens, I think, Maybe I could have stopped it. What if I'd read his cards? Left my hand to linger on the back of his head? Made him feel a little more cared for?

I think Roger must have had a way about him. Maybe he had that way John had, a tenderness to his touch, a way of cupping a woman's breast by first smoothing the heel of his hand up her body, over the soft upward slope of her ribs as if pushing a small mound of snow. I think Roger must have held a woman the way John did, by first tracing her skin with his fingertips and only then laying down his palms. Where did all that tenderness go, that last night in the kitchen?

I think he wanted Laura Doherty more than anything in the world. And he wanted that family, that one-souled creature, all those loaves of bread and startles of laughter. Why wouldn't he want them, those four laughing girls in the photograph, those pretty dresses, that sunlight slanting down? Why wouldn't he want those beautiful, dark-eyed children, all those well-mannered boys? I think he wants to josh around with the other husbands, throw a ball to the eight sons. So he marries her, because she is warm and beautiful and makes him feel loved. Then he changes his mind. He discovers he can't extract her from the bread and the children and the sisters, she's a package deal. It's all or nothing. He comes to fear them, the sisters who call twice a day, the genial husbands who are neighborhood fixtures, who make a mean chocolate cake, who make everything that comes hard to him look easy. He doesn't know what to do with all these relatives, doesn't know how to fold himself into their rituals. He loves his new wife, wants his new wife, and when he finds he cannot extract her from the bread and the children and the mother and the sisters, he makes the new rules.

The family, like all threatened creatures, raises its hackles. They snarl and hiss a bit.

His wife has made her corner, her own private corner with him. But she still loves them. She is still the hub, the glue. They need her and she goes, again and again. Not like before, but still. She is not entirely his. She could go back. He fears it every moment of every day, fears the loss of her pliant body, her reassuring voice, her listening, her welcoming. When the baby comes, his fear increases, he feels it in his gut all the way up to his throat, *I'll lose them.* The pills he skims from those plastic bottles don't help fend off the ferocious forward motion of her life wish.

Is this how Layton felt sometimes, jiggling the ice in his glass? There was so much I wanted. He couldn't extract me from what I wanted.

So here they are, that last night in their kitchen. Aileen will be three. There will be a party.

It's just a little party, Roger. Why are you acting like this?

I want to move. We can start looking at houses tomorrow.

Roger, this is nothing, just a birthday party.

Like the baptism was nothing, and her first birthday, and her second, and Christmas and Easter and every goddamned Catholic—

They can't help it. She's their only girl.

I'm the father. I'm the husband and the father.

Stop it. You'll wake Aileen.

Oh, they terrify him. How easy they make it seem, the family stitched together like a bed quilt. He looks like a hermit compared to them. A hermit who's bad with kids. He is standing there, looking at his wife's pale throat, the white tiles of their kitchen, the child's toys clustered near the doorway. Does he see all his riches? No. He sees what he stands to lose.

She presses on.

It's just a party. It's not a plot to make you invisible.

The hell it isn't.

We're not moving. They need me.

I need you more.

You took something. You took something, didn't you?

No.

Layton, you said you wouldn't. It's not good for a baby, Layton. It makes for an unhealthy environment.

Now I'm mixing up my stories. What did Layton see all those times he looked at me? He'd tilt his head, slightly drunk, steeling himself against—what? The things I wanted must have seemed like a cast of thousands.

Laura gives up.

I won't talk to you when you're like this.

The way she is looking at him, does he see that she is fading from his life in a way he can't quite grasp? Searching her face is like trying to find the spot where the river becomes ocean or the dusk becomes dark: She is not quite absent, not quite present. He is so afraid.

There's the difference: Layton was never afraid to lose me.

Does she rub her face, turn her back, does he get a whiff of her hair?

I'm going to bed.

She turns away.

Laura! Get back here! I'm not done!

Does he hear his own cry? What does it sound like? If it had stopped here, if he had only said what he meant. Don't leave me, is what he was saying. Don't leave me.

She flicks on the radio to cover his voice, which is loud and thick and gravelly, not his usual voice. *Look at me!* he shouts. *Look at me!* His love and need are boiling now, a churning hotness. And all those pills. Does he see her now through a mist, the scent of her hair turning up a yearning in his stomach? And her face shutting down, leaving him, the fierce blue irises full of regret, defiance, disgust? He is beyond words now, his eyes are locked on hers. She looks at him but does not see him. His arm comes up. His fist curls.

This is how it ends. And begins.

14

Back when Alton had a town square—a patch of well-trod grass and some park benches, not the stage-set gazebo that's there now—I spent many an evening there, watching for Layton's car to turn down our street. The lot at the end of Main Street had been reduced to white dust, a big bright COMING SOON banner stretched over the staging. Coming soon. I would wait on one of the benches, the concrete dust laced over the grass like hoarfrost. By this time I had stopped pretending he might be dead in a ditch or stranded without a jack.

At these times, toward the end, I used to reel back through time in order to keep my mind off my waiting. I'd sit on a bench and remember a conversation I might have had with a customer a week or two back, or I might remember my two years at Alton Insurance, that ringing phone, the bright overhead light.

Sometimes I went far back, to my mother's little speeches at the dinner table, directed mostly at Darla but at a volume such that I could also reap some benefit: *Go ahead, Little Missy, wag that backside some more, let the whole town know you've got nothing to offer a God-fearing family man.*

I don't want a God-fearing man. I don't want to be like you.

What exactly is that supposed to mean? Rita, tell me what in God's good name does your sister mean.

She means she doesn't want to get married. She wants to be a ballerina.

Rita, shut up. I never said that.

You want to be a ballerina? Is that what you want?

No. Yes. I've thought about it, is all.

And you without so much as one dance lesson?

She wants to take the world by storm.

Am I hearing this right, Darla? What your sister said? You want to take the world by storm?

Yes. I do. And I will, too.

Your daughter wants to take the world by storm, Frank. You hear that?

I hear it.

So far as I know, young lady, there's no ballerina in the world who took the world by storm. That goes for you, too, Rita, just in case you're getting some of your sister's wild ideas. Frank, talk some sense into them.

Why not be a missionary? You don't want to get married, be a missionary. This sorry world could use a few good missionaries.

All this time my grandmother is chewing, slowly, because the meat is tough and her dentures don't fit right. She is listening, chewing on food she doesn't like and never did, but what choice does she have, barred from another woman's kitchen? All those years she baked pies and casseroles, won ribbons, and now she has to look down into overcooked Baptist food on another woman's dishes. "Isadora Duncan took the world by storm," she says. She finishes chewing. "Anna Pavlova. Now, those were two stormy ladies. I bet I could name a dozen others."

Nobody asked you.

May I be excused? Rita, you big-mouth.

Sorry. I was trying to help you, Darla.

Some help.

Why don't you take the world by storm by being a good girl for a change? I can't hold my head up in this town anymore.

And around and around. It always amazed me, how we spoke, like poisoned darts passing back and forth in the dark, missing every target. No one ever understood one thing somebody else was saying, except Gram, who understood everything but couldn't get herself listened to. "The girl is speaking of dreams, Frank, remember those?" she might say, but by then Darla was crashing away from the table, an upended chair in her wake, the shepherdess figurines on Gram's crowded highboy shuddering against the slamming door.

Still and all, Darla was wrong about there being no love in that house. After one of these scenes, my father would rub his face so hard he'd look slapped for an hour afterward. My mother would go quiet, clear the table, wipe down the kitchen, refusing any help Gram and I offered, her bony shoulders working back and forth over a pan of soapy water. Gram would shuffle to the screen porch if the weather was all right and clutch her cards, tell me a story about the pie-baking contests at the Kansas fairs, and we'd sit like that until it was time to go to bed. We would all kiss one another, a little peck on the cheek, even Darla if she wasn't still ramming around town in some boy's father's car. It was just something we did, this family that couldn't talk or listen; we kissed.

I was telling John some of these things as we drove to Portland on the following Saturday, an overnight bag in the backseat, some books and paints, some sheet music, a few hair baubles shaped like stars and flowers. It was not a long drive, a little over two hours, but it seemed longer. I was going over my whole life, almost like a good-bye, exchanging one life for another.

My ring caught snags of light as John weaved in and out of traffic. Ordinarily he was a careful driver, but that day he drove the way Layton used to, as if he couldn't get to the next moment of his life fast enough. My ring was simple—a glinting diamond set flat against a band of white gold, the opposite of my first engagement ring, a show-offy heap piled high on my finger. I sold it after the divorce, exchanging it for new tile in my salon with a little left over for a good deep sink.

"I wonder how the funeral went," John said, reading my mind.

"What does it mean when a funeral goes well?" I wondered. "That the deceased didn't spring out of the coffin and say boo?" I glanced out at the disappearing traffic. "Not that it would surprise me, in Vicky's case."

He looked at me. "Are you sad about her?"

"She said something kind to me once. She said Layton didn't deserve me."

"He didn't." Ahead was the entrance to the Maine turnpike. "I don't either, but at this point I'll take whatever God sees fit to give me."

I slid my hand across the seat and he folded it into his. We took a ticket at the tollbooth, then headed straight north.

"In forty-five minutes," he said, "we'll be there. Oh, honey, thank you for this."

There we were, hurtling toward that little girl, that curled-up family, that neighborhood with a view of water. My life had found its true direction at last, I was thinking. Happy days were here again. I believed I had done all I could for John, that I had fulfilled the demands of my dream, that whatever happened next was up to him. I was truly the helpmate now, not the shepherd. I liked that he was driving fast, and he seemed to know it, glancing at me, a smile forming at the edges of his lips, as if to say, *Stick with me, kid,* all proud and Bogart-y, as if he'd finally turned into the man he hoped he might become back when he was eight and his brother was buying his piano lessons.

We arrived in full sun, an afternoon breaking with the promise of spring. Dirty tuffets of snow lingered in the low spots in the yards. Tulips were beginning to muscle through the earth. A few forsythia blossoms swelled on their branches. The street was quiet, the bakery nearly empty. A dog waddled by. John turned to me. "Here it is," he said, squeezing my shoulders. "The end of the yellow brick road."

I smiled, following him out of the car, and I couldn't help noticing how strong he looked, how resolute, a man who could walk straight into the heart of a happy ending.

Beth and Aileen stood on the first-floor landing, gazing at us. None of the others appeared. Across the street the twin houses looked blank and silent, like paired headstones.

"Hi, Rita," Aileen said.

I waved mightily. "We meet again!"

She smiled at me briefly, then fixed on John. She was so thin as to be nearly invisible, despite the sweatshirt with *Cathedral School* scrolled across the front, the hardy-looking blue jeans, the thick white sneakers. A fragile vein pumped across her translucent forehead.

John lifted his hand to her, a gesture filled as much with wonder as welcome. She stepped off the landing to see him better.

She watched his hands. Her hair flamed in the afternoon light. She seemed otherworldly—a vessel filled with magic, or grace, or God's apology. Her eyes moved over John's face, and his over hers, their mouths stretched to breaking.

"I'm your uncle John," he said, his hand lifting again.

She said, "I remember you."

He drew a long, shuddery breath, the kind you take after a hard cry. They shook hands briefly, his fingers covering hers, then stood a pace apart, regarding each other with the calm of old friends.

Beth lingered on the landing, allowing Aileen whatever the moment held. I could see that she had fought hard for this moment, which was both a letting-go and a sort of claiming. By letting that child step off the landing and hold out her hand to her father's brother, to a mystery, to a new fact of life, Beth was calling that child hers. She might as well have stepped into the middle of the street with a bell, crying *I'm the guardian. I have all the rights.* A few doors down, the twins appeared outside the bakery door, and a couple of the boys, and one of the husbands. They looked bunched and afraid. Owen, the youngest boy, started toward us, but his mother collared him back.

I did not move, or talk. I simply stood aside, twisting my ring around and around, watching John and his niece not talk, not laugh, not ask questions, not wonder why. They stood comfortably, within reach of each other, their arms slackened, relaxed at their sides. They stared at each other, smiling, filled with awe.

In no time at all I would be her aunt, is what I was thinking, twisting and twisting my ring. In no time at all. But for now, on this April afternoon, the white light of early spring pooling on the asphalt at our feet, I was no one. No one's mother, no one's aunt, no one's wife. Of the four of us standing in the cool, whitewashed sun, I alone had nothing to claim.

"We could start with a walk," Beth said. We walked.

And that's how it went, all through that Saturday and Saturday evening and then the next morning and afternoon and evening. I expected, of course, to get to know the child, to peek under her thinness and quiet and one pulsing vein, but it was John I discovered. He had a knack for charming children. He laughed more easily than I realized. He knew the difference between a chipping sparrow and a house sparrow. And he could whistle like a champ. The two of them walked along the Eastern Promenade, her hand tucked shyly into his as she called out her favorite tunes—"Nothing Like a Dame," "Old Man River," and "Amazing Grace"—prompting him to purse his lips for a melody that would make a nightingale swoon. Beth and I watched from one of the benches scattered over the winter-weary grass.

"You were right," she said. "She needs him."

So we walked, we fed squirrels, we played Junior Scrabble, we baked cookies in Beth's kitchen. Beth accompanied us through the weekend, the chaperon, though no one used that word. I believe she enjoyed our company. She liked John's whistling. She liked taking walks. She liked watching John and Aileen. She told us stories about being a school nurse, about broken bones and chicken pox. On Saturday evening, just before supper, she let me read her cards. Transformation, I told her. Wands everywhere. Then she fed us.

We left for our hotel late, after Aileen had gone to bed. John opened the overnight bag, where our clothes lay together, all a-tangle. "You and me," he said, and I felt married the way I never had with Layton. John laid out my nightgown and watched me put it on. I laughed, running to the window where the city spread out below us like a picnic blanket. "I feel like I'm on vacation," I said. "The best vacation of my life."

He came to the window and held me. "We start from here, then. Is that all right?"

"We start from here," I agreed.

"And here," he said, squeezing my wrists, "and here," petting my shoulders, "and here," tracing my hips.

"John Reed," I said, "I believe I have woken a lion."

"I hope so," he said, leading me to bed.

Our sleep was fitful but dreamy. We woke many times, smiled at each other, then fell back asleep.

In the morning we had to wait until they had finished with morning Mass at the Cathedral of the Immaculate Conception, which rose like a prayer at the foot of the hill. Organ music gusted into the car window, and the churchgoers began to spill out over the sun-drenched steps. Among them flocked the Balzano family, Aileen snugged into their center.

"The church my father took us to had ten pine benches and a tippy lectern," I told John as we drove past. I felt a little awed by their church, its weight and beauty, the glimpses of gilding I caught through the open doors.

We waited for them in front of the closed bakery, where the family converged for coffee and biscuits. Aileen broke away when she saw us, running over to grab John's hand. Beth guided us through the door, offered us coffee, took our coats, all with an impressive amount of grace, I thought, under the circumstances. The twin sisters and their husbands sucked in all their breath and moved with the poise and menace of a nuclear missile still in the silo. *We're doing this for her,* is what they said through their narrow mouths, their squared-off shoulders. *It's for her sweet sake.* The sisters brushed their eyes over me the way Vicky used to, lingering over my fingernails, my bangle bracelets, my blue shoes, and I suddenly felt like one of those gum-popping, beehived hairdressers the filmmakers are so fond of depicting, some draggletail in spike heels from the wrong side of the tracks. *I've read the Canterbury Tales,* I wanted to tell them. *I'm an informed voter.*

The younger boys came around to our table, curious, eating their raspberry muffins like cud-chewing calves, staring out the sides of their eyes. "Hi," I said to one of them, and he lowered his long, blue-black eyelashes, as if maybe I'd had a hand in the killing, as if I'd held Roger's fist and brought it down on her myself.

Aileen asked for nothing. She harkened like a perched bird to everything John said, listening between the lines. You could almost see thoughts crossing those navy-blue irises: *Maybe my father was like this. A nice man who liked squirrels.* Sometimes she would say something that made him laugh, and then say it again, just to hear him again.

She watched him and watched him.

All this in one Saturday and a Sunday, a weekend that felt like a week. John whistling behind the wheel as we drove to and from our hotel, each loop back from Morning Street leaving him more in love than the last.

I loved her, too. But it was not me she watched for signs of her erased life.

At long last a moment came. Sunday evening, as Beth and John talked in the kitchen, Aileen took me to her room for a tour of her possessions. I sat down on her bed and breathed that moment, hoping never to forget it.

"This is my room," she said.

It was a nice room, a little girl's room. Pompons trimmed the pink bedspread and pink throw rug and pink curtains; stuffed bears crowded near her pillow. On a shelf over the dresser stood a line of small plastic people—cake decorations for specialty occasions. She had them lined up in the same configuration as her family portraits, each family member encumbered by exactly the same molded-plastic face with the same painted features. A nurse, a seamstress, a baker, a gardener, another baker. Aunts and uncles. Then the cousins: three hockey players, two basketball players, a soccer player, a guitarist, and a boy figure holding an artist's palette. There was no girl.

"Uncle Pat gives them to me," Aileen said. "Those are my friends, over there." On another shelf were lined up a few girl figures engaged in various hobbies.

"Where are you?" I asked, looking again at the family gathering.

She shrugged. "I can't pick myself out, just other people."

"Well, it's a nice room."

"I have one just like it in Aunt Callie's house, and Aunt Susanna's."

Everybody Loves Me.

"Same thing exactly?" I asked.

She looked around. "Mostly." But I could tell by the way her voice wrapped around the word *mostly* that she considered this room, in Beth's house, her real room.

"Did you know my father?" she asked me.

I shook my head, watching the color of her eyes fade just a shade, losing interest. But she perked up again when I asked her about the tin box atop her dresser. "That's my button collection," she said. "Do you collect anything?"

I nodded. "Hair."

She made a face. "No, really."

"I mean it. I collect hair."

"Why?"

"Why do you collect buttons?"

We were smiling at each other. I was so happy.

"In case I lose one," she said. "Then I'll have all kinds to take its place." She tipped out the buttons and swished her hand through them, making a sound like hailstones on a window. It was nice.

"Once I lost a button on my sweater," she told me. "I looked and looked but couldn't find a match. So I asked Aunt Callie to sew on all different ones. She's the one who sews. Aunt Susanna gardens. Aunt Beth cooks." She grinned. "So Aunt Callie sewed on buttons all different, and then all my friends at school wanted the same thing. I started a new style." She dug into a drawer and showed me the sweater. It was a small cardigan with reindeer prancing across the front. "I was seven," she said. "But I didn't throw it away after."

On a white nightstand stood a framed photograph of Laura holding a red-haired baby. Next to that, a plastic hairbrush, which

I picked up. "May I?" I asked, unwinding one long, red hair.

She nodded, watching as I curled the hair around my finger and tucked it into my skirt pocket.

"Do you have a box or something?"

"A jar."

"That's neat."

The aroma of hamburger drifted in from the kitchen, where Beth and John were consulting on supper.

"I'm guessing your father was just like your uncle John," I told her. "A nice man."

She lowered her eyes, then lifted them again, then looked quickly away. "He killed my mother dead," she whispered.

"Well, yes, I know that. But imagine how sorry he was."

She began to put the buttons back in a tin box, one at a time. Each one sounded like a little gunshot.

"Can't you?" I asked her. "Can't you imagine how sorry he was?"

She nodded.

"You think of that," I said, "when you think about him. You think how sorry he was, and how much he was like your uncle John out there. Except for that one thing."

Bang, bang, went the buttons. "I don't remember it," she said quietly. "I was three. But I remember Uncle John. He brought me a toothbrush once." She was eight, but seemed so much older, and younger. "Sometimes I wish I remembered everything."

"That's what I try to do," I said. "I try to remember my whole life." I picked up one of the buttons and looked at it, a gold-speckled thing that might have come off the back of a cheap ball gown. "Remembering isn't always so easy, though. You tend to recall things in pieces. You remember this one as bad, that one as good. When I think of my ex-husband, I think, Drinker. Gambler. But he was also very hardworking. And charming. Just thinking about him used to curl my toes." She was looking at me, puzzled. "All I'm saying is, people are more than one thing."

I was a little disturbed by the three identical rooms. How a person was supposed to be more than one thing in such circumstances I couldn't imagine. And I didn't like the boxes she put her aunts in: seamstress, gardener, cook. Not that I gave two cents about the twins, but Beth was more than a cook, I could certainly see that. And I didn't want to get tucked into a box labeled hairdresser.

She didn't say much for a while. I waited while she finished putting each button back in the tin. Then she replaced the cover and held the box close to her chest, the way I liked to hold my jar of hair. "I like how you dress," she said. "I like flouncy clothes."

"In no time at all I'll be your aunt," I told her, flashing my ring.

She looked at it. "You're going to marry him?"

"We haven't set the exact date, but yes."

"I thought you were his friend."

"I *am* his friend," I said. "Also his beloved."

She looked away shyly. "I have three aunts already."

How I wanted to fling my arms around her! "You don't have room for one more aunt?" I asked.

She stood before me, her box of buttons clutched to her chest, her feet perched exactly side by side. "I think Aunt Beth should marry him," she said. "Then you can marry somebody else." She smiled suddenly, all our problems solved.

I suppose her desire was the most ordinary thing in the world. Beth and John would be the next best thing to calling Roger and

Laura back from the dead. Two brothers marrying two sisters. It was already a family tradition.

"But then who would *I* marry?" I asked her.

"You're so pretty," she said, placing her box of buttons back on the dresser, "you could marry anybody."

"Boy, have you got some learning to do," I said. "In about twenty years you'll find out for yourself."

"There's lots of nice husbands," she insisted. Her eyes opened in a way that thrilled me. Her irises separated into two layers: Closest to me was a fine sheen of color, which I took for the innocence of childhood; beneath that pulsed a fiery undercoat, which was the single-minded burning of her life wish. Her narrow teeth glistened.

"People can't help who they love," I told her.

"Yes, they can."

Her insistence surprised me a little, but not for long. Her face burned with desire. Don't all children want divided parents back together? It made a gruesome kind of sense, her wish to haul Roger and Laura up from the grave. I knew how it felt to want things so wholly, how certain desires could register in your body like an electrical current.

I stood up. "Well, I don't blame you. This street is lousy with aunts anyway. How about if I just be your friend for now?"

"Okay," she said. "Can I see your cards?"

I took them from my pocket and showed her. She picked one, the Page of Cups. "What does it mean?" she asked.

"It means you're a wonderful girl."

She laughed.

"For now," I said, touching her hair. "I'll be your friend for now."

And this is what I had to content myself with as John and I drove back to Alton in the rain that night, John's whistling coming down like more rain as I leaned against his shoulder. We spoke very little. "You're crying," he said to me at one point, and I smiled and said, "Yes." When we arrived in my driveway, he said, "I've never been this happy." We went inside, said hello to Sheldon, and collapsed into my bed.

John fell asleep instantly, the sleep of the newly loved. I lay long awake, looking out at the sky, which was tinged with orange from all the new lights in town, the trail of fake prosperity that traveled up the old Main Street and around the curve to the new Main Street, which was being dug up at night, as if in secret, and from where I lay I could hear the distant whine of a backhoe. I was thinking of the three identical rooms inhabited by that translucent little girl, who, unlike the child brought before Solomon, had been allowed to be divided, not once, but twice, with no true mother to step between the knife and the flesh. So they made three girls out of one, three versions of their dear, dead sister.

Perhaps it was then I first let go of her, not wanting to divide her again. This is how I was able to comfort myself, fill that still-empty hole.

I was nearly asleep when the phone rang. It was Darla, who needed me.

PART 4

the moon

15

The no-ceiling waiting room was empty. The trees seemed taller than when I'd seen them last, and their leaves, fat and spongy, looked freshly waxed. My heels clacked against the hot, hard tiles.

"Hello?" I called, and one of the assistant swamis came hurrying out, his hair slicked back like an otter's. He had a soft, slippery face, normal clothes. Darla once told me they had a botany teacher and a pediatrician in the ranks; maybe this was the teacher, I thought—he looked swamp-fed, a tad unformed, the type of person who might like to study slime.

"I came to get my sister," I said. "Darla Cooper." He stood there, waiting for me to say her new name. "Get her," I told him.

He tipped up his palm in that aggravating salute, then spun around and left. After a few minutes he reappeared along with two other swami-helpers—another guy who could have been another botany teacher, and a youngish woman in a blue tunic. They stepped aside nervously, and then Darla slipped through the open doorway, wearing the dress she had worn to my wedding and a pair of loafers a size too big. She carried no luggage except a woven cloth bag the size of an eggplant, which she held by the drawstrings. It had nothing in it but twenty dollars and her driver's license, which she'd had the presence of mind to renew annually, though she hadn't driven a car since she left home. The whole thing looked like a scene in a movie where the lifer gets out of prison with nothing but a bad suit and a bus ticket.

She lurched over to me as if attempting a hug, but stopped just short of touching me. "They kicked me out," she said. "I had no one to call."

"Darla," I said, stretching out my arms. "You look—" She looked awful, is what. I left my arms out but she didn't take them. She seemed not to know what to do with the offer. This place had eroded my sister's physical charms—she was skinny and bug-eyed, and, except for her sun-reddened hands, so painfully white that I half believed they'd replaced her blood with tap water.

So there I was, stranded with my arms out in the sticky San Diego heat, standing in a waxed tile courtyard under a high, high sun, staring at the wisp of hair and flesh that once upon a time was my vibrant, mutinous, infuriating sister, Darla. The dress hung on her like a shroud, though I could still conjure a vision of her at my wedding, the subtle swell of her hips and chest making that pink dress seem to move on its own.

The assistant swamis huddled near the door, shuffling their feet, clearing their throats none too subtly, like hosts trying to get the dinner guests to leave. Suddenly Darla turned around and spat into the doorway. They edged back, their eyes draining instantly of pious regret and filling with an ugly mix of contempt and fear.

"Fuck you! Fuck you! Fuck you!" Darla hollered. "Fuck the shit out of every goddamned two-faced one of you!"

The woman in the tunic looked at me: *Do something.*

"I'm just visiting," I said.

The first botany teacher nudged the second botany teacher, who nudged the woman in the tunic, who said, "There's nothing we can do, Patience. This is Kenneth's decision."

"Fuck you!" she screamed again. "Fuck you, *Tammy!*"

Poor Tammy—who clearly had since taken another name (Humility or some-such)—recoiled as if shot at. It didn't take a card-reader to guess what was going on: The second botany teacher was none other than Dance, my sister's fiancé, and Tammy had apparently horned in on the action. Proving my hunch, she edged toward Dance and placed her hand on his shoulder like the bride in a turn-of-the-century wedding portrait.

I was suddenly enraged on behalf of my sister, my poor, pale, shadow-of-her-former-self Darla. And I was enraged on my own behalf, too: These people had stolen my only sister and left this vessel of bones in her place. She still had some zip left in her, though; she cursed and wailed, sounding a lot like the Darla I once knew, the girl in tight skirts who made men howl in the street.

"He threw you over?" I asked her.

She nodded, rattling her skeleton bones, crying these awful, grinding, phlegmy sobs that sounded like a bridge collapsing.

"For *her?*" I asked. "He dumped you for *her?*" Not that I couldn't see why. The other woman, or girl, was fresh off the farm, curvy and pink. Her nail polish hadn't had time to completely chip away. "That's some sacred trust you've got going there, Dance," I said. He looked up, startled at the sound of his name. "Little

Tammy here, she's been amongst the fold, oh, I'm guessing ten days?" I curled my arm around Darla, careful not to break any bones. "Ten days, am I right?"

Suddenly they all seemed afraid of me. "We can call the police," the botany guy said.

"Go ahead," Darla shrieked, flinging the twenty out of her bag and onto the clammy tiles. "Tell them what you did with my money."

"Give her back her money," I said.

"Liars!" Darla yelled. "Liars, liars, liars!"

"Patience," said the two-timer. He looked scared to death. "You have to go. We wish you peace."

"Wish my ass," she said, grabbing up the twenty. "Come on, Rita, let's go."

For a second I thought I might be having another dream where people show up as something other than themselves. Darla was a person I was barely acquainted with and wouldn't have recognized on a busy street, and yet I *knew* her despite the disguise of her bony wrists and her sad brown shoes and her twenty dollars wilting in her bag. Her true self shimmered, somehow, still, beneath those poor changed bones. She grabbed my wrist and dragged me out to the street. Though she was frail, she moved the way she used to back when her dearest pleasure was to snarl through our apartment like a trapped cat. When I opened the door to the rental car parked at the curb, she shook off my arm and hauled into the front seat, fuming, flexing her fingers as if she might be looking for a gun.

The first botany guy trotted out after me. "Where are you taking her?"

"To a hotel," I said. "She looks like she could use a rest."

"Take her to a hospital," he said. "She's ill."

I glanced into the front seat, where Darla sat like a convict strapped to an electric chair, breathing hard. I hoped there wasn't anything wrong with her that a few high-fat milkshakes wouldn't cure.

"Nobody tells Darla what to do," I said.

He seemed surprised. "She was perfectly obedient up until last week," he said. "When Kenneth amended the match between Dance and Patience, she wouldn't accept it." His face came closer. "She questioned his authority."

"The nerve," I said.

"Take her to a hospital." He laid his mildewy hand on my arm. "I'm a physician."

"Oh, really. And where do you practice?"

"Here." He looked genuinely sad. "Obviously I can't treat her here, under the circumstances."

"What's wrong with her?"

"Malnutrition, is my guess. She always took the fasting to extremes. It tells after a while."

Darla banged on the window, which startled the good doctor and sent him scampering inside.

"He says I should take you to a hospital," I said, getting into the car.

"They can't kick me out," she groaned, banging on the dashboard. "They're my only family."

I peered into her face. "Listen to me, Darla Cooper. I'm *this* close to finding my little lost child, but instead I fly three thousand miles to haul you out of, I'm sorry, a loony bin. What does that make me if not your family? Listen to me. I'm your family. You *have* family."

"It took you long enough to get here."

"Excuse me. I had to reschedule about four million appointments."

Her forehead crinkled. "You lost a child?"

"Not literally. I didn't mean it literally. It's actually somebody else's little lost child."

"I didn't know you had a child."

"I don't."

Then she leaned over and coughed up a bright spot of blood, so I opened up a map of San Diego to find a hospital.

Darla didn't say boo during the ride. I found myself wondering what might have happened if the mill hadn't closed all those years ago. Darla and I might have worked there a couple of years, saved our money, then left Alton to study economics or Chinese poetry on a campus somewhere with big trees. Maybe I would have been sitting across from her in a café in St. Paul or Atlanta, visiting the way sisters do, instead of thicking my way through the San Diego traffic and trying not to panic about the way she was keeled in the seat, the hem of her dress bunched in her hands and pressed to her mouth.

They took her into surgery within hours of our arrival, to repair an ulcer that had bled nearly through. After that she sulked in a six-bed ward, recovering, refusing to believe her ulcerated, malnourished self had anything to do with her so-called friends at the House of Peace. They put her on IV antibiotics, and a tube-feed to avoid contaminating her stomach. She was some kind of mess, bile shooting out one tube, urine out another.

In all, she was there nearly four weeks, and because of the way admissions and discharges went in that place, I was gone a total of five weekends. With the twice-monthly visiting schedule Beth had given us, that made three weekends for John to go to Portland without me, to bake cookies and take walks and go to movies and whistle. We talked on the phone every couple of days, but it sounded like very long distance.

It was rough going. After Darla's initial burst of rage, she seemed too exhausted, or frightened, to fully return to her old self. She shimmied down into those clean sheets, looking for all the world like a snake trying to get back inside its shed skin.

"Morning, Darla," I would say, entering her room first thing each day.

She wouldn't answer. Instead she did that tipped-palm thing.

"Quit doing that," I said finally. "You're giving me the creeps."

"It's God. There's nothing to be afraid of."

"God?"

"Yes," she said doubtfully. "The breath of God."

"Coming through your hand?"

She folded her hands. "*Yes.*"

"God has better things to do than blow all over innocent bystanders."

"Think what you want."

"They probably got it from an old episode of *Star Trek,*" I said, fluffing her pillow. "Those lunatics sold you a load of bullshit, Darla, and the sooner you realize that, the sooner you get better." I bent down to check her feeding tube and her catheter. It wasn't the greatest hospital on earth, to be honest—there was a nurses' strike on, and they'd imported people from God knows where to man a skeleton crew on the wards. I kept having to go out to the nurses' station to remind them to refill her food bag.

She wouldn't let me call our parents, didn't want to give them the satisfaction of knowing her spiritual journey had landed her in a hospital, which my mother had actually predicted once, way at the beginning. I did call the alleged House of Peace and threatened them with the police if they didn't pick up Darla's hospital tab. Turns out they had some kind of group insurance, so they agreed to pay, which Darla took as a sign that they were willing to take her back.

"There's nothing for you there," I said. "Darla, don't you see what happened to you? Your old personality came roaring back when somebody crossed you. That two-timing soul partner of yours wheeled a deal with the swami when Miss Oklahoma waltzed in there twitching her bee-hind."

She glared out the window. "I don't have any choice than to take this from you," she said. "Every friend I have is in the House of Peace."

"Some friends," I said. "You show the slightest shred of your actual self and they put you out on the street."

"That wasn't my actual self. This is my actual self." With that she closed her eyes. Inhale, hold, exhale.

"Darla—"

"I told you not to call me that." Inhale, hold, exhale.

"I'm not calling you that other name," I said. All the nurses were calling her Patience, which is how she checked herself in. Her driver's license, I noticed, still said Darla Cooper.

"Why did they make you change it?" I asked.

Inhale, hold, exhale. I could see her going back to that place, to those hot gardens and quiet halls, the palm trees lined up like skinny women in bad wigs.

"Sometimes," she said quietly, "you have to cover your tracks if you want to move forward. You have to let birds eat the bread crumbs." She closed her eyes. "He was the real thing, Rita. My mate. Kenneth brought us together, he matched us. Then Dance saw that girl and Kenneth changed his mind."

"He's just like any other man. Some cutie fills up a tunic just so, and boom, you're out like an old shoe. Those people are no more holy than my parakeet." I adjusted her blankets. "And I will *not* call you Patience."

"Fine. Then don't talk to me at all," she said. Which I didn't. I borrowed her tray table and dealt out some cards, trying to calm myself. Every time the King of Cups turned up, I'd heave a little sigh.

"Are those Gram's old cards?" asked my supposedly not-talking-to-me sister.

"Uh-huh."

Her eyes slid sideways. Her lips pursed.

"What," I said.

"She ruined our childhood."

"Speak for yourself. She saved mine."

Darla sat up a little, wincing with the effort. "After Gram came to live with us, Mom and Dad started fighting."

"Out loud," I said. "They started fighting out loud. Personally, I thought it was a relief."

"They never fought before she came."

I gathered up my cards and stuck them in my purse. "Darla Cooper, you have the most selective memory I have ever come across in my entire life."

"I'm not talking to you," she said, remembering.

Fortunately, we were halfway through April, and the NBA was gearing up in earnest for the play-offs. Boston was long out of it, so I had no real loyalties. We watched an afternoon game—L.A. versus Utah—and I careened back and forth, rooting for whoever was losing. The game was exciting in a nineties sort of way, lots of flying and dunking, but I found myself missing the old days, the journeyman's game, when free throws actually were free, when the pick-and-roll was a beautiful ambush rather than a body slam by a guy who used his torso like a refrigerator on a dolley. After about three quarters I even started to miss the old flat-footed set shots. The game was close; the score went up and down and up again, so I had to switch sides about two dozen times.

"Whose side are you on?" Darla asked me once, forgetting her silence.

"Whoever's losing," I told her.

"And what's the big deal about this one?"

"They're going for a play-off berth."

At the end, I was exhausted. Up went the score, down went the score. My heart rose and fell for both sides. This is no way to live, but I can't help it.

After the game was over, we watched the postgame commentary—the same old bladdy-blah they always say about stepping up, showing what you're made of, poise in the clutch. I hoped Darla was listening, that she had enough of her old self left to make a connection between the game of basketball and the game of life. She was staring out the window. But she could have been listening. She could have, for once in her life, been listening between the lines.

I switched off the TV. We hadn't seen so much as a nurses' aide since tip-off. Two of the other beds were occupied by weirdly tanned older ladies hooked up to oxygen. For obvious reasons, neither of them had made the slightest attempt to strike up a conversation.

I inspected Darla's urine bag again, and her food. I laid my hand on her forehead, checking for fever. "Why did you keep renewing your driver's license?" I asked her.

"What's that supposed to mean?"

"Your driver's license says Darla Cooper. And it's current."

"I had to work. To cash checks."

"I thought you worked in the community garden, or whatever."

"I did. I also worked in a copy shop two days a week. It's right next door. They employed quite a few of us."

I removed my hand from her cool, narrow forehead. "Why didn't you change your name to Patience on your license?"

"It's a big rigmarole."

"This is California. People can pay twenty bucks to a court clerk and in ten minutes change their name to Supreme Ruler of the Planet Krypton."

Inhale, inhale, inhale. I thought she might be getting ready to laugh, which would have been a strange and welcome sound. But I was wrong. "My life's a waste, is that what you're saying?" she blurted, out of breath. "That I'm thirty-seven years old and have nothing to show for it?"

"You can come home with me," I said. "You can enroll in community college, learn a skill."

"I can't go back. I *left* there."

"Darla," I said. "Really. I want you to come home."

"I suppose all this gives you a chance to feel superior."

I stood up. "I came because you asked me to, and you're my sister. That's why I came. If you want to know the truth, this is costing me a fortune, I have people waiting for me back home, and sitting here with you acting like we did back in high school is not making me feel superior, it's making me wish I'd never left. I have things to *do* there, Darla. Important *things.*"

With that, I stomped down to the cafeteria for my umptieth cup of coffee and cinnamon roll. The kitchen staff was not on strike, but you couldn't tell by the cuisine.

When I got back, she was sitting up in a chair. "I asked them to get me up," she said meekly. "The sooner I'm better, the sooner you can get back home." She kept glancing out the window, fidgety as a sparrow. "I could stay here, actually," she went on. "I could move north a bit, maybe up to San Francisco. It's nice there, I've heard."

"You've been in California all this time and never saw San Francisco?"

"I've never even seen L.A."

"They wouldn't let you out?" I asked. "Just for fun? A little sight-seeing? Not ever?"

"The path to God is a narrow one, Rita." She shifted in her chair, which looked big as a lifeboat around her frail self. "Anyway, I'm sure the copy shop would take me back. They have branches everywhere. I was thinking maybe you could help me look for an apartment, or a room somewhere, and maybe lend me a couple hundred dollars, and then I'll be out of your hair for good." She glanced out the window, at me, window, me, window, me. "Rita," she said. "I'm all alone."

I went over to her, patted her back.

"I'm all alone," she cried, her thin sunburned hands shaking, covering her face.

"Shh. Don't cry. I'm right here."

"I'm so embarrassed, Rita. I wasted my life."

"No, you didn't. You've got plenty left. I know a guy back home who's just starting his life and he's a whole year older than you."

I let her cry for a little while as I sat next to her, patting her rickety back. When we were small, she used to crawl into bed with me when I was sick so we'd both get served soup and crackers. Despite her less-than-stellar motives, I loved those times, the warm scent of us beneath the covers, the coolness of her arm across my feverish neck.

Darla dried her eyes on her johnny—which in this hospital sported ghoulishly cheerful magenta and orange checks—and composed herself. She raked her fingers through her hair, which hadn't been cut in years and was dry and split from Darla's diet of seaweed and what have you. I was just beginning to believe that I would never see my sister again, that her life wish had died in that place, that her spark of fire in the courtyard was some kind of death rattle, when she turned to me. Looked at me.

"You have a parakeet?"

"Name's Sheldon. He likes to sleep on my shoulder."

"He must be getting hungry."

"He's all right. John's feeding him."

"John your fiancé?"

And in this way, we pieced together the last two decades of our lives. Or nearly. She didn't mention my lost child again. I didn't ask whether she fasted on purpose or was deprived of food. We stayed away from the tender spots. Mostly we talked of our parents and uncles and cousins, the changes in Alton, people we used to know. There was nothing else to do except wait for her cheeks to fill out, to watch the sun burn outside the hospital window, to imagine the arrival of spring back home.

16

I wonder sometimes—not often, but sometimes—what would have happened had I not gone out there to get my sister. Surely I had that choice. I could have stayed in Alton, left Darla to her own pitiful devices and gone tripping up to Portland with John every other Friday, shown myself as his other half. The package deal. Wouldn't they have thrown me in with him, reacted to me the way they reacted to him, melted toward me at the same rate as they melted toward him? It would have taken longer, of that I'm sure. It would have been a long wait. But at the end of that wait, there we would have been, side by side, a couple. His and hers.

But I did go out there to get my sister. And John kept spinning forward on his own momentum, without me. Alone, he must have seemed a soul even more lost than he was. Maybe he woke the mother in them. Alone, he must have seemed less large, less looming, less like his brother. To Aileen, he must have looked like a missing puzzle piece, the one you find the next day, or a week later, or years later under the linoleum or between the sofa cushions. One last piece. Just one.

It's not so much, what I wanted. To marry a good man, to love a little girl, to live in a town that hadn't killed its own history. I could have left Darla in San Diego to wander the streets in those pitiful shoes. But I couldn't bear the thought of my sister, alone, groping her way toward home, wherever that was. And it was more than a feeling of obligation, I think. At least I hope it was. I hope it was my own missing piece. If it was, I didn't know it right then, just as you don't know what you're looking at when you reach for the funny gray shape behind the sofa cushion, you don't know what you're looking at until you turn it right side up and recognize that silly, missing piece of sky. Or ocean. Or flower petal. Then you know. If the puzzle is still set up someplace, on the kitchen table or the patio floor, you hurry over, pop it in. *There. Hah.* You feel almost ridiculously satisfied. And if the puzzle has been taken apart and put away, you go to the closet, slip the piece into the box, satisfied to know that should you ever think to assemble that puzzle again—even knowing you won't, probably, not until you're an old lady with nothing better to do—you will have everything you need to reconstruct the picture exactly.

We returned to Alton on a Friday. On the ride back from the airport, Darla kept her face pressed to the window, looking.

"You won't find it," I said to her. "It's mostly gone."

"Where's our house?" she asked.

I circled around River, slowing down so she could see the heap of nothing where the mill once whistled three times a day, then made a left on Broad, which was now a divided throughway with planters full of pansies set down every few hundred feet. I pulled into the parking lot of the pasta store and got out. "The oak tree was here," I said, pointing to a green Volvo. "And right there was our screen porch, where Gram and I did business. Our bedroom was there, where the door swings open."

"How do you know that?"

"Spatial perception," I said. "It's a gift."

She narrowed her eyes, checking out the Volvo. "I don't believe you."

"Follow me," I said, and she did—through the antiqued front door with the jingle bell on the handle, past the proprietress, a Shazaam client with a bad-on-purpose dye job. Her aqua contact lenses glimmered over me, then rested on Darla, whose straggle of hair had gotten caught up in the zipper of the windbreaker I'd bought for her in the San Diego airport, which had been nearly arctic with air-conditioning.

"May I help you?" she asked.

"Just browsing," I said, which was what I always said. She suspected I was a shoplifter. From time to time I'd go in there to take a self-guided tour of my childhood home, but so far I hadn't bought so much as a stick of spaghetti.

Darla eyed the place furtively, an animal in foreign territory. She followed me to the back of the store. "Dad's blue chair," I said, pointing to a display of Sicilian spices. "The rest of the parlor's in the back parking lot."

She didn't answer me, but stood near the spices, her feet settling in. "The door was there," I told her, "and the kitchen table was right about where those striped macaronis are."

She followed me all through the store, looking at gallon jars of biscotti taking up space once occupied by Gram's highboy, a rack of 100 percent cotton KISS THE COOK aprons where Darla had kept a fresh line of chalk traced around my tiny share of her bedroom.

"I don't like this," she said, and I knew what she meant. The pasta store was exactly like our old house in the way you had to move through it. One drawback to carrying an inventory of three thousand flavors of imported pasta is that it tends to narrow your aisles: Darla and I had to squeeze single-file, dodging shelf corners and bulging drawers as if they were the dark, oaken shapes of our grandmother's furniture.

"I want to go," Darla said.

We filed to the front and opened the door. "Thanks for coming," snapped the proprietress.

Darla didn't get into the car right away. She glanced around at our made-over town, at the budded cherry trees, the white sidewalks, the Nautilized professional women shopping with mesh bags. "It was an ugly place anyway," Darla said. "Good riddance." But then she kind of stood there, fluttering her hands a little at her sides, as if looking for someone familiar to wave at.

She liked my house, which in my absence had developed a skirt of leaves from the perennials I'd planted all around the foundation. Spring had popped up every which way. I leaned down to inspect the leaves, feeling their shiny newness, feeling grateful for this one thing. The plants were from Vicky, who showed up one day long after my divorce with a truckful of samples from the garden she was digging up before moving to a smaller place. She had lost weight—wattles of skin hung from her face and arms like some sort of primitive jewelry. We barely talked. She got out and unloaded the plants, never even stayed for coffee. "You've got this big grassy lot," she said. "It's a crime not to garden it." That's the last I saw of her.

But life is full of surprises. There I was, a few seasons later, feeling a delayed sprig of gratitude that she'd thought of me. Bringing Darla home was something I'd wanted to do for a long time, and Vicky's unfurling plants, to me at least, made a ceremony of it.

"Didn't the Sturdevants used to live here?" Darla asked. "Nancy was in my class."

"I do her hair," I said. "She teaches third grade."

"Then not everyone's gone."

"Not yet," I told her. "The School Street neighborhood's mostly still there, and some of the old places on North River. But every middle manager from E. F. Hutton who moves here from Boston, property taxes go up a half-percent."

Darla stood away from the house, looking right and left, bewildered. My house—an asbestos-shingled two-story stranded between two not-very-neighborly-looking neighbors—suddenly reminded me of an abandoned animal. A poor baby woodchuck, or a lost skunk. "This would make a good postcard," Darla said, then followed me inside.

On the kitchen table was a note from John, who had already left for Portland. I read it through. He signed it "love."

"Who would've guessed?" Darla said. "Alton's been gentrified." She put her finger out and Sheldon stepped onto it like a self-conscious ballerina. Darla laughed. It was her old laugh, throaty and full of sand.

"I'm the last holdout on the street," I said, folding the note. "They want to turn me into one quarter of a food court."

"Did he leave you?" Darla asked, looking at the note.

"No," I said, whirling around. "Whatever gave you such an idea?"

She shrugged. "Do I sleep in there?" she asked, pointing to the guest bedroom off the kitchen. It was the room I was holding for Aileen, already cleaned, with a new bedspread—not pink, not pomponed, but bright green, a change I hoped she'd appreciate. Her geography notebook sat on the bedside table, waiting for her to add to her chronicle of discovery.

So I took Darla upstairs to my one spare room, which was filled with remnants from my adult-ed courses. The bed was half obscured by blue-and-white samplers, crewel patterns, embroidery cloths, and a pile of knitted squares for an afghan I was making for my mother. In the closet was a folded-up easel from my oil-painting class, a block of cherry wood and a sack of carving tools. The top dresser drawer overflowed with seashells, pine cones, bird feathers, and dried leaves from my urban-naturalist classes. The bookcase contained books on perennial gardening, McCarthyism, William Butler Yeats, and fly-tying. There wasn't much room, I'll admit, for one skinny sister.

"Some view," Darla said, looking down on the back side of an Eddie Bauer, its loading ramp poised in the load position. "Please, God," she wailed, heaving her body over the only cleared space on the bed. "I *wanted* him." She turned over and flung out her arms, exposing her body like a throw rug. "I *wanted* him, Rita."

That's my Darla, I thought, a spark of hope thrilling through me, the first since I'd gotten the phone call. That's Darla, mad with desire. Life wish intact.

"I'll clean this place up," I told her. "You can stay as long as you like." I went to get storage boxes from my shop, with Sheldon, who had missed me, nestled beneath my collar. When I returned, she was sitting by the window, her eyes closed, her newly filled-in face composed and really quite pretty again. Her hair was another story, and she was wearing one of my dresses, which was small but still big for her.

"So," she said. "John Reed. Happily ever after."

"That's the plan," I said, shoveling some instructional pamphlets into a box. "And I don't mind admitting he thinks he's the luckiest guy on the face of the earth."

"You can't know what a man thinks," Darla said.

"I know enough," I said. John Reed had been lying dormant through a very long winter, but I had faith there would be a blooming, had seen evidence already in the way he held me like a bunch of daisies, the way he clowned for that little girl. He had the makings of the long haul. This I knew. I told Darla this, and she fixed me with a look I didn't like one bit.

"You don't think it's a little too late for him?"

"No, I don't," I said. "I'm discovering all sorts of things. He's wonderful with children. He can whistle."

"Well, it all sounds hunky-dory," she sighed, flinging herself onto the bed again. "You're lucky."

"It's not too late for you, either." I started to clear off the bed, picking my way around her body. "You could start by calling Mom and Dad. They'll be wondering why they haven't heard from me."

She opened her eyes. "They'd be up here in a day. I don't think I'm ready."

This was the last thing our parents would have done, though I kept that information to myself. "Actually, they're afraid of flying," I told her, which was true, but the other truth was that they hadn't so much as mentioned her name in five years. "I visit them once a year for a week, in October. They're practically rooted to the ground. They love the heat. Uncle Ralph and Aunt Alma are down there now, and Uncle Lenny moved there last fall." I looked at her. "When you're feeling better, maybe you can go down there for a visit."

Darla was sitting up now, blinking hard. "They haven't seen me since your wedding. You're telling me they wouldn't get on a plane?"

"It's a little more than that, Darla. They can't bear to look at this place anymore, their old life paved over."

She continued to blink at me, arms folded.

"You have to imagine how they'd feel," I continued. "Coming back here, seeing you so changed in a place that's also changed."

"That's always been your big problem, Rita," Darla said. "You can imagine yourself as anybody." She fell back on the bed and began to cry. And continued to cry, off and on, all through Friday and Friday night and Saturday morning.

Saturday noon, she drank a glass of milk.

Then she slept a little, and cried some more. And slept and cried. She was still in this state when John came back on Sunday night, glowing. His face looked big and loose and innocent, like a child's drawing of the man in the moon. He seemed like a different person: The dental-supply salesman had vanished and a musician had turned up in his place.

"I take it things are good, long-lost unclewise?" I asked him.

He laughed. "We've switched to weekly visits," he said. He kissed me.

"Well, I'm glad," I said, but really I was scared. I had thought he would need me more, that my presence would be required to cushion the prickly looks, the needled words, all the thorns and brambles in that thistle patch of a family. Isn't that the helpmate's job? Well, he had done just dandy all by himself. They saw a horse in a field, they made cookies with red hots in them, they played softball on the Eastern Prom with some of the boy cousins. "Not that I was ever any kind of athlete," John was saying. "That was Roger's department." His brother's name rolled out like a red carpet. "But I held my own. Me and the other uncles."

The other uncles. Already he had heaped himself in with them. His voice bounced off the ceiling, each word releasing a bright balloon of sound. From above us came the staggery drift of Darla's hiccupping from beneath the bed covers.

"Darla won't stop crying," I told him.

"Well," he said. Pop, went the balloons.

"She won't eat. I don't know what to do with her."

Pop, pop, pop.

"Maybe she needs to see a doctor," he suggested. "She's been through an awful lot."

"She just got *out* of the hospital." I rested my face on his shoulder. "Did you miss me?"

A brief pause, which I took for shyness. "Yes," he said. "I missed you."

When I led him upstairs and introduced him to Darla, she lifted her damp hand from the blanket and laid it in his like a sardine. John tried to smile.

"Are you Prince Charming?" Darla asked.

"No," he said. "I don't know."

"I'm not myself," she said, taking back her hand. "This isn't me."

"Oh," he said. "Well. That's terrible."

Darla turned over and closed her eyes, so I led John back into the hallway.

"She seems a little unsettled," John whispered. Scary, is what he meant. "What's wrong with her?"

"Broken heart," I said. Then I hugged him, smelling fresh bread, a child's room, a woman's kindness.

He started talking again. "Beth showed me some old photos of Roger and Laura," he said, "and we all three looked at them, sitting there at her kitchen table like normal people. I couldn't believe it, Rita. I actually got to the point where I told them some nice things about him." His face looked wiped clean.

"She kept pictures of him?"

He nodded. "For Aileen. Her sisters destroyed every scrap of Roger they could get their hands on, but Beth is different. You should have seen her leafing through those pictures, her fingers touching the edges so as not to smudge them. She wants to do what Laura would have done." He closed his eyes. "Laura would have forgiven him. And she would never have turned me away."

I took his arm and led him down to Aileen's room. "I thought about her the whole time I was in California," I said. "Her sweetness. Those steady eyes."

"I noticed that, too. That steadiness. She's rock solid."

I looked at him. "I meant Aileen."

He reddened and looked away, glancing upstairs. "This will pass. Don't all hard things pass?"

"I hope so. I missed you so much, John. I missed our—" I scouted around for a word. Our mission? Our undertaking? Our scheme? "Our project," is what I finally settled on.

He laughed, that spangled silver. "Our *project* is alive and well, Rita. I visited her classroom on Friday. Career Day for the fourth grade." He made his little bow. "I was introduced as a musician." He sounded humble and sweet. "Rita, it's happening just the way you said. We had a ball game, can you believe it? I'm not saying it's a bowl of cherries yet, it's not. Beth and her sisters, you can see them walking on eggshells. But they won't cross her. She's a lot mightier than she thought she was."

"I saw that from the first," I said.

"Whether they're doing it just for her or they're genuinely bending toward me a little, I don't know." He lowered his voice. "But I think they can see I'm good for her, just as you predicted."

Not exactly, I thought. I had not predicted this, exactly.

"I didn't even know how much I needed this child in my life until I met you." He looked happy, enthralled. "I've been lying awake at night feeling so astounded—so *astounded,* Rita—that it's my brother this goodness came from. Rita. I believe in happy endings."

I had to smile. "I saw that from the first, too."

We sat on Aileen's bed the way Layton and I once sat in the nursery on Lilac Drive. "She'll sleep in here," I said. "She'll feel right at home."

A low, eerie moan spooled down from Darla's room. John got up and peered around the door.

"Tell me everything," I whispered, following him. "Tell me what she was wearing, everything she said."

But he didn't. Darla was skulking down the stairs, looking like she'd just broken out of a coffin to commence her nightly rounds, her moth-eaten hair dragging over her shoulders.

"If you don't mind," she said quietly, "I'd like a word with Rita."

"Certainly," John said, ever the gentleman. "Certainly, of course." He hugged me self-consciously, whispering into my ear: "I'll call you before bedtime." And then he was gone.

"Darla," I said. "You could use a semester or two in houseguest school."

She was standing on the stairs, heavy-lidded, her lips swollen from biting them. "He's in love with that woman," she said. "He remembered how her fingers looked on those pictures. They were pictures of his dead brother, but he was looking at her pretty fingers."

I stood there looking at her, fighting a feeling like bees filling my head.

"I'm sorry, Rita," Darla murmured. "I know how you feel. Really. I know exactly."

"He's a faithful man," I said. "He said he'd marry me, and that's exactly what he plans to do." Which was the truth. It was the plain truth, and I hung on to it.

She smiled oddly. "*Faithful* is a beautiful word." Then she put her hands to her face. "Don't look at me, Rita. I can't bear to be looked at. I'm a grown woman with no possessions. I haven't made one single decision for myself since I was nineteen." She sat in a heap on the stairs. "Was that love? Did they love me?"

"No," I said, as gently as I could. "But maybe it was close enough."

"I think I need help," she said.

I walked her back to bed and sat with her until she fell asleep. Then I stole downstairs, into Aileen's room, and slept there, on top of the green spread, in my clothes. Darla's weeping woke me a few times, and in the meanwhile I suffered terrible dreams, the kind children have, with monsters that make you wake to your hammering heart. In the morning, when she still wouldn't eat, I found Darla a psychiatrist, which the new Alton, for all its pickets and gazebos and tulip beds, turned out to be chock full of.

17

I had Rodney in the chair, Mrs. Rokowski waiting none too patiently, and a walk-in hovering near the counter. "One sec," I said to Rodney, who was studying his cards while I cut his hair. I laid down the scissors and went to the counter.

"Can you fix this?" said the walk-in, a teenaged girl with a skunk streak down the center of her glossy dark hair. "My mother told me you could fix this."

"Let me guess," I said. "Hair Tomorrow."

"Angelique," she said, her lower lip trembling. "She said it would make me look— Oh, I forget what exactly."

What she looked like was the wicked witch in a cartoon movie. "You'll have to wait half an hour," I said, "but I think I can manage it." I patted her hand. "Don't worry, you'll look like your old self—which you might remind yourself was plenty good enough in the first place."

I took down her name—which was Teresa Sharron, a lovely

name that should have clued Angelique that out of four thousand options for a new look, the skunk streak should have been Option Number Four Thousand—then released her to the waiting area, where she shrank into a chair under the withering gaze of Mrs. Rokowski, who had spent enough time in my shop that she could spot a Hair Tomorrow experiment fifty miles off.

"Where were we?" I asked Rodney, picking up the scissors.

"The Eight of Wands," he said. "That's a journey by air, isn't it?"

"Not necessarily." I finished cutting and looked at the spread of cards. The Eight of Wands was sitting right next to the King of Pentacles, who I took for Rodney's supervisor at the plant. "Did you put in for that foreman's job?" I asked him.

He nodded.

"Well, guess what? I think it's yours."

"Really?"

Rodney preferred prophecies to leading questions, and because he was the type who liked to make his own destiny, I didn't mind predicting. He grinned at the cards, already hatching a plan to snag that job and make me look like a genius; then he looked up, his face falling. Darla was stealing in from the door that led to my upstairs. Swaddled in a bathrobe, she lurched into the shop, her hair a sight, her eyes looking stung by killer bees.

"That's my sister," I said.

"The one from the cult?" he whispered.

"It's not a cult," Darla said. She shuffled across the floor in her bare feet, picked up a magazine from between Mrs. Rokowski and the teenager. Then she began to shuffle back, stopping at the counter to flip through my appointment book. Everyone looked at her, temporarily silent, as if a cloud had just passed over a picnic.

"I thought you said she was improving," Mrs. Rokowski said.

"She is," I said, though it was mostly wishful thinking. The psychiatrist had put her on medication, but her hands trembled, her eyes darted, and most of the time she reminded me of a lost kitten. Except for the times when she acted more like a lost wolverine.

"I called Mom," she said, settling on the stool. "They're not coming."

"It's nothing personal, Darla. They're afraid of planes."

She didn't answer, just kept flipping through the appointment book, her hands trembling ominously.

"This is Mrs. Rokowski," I said. "One of my longtime customers. And this is Rodney, another old-timer."

"Rita saved my life way back," Rodney said, getting out of the chair. He loped over to her, hand extended.

"Nice to meet you," she said. Her small hand looked lost in his. He gave her some bills, and she took them, stuck them in the cash drawer, smiled at him.

"Have a good one," she said, like a secretary in a Jimmy Stewart movie. Heads swiveled over. She tightened the tie on her bathrobe and took a couple of deep breaths, eyes closed. Maybe she was praying. Despite the medication, you could see how much it was costing her just to go through the motions of civilized life.

The phone rang and Darla picked it up. "No," she said into the phone. "She's *busy.*" By the look on her face—which was exactly the same look from back when she used to hold it against God for dropping her into the middle of a family such as ours—I knew it was my mother calling. "I told you," Darla snapped, "she's *busy.*"

I motioned Mrs. Rokowski to take the chair, then I grabbed the phone.

"What in Sam Hill is going on up there?" It was my father, on the bedroom extension, shouting over my mother's high questions.

"Darla's home," I said.

"Bring her down here," my mother said. "I want to see her. Is she all right? Is she still one of those people?"

"Listen," I said. "She's fine. She left the—people. Think of it as a change of address. No big deal."

"Can you bring her down here?"

"Mom, I've got a business to run," I said. "Besides, you're perfectly capable of flying up here."

"There was that crash in the Everglades last year," my mother said.

"After all she's put your mother through?" my father boomed, his voice exploding into the shop. Mrs. Rokowski was all ears. "She can jolly well get her keester down here and see your mother."

"She's had kind of a shock," I said. "She's not at her best right now."

"She breaks your mother's heart a dozen times, the least she can do is get on a plane."

"She didn't break my heart, Frank. You don't know what you're talking about. Is she all right, Rita? They didn't do anything to her?"

"She's fine," I lied.

"Thank God I had two children," my mother said.

"She broke *my* heart, then. How's that?"

"Frank, stop it. This isn't helping anything."

And etcetera. When I finally got them off the phone, the Hair Tomorrow refugee had left, apparently deciding that a skunk streak looked pretty good compared to my family miseries.

Darla was shaking her head. "I know how they feel," she said, aiming each word at her hands.

She sat there the rest of the morning in her bathrobe and

fright-wig hair, answering my phone, sweeping up, neatening the magazines, folding towels. At noon she went upstairs and brought me back a sandwich. At three she put on one of my old raincoats, went out, and came back with ingredients for a casserole. All told, she was quite a help, though she never bothered to put on anything that might be considered day wear.

"I'm trying to be normal," she said.

At least she had stopped crying. This is what I kept telling myself. I assumed this was an improvement. "It might help to put on some clothes," I suggested.

"Would you pay me if I worked here?" she asked.

"You're getting free room and board," I said, as nicely as I could. "Plus I'm paying what the insurance won't cover."

She glowered at me. "Well, touché to you."

"I'm just saying, this is real life we're living now, Darla. Really. We don't eat our seaweed soup at the stroke of sundown. I'm doing my best here."

She lowered her eyes. "I know. Thanks."

"It's all right."

"This isn't my life," she said, looking up. "I miss my life."

"I know that, I know you do, Darla, but you have to stop thinking about them. You think old Dancy-pants is losing an ounce of sleep worrying about you?"

"He could be."

I squared her by the shoulders. "He *isn't.* You're home now, you can start over. So you made a false step out there, so what? It's not too late to regroup. We'll take baby steps. I'll help you."

I cashed out, showing her how to store the day's receipts. It turned out that manning my phone and cash register wasn't much different from her job at the copy shop. As I watched her nimble, quavering fingers counting out ones, I was thinking: musician, surgeon, hand model. All her lost chances made me feel a little bit like lying down.

"You're hired," I said. "But first I'll have to cut your hair. I need you for advertising." This was the most diplomatic way I could think of telling her she looked like she'd just climbed out of a flooded manhole.

She grumbled a bit while I had her in the chair, but at the end her hair curled just below the chin, her greenish eyes opened beneath a fringe of bangs. I thought about adding a titch of color, but decided not to push my luck. I turned her around to face the mirror.

"This is the haircut I had in high school," she gasped, grabbing the sides of her head. "I look like a *fossil!*"

"You look like my sister again," I told her.

She flung herself out of the chair. "I don't want to look like your sister again! It's like saying my life never happened!"

Poor Sheldon was cowering on one of the hair dryers. He was going on seven years old and didn't like sudden noises, loud voices, or any change in temperature. A little old man of a bird, one more thing I had to worry about. I opened the door to the upstairs and he fluttered through.

"I'll cut it shorter," I offered. "I'll make you look any way you want."

Her face crumpled. "I wasn't in a coma for all those years, Rita. I *lived* there. I lived a life of the spirit. I had friends. People loved me."

"I know," I said. "I'm sorry."

"Rita," she cried, collapsing into the chair. "I *lost* something."

By this time it was nearly six. John's car rumbled on the street, a noise I had come to hear as a balm. After his initial scare, he'd come around to the point where he could actually sit within ten feet of Darla and not look like a trapped rat. This in only a few days. Truly, he was a decent soul.

He came in through the street entrance, which I didn't like. When he used the house entrance, I felt better, listening to his shoes on the floor above me, watching him enter the shop from the stairway after having passed through my hall and kitchen and picked up on his clothes some homey, invisible things—a bit of dust, maybe, or the smell of cooking.

"Don't you look nice," he said to Darla. When she didn't answer, he turned to me: "How is everyone tonight?"

"Perfect," I said.

Darla was picking up fistfuls of her cut hair and flinging them back to the floor. He gave her a wide berth, as if she were a breed of animal he wasn't familiar with. "Maybe we could all go out for a bite," he said. "My treat."

"Actually," I said, "Darla made a casserole."

He tried to smile, then figured that for the wrong reaction, so he clasped his hands together like a preacher and stood there gravely. She ignored him, dropping the last of her hair on the floor and peering into the mirror from a distance of about one inch. She fluffed up her hair, smoothed it, fluffed it. She turned one way, another way. She reached into a big basket where I keep my bracelets out of harm's way and put on three bangles, four, five. She lifted her arm and the bracelets shimmied down, making the sound of a dragging chain.

John followed me upstairs. "I thought you said she was improving."

"I'll admit she's running a little hot and cold," I said. "But at least she's consulting a mirror. You have no idea what a good sign that is."

"And she's not crying," he said hopefully.

"Right, that's good. We have to think positive."

I hauled the casserole out of the fridge and put it in the oven. It was green and orange. Darla had taken my wallet to the pasta store, which was a good two-mile walk round trip, and there wasn't a blessed thing in that casserole I could identify except macaroni, and even that had polkadots. Unfortunately, she'd made enough for a traveling circus.

John was staring mournfully at the oven door. "Rita, I have to admit to you, I feel just a little over my head here."

"No need," I said cheerfully. And truth be told, I was feeling cheerful. His color was high, his step light, despite Darla's gloom. I charged these gifts to myself; without me he'd be sitting in a church basement, drinking bad coffee. "She'll be her old self in no time," I said. "Of course, her old self was wound pretty tight, too. But in a good way. Darla Cooper knew how to make things happen."

He rested his hand on the stove, looking suspiciously casual. "What I'm saying is, I'm kind of up to my eyeballs in people's sisters right now."

I turned to him. "I'm not *people.* Beth is *people.* I'm not *people.*"

"I didn't mean that." He looked toward the door, where Darla was clanking up the stairs like the Ghost of Marley. She looked us over, then snatched Sheldon from the top of his cage and went upstairs.

"She's spent her entire adult life with kidnappers who believe God breathes through their palms, John, you think she's not entitled to a few adjustment problems?"

"Of course she is." He looked upstairs, suspecting rightly that Darla was crouched and listening.

"Look, I'm the first to admit that my sister's one holy mess," I said. "Which brings me to my problem. You're going to Portland next weekend, I assume." He nodded, his face looking lighted from within. "I'd like to come with you—"

"Well, of course, Rita, I never said—"

I put up my hand. "I'd like to come with you, but obviously I've got my hands full here. So I was thinking, maybe it's time you invited Aileen down here for a visit. You could drive up and get her on Saturday morning, bring her here for the night, then bring her back on Sunday."

He looked at me blankly.

"Why not?" I said. "The road runs both ways."

"Rita," he said. "You're not thinking this through."

"I've thought it through," I said. I yanked open the silverware drawer and began to set the table. "Through and through and through. I've got her room all ready."

He watched me plink down the forks. "Beth isn't going to let me take her," he said. "Not at this stage."

"How am I going to see Aileen again? I'm kind of stuck here with Darla for the time being, in case you haven't noticed. How do I get to see her?"

He shook his head. "I've been going so slowly," he said. "Making little inroads, trying to manage a very delicate situation up there. I can't go throwing a monkey wrench spank in the middle of everything. Besides, even if I did ask her, even if she did say yes"—and here he lifted his chin toward the stairs.

"You don't think it would be nice for Aileen to meet somebody who's not marching in time? I'm not saying Darla will ever be all sweetness and light, she never was. She'll never be one of these chim-chim-cherees who wake up singing." I set down three plates, not that I had any hope that Darla would want to eat anything or that John would want her to join us, but because I wanted my table to look full. "But she's always had a different take on things. And talk about your oddball life experiences. Aileen will love her."

"Things might not work exactly the way you planned them, Rita. The things you want might not be possible." He petted my arms. "Honey," he said quietly. "I'm her uncle, not her father. There isn't a card in the deck that can alter that one fact."

I waited.

"One visit," I said. "Is that so much to ask?"

"We should discuss this somewhere else," he said, glancing upstairs. "Why don't I take you next door?"

"I wouldn't be caught dead in that restaurant, it used to be my second-grade teacher's house. Besides, I can't leave Darla in this condition. She could burn my house down, the condition she's in."

"Now, see, that's the whole point I've been trying to make."

"Accidentally," I said. "I didn't mean she could do it on purpose."

"Rita," he said softly. "Honey, are you listening?"

"No," I said, which wasn't quite true. I was listening, all right. Listening between every line he spoke, afraid to hear the sound of my second chance fading. "You told me you loved families," I said, setting down three glasses. Plink, plink, plink. "I. Love. Families. That's an exact quote."

"*I do,*" he said. "I *love* families."

I pointed upstairs. "What do you call this?"

He followed my finger dumbly, not saying what he was thinking. So I said it for him.

"We don't look much like the Morning Street crowd, I'll give you that."

"I didn't say—"

"Not all families march together like an occupying army. She's practically all I've got."

He stared at the table as I threw some napkins down. "I'm sorry," he said. "That's not what I meant."

"She's seeing a guy twice a week. He put her on some pills."

"Now, see, that's good. That's a good thing." He looked genuinely anguished now, and I have to admit it gave me some measure of comfort to realize how pained he was to refuse me something. "And I hope she comes out of it. I sincerely mean that. But I'm trying to get the long view here, Rita, and I don't see Darla as part of the overall picture."

It struck me then that Roger and Laura must have had some version of this exact conversation. Why are your sisters always here? Don't they have homes? Can't they take four steps without consulting you? I wonder if Laura felt what I felt then—torn between obligation and desire.

"You're willing to take on those sisters in Portland," I said. "You're all but standing on your head to win them over, if I'm reading between the lines correctly."

"I wanted this to be simple," he said, rubbing his face. "That's all. Rita, you opened up this beautiful road to me, and now you're blaming me for taking it."

"You want simple?" I asked. "What, in all your experience of this consolation prize we call *life,* have you found to be simple?" I stood there like a schoolmarm, tapping my foot. "I dare you to name one thing."

He looked away, but not before I saw what he saw: Beth and Aileen, standing on a set of stairs. I leaned down and squared him by the shoulders. "Beth Doherty isn't the answer to your prayers, John. I am."

He rested his eyes on me. I could see her in his burning cheeks. He was a man who could be wooed by the simplest act of kindness. And who could blame him? I had a whole list of people who had made me feel that way.

"What she's doing for you is what any decent person would do," I said.

"It's more than that, Rita. You know it is. I've cost her something. It wasn't easy for her to stand up—"

"She's been waiting years to stand up. You can't see that? We *helped* her."

"She could have taken the easy road, she could have told us no and that would've been the end of it—"

"She did tell us no. That's just what she took, the easy road. If I hadn't gone back there—"

He looked at me hard. "Rita, give the woman her due."

My mouth opened, and here is what came out: "She could have saved him. He was still alive."

I sat down and covered my face, ashamed. My grandmother had always trusted me with secrets. I alone in our household knew about the window boxes she missed so badly, about her dishes and linens handed off to a church, her two cats given to a neighbor. And now here I was, swollen with jealousy, betraying another woman's secret.

When I lowered my hands, his face was close. "I already know. She told me." He kept looking at me, his eyes wet and curious, as if trying to match me to the person who had washed his hair back when the year was new.

"I shouldn't have said anything," I murmured. "It wasn't mine to tell." I looked up. "It must have been quite . . . emotional."

He didn't say anything for a while. Maybe he was remembering her tears and sorries, his hand on her back. "He would have died anyway," is what he finally did say. "He'd lost a lot of blood. I don't blame her for what she did." He got up.

"I don't, either," I said quickly. "Really. I never blamed her. I told her that." I went to him then, resting my face on his chest. He had no choice but to put his arms around me. I took in the laundry scent of his shirt, pressing myself against his sweet, soft middle. He smelled so ordinary, so husbandly and picket-fencey. For a moment I tried to believe it really was simple: just the two of us in the world, and that little girl waiting.

"My brother left me something absolutely decent and pure," he said softly. "Can you imagine that? My brother, who I loved."

I lifted my head to look at him. "I'm sorry I told."

He gave me a squeeze. "You've had a bad time here, Rita. I know that. I'm sorry, too." He patted my back. "You're going to have to wait, honey. That's all. When Darla gets better, you can pick up right where you left off."

"Which is where, exactly?" I really wanted to know.

"Right beside me."

"I'm tired of waiting."

"I know, honey. But that's what life is, mostly. Waiting."

This is how he was. Gentle. As accommodating as he could be. He never once shamed me for the things I wanted.

Darla came downstairs, returned Sheldon to his cage, and sat at the table. She was wearing the dress I'd worn the night I'd met John. "I'm starving," she said, pushing the bracelets up her arm.

To my relief, the casserole didn't poison anybody, and Darla made one or two normal-sounding contributions to the table talk. It seemed that my life might wheel along according to plan, after all, despite the unscheduled detours.

At evening's end I walked him out, past the plants with their folded hands. "That's you," I said. "Ready to burst."

"Thanks to you," he said. Then he kissed me. "Rita, I love you so much."

"I love you, too," I sighed, relieved, and it wasn't until he'd gotten in his car and pulled away that I realized the word he'd spoken was not "love," but "owe."

Rita, I owe you so much. That's what he said.

I stood by the gate as he pulled into the street. It took him forever to make the turn onto River; he was cautious around the construction. Or maybe he was aware of me standing there, watching him, my heart breaking.

He had forgiven her. Now there was that between them.

PART 5 giveth and taketh

18

Come Friday I decided that if Darla really did burn my house down, it would be worth it just to see that little girl again. Already her blue eyes were fading in my memory, her exact shade of red hair was dimming. "I'm coming," I said to John, and arranged to meet him at his place, leaving Darla with no car, which I thought was safer.

"There's the rest of that casserole in the fridge," I told Darla. "Don't put it in the oven. Use the microwave."

"They allowed ovens, Rita," she said. "I can light an oven."

"I know you can," I said. "But don't." I gave Sheldon a little kiss on the beak. "He has to have his water changed every other day or he dumps it. There's a basketball tape in the drawer if he gets bored."

"What about me? What am I supposed to do here all weekend by myself?"

"You do what normal people do."

"Rita," she said. She looked scared. "I don't know what that is."

I set down my overnight bag and took her by the shoulders. Very gently. She didn't mind. "You get up and take a shower. You come down to the kitchen and say hello to Sheldon. Get yourself some juice, a little bowl of cereal. Take a walk. Read a book. Etcetera." I thought this was a pretty simple prescription, but she was looking at me as if I'd just given her quickie instructions for assembling a lunar module. "Darla. Sweetheart," I said, giving her shoulders a quiet shake. "Quit thinking and start living. Just live. Do you think you can do that for two days? I'll be back on Sunday. I'll call you every night. Now. How do I look?"

"Like you're trying too hard."

"John likes ruffles," I said, smoothing my skirt.

"It looks kind of Miss Muffetty to me."

"Excuse me, but you've been wearing a cotton tunic for twenty years."

She shrugged, trudging back up to her room. "A shower," I called up to her. "Start there."

Then I was in a car again, speeding toward Maine, my fiancé installed behind the wheel. And there was that feeling again of the world dropping away—Darla's moods and my mother's phone calls and the letters from the greedy-guts at Danforth Outlet Centers, Incorporated, who still wanted to buy my house. There was just us, and our future.

"I'm wondering about a big, old-fashioned wedding," I said. "It's the nineties. People go all out the second time around."

John smiled over, which comforted me. "How big can it be?" he asked. "We're not exactly social butterflies."

"I'll invite my uncles, and my cousins. Well, some of them. And there's Audrey, of course. And Mrs. Rokowski and Rodney and Amy Chang, and Kenny Batchelder and the Dornan sisters. We could fill half a church, easy, just with my regulars." I snapped my head over. "And we'll fill the other half with the new wing of the family."

He kept his eyes on the road. "They won't come to our wedding, Rita."

"You don't know that," I said. "We've got time."

He felt for my hand. "A nice small ceremony would be fine with me. Just you and me."

"Aileen could be the flower girl," I insisted. "Somebody'll have to drive her here. And as far as I can see, where one goes, everybody goes."

I envisioned the head table, which went on for miles, each place marked with a little cake person from Aileen's collection. What a picture it would make, all those handsome boys sitting side by side, their parents dressed up, Aileen at my left hand, John at my right. If my parents didn't make it, who would notice?

"It would be so much more than a wedding," I said.

He didn't say a word.

Then I said, "Think of it as the official joining of two families. Romeo and Juliet with a happy ending."

"We haven't even set a date."

"How about September? A fall wedding. I see earth tones. Hunter green, harvest gold, cream—it'll be stunning."

"But it's already May. It's practically June."

"January, then," I said. "It could happen, John. It could happen just that way. Darla will be all better by then. Everyone will be friends."

I turned to the scenery outside, which whipped past in pretty spring greens. I couldn't wait to see them again, to try my luck, to make up for lost time.

As we crossed the Maine border, he said, "You're presuming a lot, honey."

I looked at him.

"I don't want you to be disappointed, that's all."

"I won't be," I assured him. "I promise you."

When we got there, no one answered at Beth's door.

"She's probably out running errands," he said, and I don't mind admitting how that note of familiarity chilled me, that inside knowledge.

We tromped downstairs and walked over to the bakery, where Susanna was sweeping the sidewalk. She smiled at John—brief, noncommittal, but friendly enough.

"Beth's at the store," she said. She flicked a glance at me, not enough contact for me to look back, show my teeth, ingratiate myself. Tucked into the crook of my arm I had a bag of presents for all the children, even the biggest boys.

Aileen burst out the doors and barreled over to John, throwing her arms around his neck.

"How's my girl?" he crooned, dropping to his knees.

"I'm good, Uncle John," she said. "Hi, Rita."

I set down my bag and held out my arms. It was an awkward moment. I was mortified, to be honest. She raised her face to me, politely, looking me over with those navy-blue eyes. I tucked my hands into my waist, bent down, and gave her a tiny kiss on the cheek, a sudden, sparking pressure, an electrical shock. Then I stepped away.

Susanna was looking at me now, her eyes nearly yellow in the spring light. Did she think I was presuming? Did presuming mean hoping that a child I loved would want to hug me? I felt the way I had in third grade, returning to school after two weeks with mumps, only to find all allegiances changed. I didn't know who to go to, which friend would want to know I was cured.

"I have a present for you," I said.

Aileen looked at the bag. "What is it?"

I handed her two cake people: a piano player and a hairdresser in a pink smock. "For your collection. The piano player wasn't hard to find, but there isn't much call for hairdressers when it comes to guests of honor."

Aileen tucked them out of sight, separating them into two pockets. "Thanks," she said.

"I don't wear smocks much myself," I told her. "My customers like regular clothes."

Callie came out. "You remember Rita," John said, and she begrudged me a smile that looked exactly like a crack in an eggshell.

"I have presents for the boys," I told her. I lifted the bag.

She considered the bag for a moment. Clearly, I was presuming.

"All right," she said. "Come in."

Some of the boys weren't there, and the ones who were didn't know what to make of my wares. I handed out a coloring book of the nation's national parks, a hot-pink water pistol, some plastic action figures with horned helmets, a watch chain, a striped bow tie, and a can of peppermint mousse.

They took their presents politely, murmuring low, boy-sounding thank yous—but I could see by their bent heads and jittery glances that I had done it all wrong, given the wrong thing to the wrong boy, each gift either too babyish or too old, so I left the bag on one of the tables and instructed them to put everything back in and take out whatever they wanted.

Instead, they held their gifts and said thank you again, then wandered off, whispering.

What did I know about children? Exactly nothing.

"Boys don't like anything," Aileen said, taking pity on me, winding her narrow hand around my wrist. It felt like butter on a burn.

She led me back outside, where there was a lot more air. John leaned into my ear, whispering, "It's all right," which I appreciated, took as a sign that my world would right itself, that the moon I'd been seeing in the cards signaled nothing more portentous than change.

Beth pulled up, her car loaded with groceries. John took two bags, I took one, Aileen took a sack of vegetables, and we walked to the house, up those steps, my breath returning, my glass filling again, my eyes fixed on the curve of this child's cheek, the comical points in her elbows, her narrow sneakers tied just so.

"How's your sister?" Beth asked when we got inside.

"Wonderful," I insisted. "All better, really. Absolutely on the mend."

She smiled. "I'm so glad. It must have been awful."

"It was," I said, and realized I'd been missing her. Beth, I mean.

It was so easy to see why John would be drawn to her company. I wanted her company myself: I'd never been blessed with lots of girlfriends. Audrey was the closest I had, but she was busy with her family; we hardly saw each other anymore except to cut each other's hair.

The whole time I was married to Layton I didn't have much to do with anybody else, except an occasional lunch with Audrey, some joshing around in the shop, a fight every couple of weeks with Vicky. In grade school there was Margaret Thibodeau, but once Gram arrived I mostly hung around with her. After she died I had no friends to speak of for a couple of years.

Not that I didn't have any friends at all, I did. I went to movies, shopping, and like that. I was in a Great Books circle for a while. I'm speaking now of friends with a capital F, the kind of people who know things about you, people who could give titles to your stories if they stopped just a minute to think. Mrs. Rokowski might qualify; Rodney, maybe. My dear ones.

John and Aileen were putting the groceries away, cozy and practiced as a Vaudeville team. He knew where everything went. My rescue of Darla had cost me some precious time, and whatever equation I'd had in mind for how all this would eventually add up had been erased from the blackboard.

The groceries were gone. The kitchen melted away. What remained: John, Beth, Aileen. A smiling trio, a child's dream. Aileen looked small and mighty, standing between them.

"So," Beth said. "Whose turn is it?"

"It would be Rita's, wouldn't it?" John said. "We've all had a turn."

"We take turns deciding how to spend the day," Aileen informed me.

"You pick," Beth said.

Probably they thought I'd suggest the beach—it was a nice day, late May—or lunch in town, or a long walk. That was just the sort of thing I might have suggested had she not been cocooned between them that way.

"How about we tour some open houses?" I said. "I used to do that with my grandmother."

"Pardon?" Beth said.

I explained, as Gram once had, that you had to pick houses that had not yet been moved out of, tricycles still tipped on end in the yard, a pile of shoes in the hall. You could study the way people arranged their pictures or made up their beds. You could sense trouble or harmony in these signs, and in some houses it was easier than reading cards.

Aileen was all for it, already scampering toward the door. This was a child who liked to get inside things. Her footfalls hit the stairs hard and noisy. I laughed, my first deep breath of the day.

"I guess it's okay," Beth said, picking up her purse.

"I thought John and I might do this with her alone," I said. "As a couple. Is that all right?"

John snapped a nervous glance my way. Beth looked at him, then at her shoes.

"We've had no time alone with her," I said. "If we're going to be part of her family, I think it would be nice to get to know her one on one."

"I understand that," Beth said. Still not looking at me. "But she's only eight."

"Are we asking so much?" I kept saying *we.* Suddenly *we* was the dearest word.

John's hand came across mine. "Rita. Honey."

But I didn't want to wait. "You've been coming up here for weeks now, John. Isn't this the natural course of things, to get a little time alone?"

"I've bent over backwards to help you," Beth said quietly.

"Rita," John said. "Let's not take advantage of Beth's good graces."

"I don't want to do that," I said, my voice a notch or two lower. "I'd just like to know why we can't spend a few hours without a chaperon."

"Because you don't make the rules," Beth said. "I do."

It was then I saw it: The longings that fueled her were every match for mine. When I got into the backseat of her car, John next to me, Aileen's red hair shining in front of me, and I heard the hard grunt of first gear, and saw the twin sisters and one of the husbands watching from the bakery door, their mouths stretched into resignation, their hands lifted dutifully in a wave, I felt the heat of her desires. I felt that gear grind beneath me, the firm hard sound of leaving, felt the street give way, the bakery shrink in the distance. Over all these weekends—these suspended jewels—she had gotten to do this one thing: leave. With her little girl beside her.

She wanted out, I wanted in. But our fervor matched up exactly.

Briefly, I caught the narrow band of her eyes in the rearview mirror. In the right light they could have been mistaken for a wolf's. She was looking at her sisters, that crowd of family. The engine made a repetitive, two-noted squeal as we cleared the turn at the end of the street: *She's mine, she's mine, she's mine.*

We visited two houses, one a brick-faced garrison with a courtyard garden, the other a clapboard Colonial with an attached garage. As we walked over the first flagstone entryway, I noticed how loosened John's motions had become, how he no longer held fast to his clothes. Aileen shadowed him, her face tipped upward, imitating his loping forward motion.

A woman in a smart red blazer asked us to sign a guest book. I wrote out my name and address. "We're just looking," I told her. Fortunately there was a couple there already who were actually interested, so the red-blazer woman spent her time on them.

"Why did you sign that?" Beth asked. "You'll get a blizzard of junk mail now."

"They get points or something," I said. "Besides, I like junk mail."

"It's true," John agreed. "She reads it all."

I took his arm, glad he knew this about me. I like thinking of the pink-lipped people who lick the stamps, stuff the reply cards into the envelopes, bale everything up for the post office. It reminds me that the world is full of people I haven't met yet.

By the time we got to the second house, Aileen was wandering around like a pro, peering into closets, turning faucets on and off. She had a natural affinity for ferreting out people's secrets.

I believe this is when she began to like me.

"You see how the coats are jammed every which way?" I asked her as we passed through the mudroom. "The people who live here don't mind the smell of each other. They don't mind each other's blunders. Forgiveness in this house rolls like silk off a spool. If somebody hurts you, you assume they didn't mean it."

Aileen nodded, hands on hips, surveying the coats.

"You remember that first house?" I asked. "Coats hung side by side, one to a hook?"

"Trouble," Aileen said.

"The worst kind."

I followed her into the kitchen. "Dog," she said, pointing to a big water bowl. "Two kids," she said, studying the photos tacked to the fridge. "No, wait. Three."

"Good work."

"What would people think if they saw where I lived?"

I petted her silky head. "My grandmother used to say that's the whole point of an exercise like this."

She composed her face, thought a few moments. "They might think I lived everywhere."

I leaned down. "They'd think you were a wonderful girl."

"Time to go," Beth said. "We've seen enough."

As we were getting into the car, she said to me, "Don't teach her anything about those cards."

"I wasn't going to."

"We don't believe in that sort of thing," she said, and got in, grinding that first gear.

Beside me, on the drive back, John kept his face bolted forward. Aileen, for her part, kept turning around to smile. It was the first time in my life I had charmed a child.

We followed Beth upstairs, stood around in the kitchen, which, I suddenly noticed, had had a little bit of a makeover. Very subtle, almost as if she meant to hide it. New paint around the doorjambs, that's all. And the commemorative plates were gone.

"I suppose we could head back tonight," John said.

Beth branched her arms around Aileen, saying nothing.

John cleared his throat. "Unless someone has objections."

"I have objections," Aileen said.

"They're busy, honey," Beth said.

John nodded. "Things come up." He had his hands steeped into his pockets the way he had that first night at the church when I plucked him out of my dream.

"I didn't mean to offend anybody," I said.

"You didn't," Aileen said. Then she carried her handful of real-estate cards and brochures off to her room.

"Look," Beth said. "We're all doing the best we can."

"I thought it would be fun," I said. "An open house is sort of like a carnival ride, except you don't get queasy."

"It was fine," Beth said. "Don't apologize."

"I wasn't."

"See you in a week?" John asked, his hands jammed so far down I expected to hear the rending of garments.

An awkward silence.

John cleared his throat again. "Or two."

"All right."

"Two weeks?" I asked. "I've barely had a chance—"

Beth directed those wolf eyes at me. "I think we all could use some breathing room."

Before I could say a thing, John said, "Fair enough, fair enough," and we were shaking hands as if closing a real-estate deal.

"I'd like to say good-bye to Aileen," I said.

I stood at the doorway of her room, John's warm breath on my neck. We looked in, together. She was arranging the real-estate paraphernalia into interesting lines on her bed. "Good-bye, honey," I said. "We'll see you soon."

She hopped up and gave each of us a kiss. I had done everything wrong without knowing how, but this little girl had forgiven me.

"Look," I whispered to John. There we were—shrunken, plastic versions of ourselves with red, turned-up mouths, standing on Aileen's dresser with everybody else.

The drive back felt long. And premature.

"You want to listen to the Country Countdown?" I asked.

"That's Sunday," John said. "This is Saturday."

"John, I'm sorry. I thought I was being delightful. I really did."

He switched the radio on and off. "Maybe if you kept some of your thoughts a little closer to the chest."

"I was trying to be fun. Like Gram always was. I wanted us all to have fun."

"It scares people, Rita, all this talk about people's inner motivations and whatnot."

"I didn't scare Aileen, did I?"

"No." He sighed. "These people are making all kinds of accommodations, Rita. You can't just go swooping in the way you do. It makes for second thoughts."

"So I brought a few presents. So I had the nerve to want some time alone with her. You've spent all kinds of time with her, but I don't hear anybody accusing you of swooping."

"I'm her uncle. There's not much they can do about me when you get right down to it."

"I'm your fiancée. That counts for nothing?" I waited. "I *am* your fiancée, right?"

"Yes, of course. Of *course*. But they don't think the way you do."

"Aileen wants you, so they have to accept you. Is that it? Well, she's going to want me, too. I can guarantee you that."

"It's a whole family we're dealing with, Rita, not just one little girl. I'm just saying, you have to go a little slower than you're used to."

"You don't understand how slow this is." I started fidgeting, tapping my feet, thinking about that family, feeling like a mouse rooting around for an opening. "I need air. Stop the car."

He pulled into a highway stop, a big slab of asphalt, a Burger King and frozen-yogurt store, some bathrooms. I slammed out of the car and he came out after me, following me as I paced. "You've had a head start," I told him, "they're getting used to you, a family like that can't keep a rift going for long, they can't stand it, they need each other too much, they can't get along without their big story." His eyes got wide as my voice rose. "But they might look around for somebody to blame for the disruption, don't you think? Those memories are hanging over them, John. Not an hour goes by that they don't think of that poor woman lying on her kitchen floor. And there you are, eating their cheese Danishes, that little girl gazing into your face, they can't blame you, they can see it's good you came back. But still, there are these *feelings.* What are they supposed to do with these *feelings?*"

"I don't know," John said, following me pace for pace. "I don't know, Rita. Slow down."

"They blame somebody, John. It's human nature to find somebody to blame. But who? They can't blame you anymore, because Aileen needs you and they can see that, they can see that they were wrong, that the sky didn't fall, that Roger didn't come back after all—"

"Rita, will you stop for a second? I'm out of breath here."

"And they can't even blame Roger, not out loud, not now that his name is back in their midst, they can't say anything in front of Aileen. And God forbid they blame Beth, she's too much part of their great big hunky-dory, one of the main appendages in that man-eating *creature* of a family—"

"Rita—"

I paced the length of the lot, breezing by the hot radiators of parked cars. "But me, what do they need me for? Nothing. They can blame me for everything that's wrong with them, for bringing you back, for ripping open their old wounds, and not miss a step. Who will even notice?" I stopped. Beyond the guardrail was a field so lovely it might have been painted there. Hill and dale, some boulders, a few trees budded with spring. I kicked at the asphalt. "This used to be a *field*," I said. "It was somebody's farm. There was a horse here, right here where I'm standing. People don't get to *keep* anything."

"Rita, shhh, it's all right." He was rocking me gently. Somehow he got me to sit, and the asphalt felt surprisingly warm, almost cozy. "Listen to me, honey," he whispered. "These are nice people doing the best they can."

Somebody Has To Pay, is what I was thinking, rocking in his arms.

On that cold January day in the basement of Trinity Congregational, I met a burdened man. I offered to unburden him; surely that's what I offered, taking him home, washing his hair. Other people's burdens weigh nothing; once handed over, they weigh no more than a tuft of hair. That's what I believed. I believed I was a healer. I believed this good man's burden would weigh no more than a tuft of hair. I believed this good man's burden had nothing to do with me.

"I won't hold you to any promises, John," I said.

"You're the only woman I ever made a promise to, Rita. I mean to keep it."

"It wasn't you who found me. I found you. I threw myself at you. Not that I'm ashamed of myself, don't think that. But I won't make you love me." I was crying now.

"I do love you." Which is what a good man says to a woman in tears.

"Well, I know," I said. "But not as much as you wish you could."

To this he said nothing. But I could see from his face that he had every intention of paying what he now thought of as a debt. He would love me as much as my heart required. As wrong as it was, as antiromantic, it touched me. A woman could do worse.

"I won't make you sorry you met me, John," I said.

"I could never be sorry, Rita," he murmured, drawing me close. "How could I *ever* be sorry?"

He drove me to his apartment in Chesley. We didn't talk much. When we pulled into his driveway, his downstairs neighbor's laundry flapped on a line like a welcoming committee of cheerful ghosts. He took me upstairs, drew me into his bed. We hadn't so much as pulled a sheet over ourselves since I got back with Darla, and though he seemed fevered and ardent, I sensed the melancholy in his lips and fingertips.

"I miss our beginning," he said. "I miss not knowing what was ahead."

"We still don't know," I whispered. "It's all in front of us still."

He looked at me with intense kindness. "Stay," he said, so I did.

I remember every moment of that night, waking to his warm form, the moonlight draining in through the window and resting like a hand across our bodies. The next morning he fed me. We took a walk through his neighborhood, which I liked, a noisy, crushed-together bank of houses and apartment buildings, a lot of cars and dogs and children. We had lunch at a coffee place on Main Street, bought a paper, sat for hours. It was like a first date, or a last.

If he was thinking about what we might have been doing, squiring Aileen around Portland, learning what books she was reading, what TV shows she liked, what she wanted to be when she grew up, he was too kind to say.

He fed me supper in that dreary kitchen, and I ate it all.

"I'm going to move out of here," he said. "I'm going to start acting like a happy man."

"Live with me. Aren't we almost married anyway?"

"Rita." He shook his head ever so slightly, the word *Darla* forming invisibly in the air.

"Oh, God, I forgot to call her." And as I got up from the table, it was like Cinderella's midnight clock, everything turning to its original form: John, the dental-supply salesman, stuck in this dreary apartment with a woman he loved but not enough.

The phone rang and rang. "I'll assume this means the house is still standing," I said. "But I don't like it that she's not answering."

Still, I was reluctant to go. Before I left I asked him to play something. I sat on his threadbare rug and listened. It was a ragtime piece that he'd written himself, a piece that started out with a clean march of notes that began to jumble on top of one another and collide, crisscrossing and barrel-rolling and then, in the last few measures, recovering that straight line.

He wiped his brow. "I wrote that for Aileen."

"It sounds it. I can hear her in there." I got up. "Thank you for this day," I said, and kissed his lips, memorizing their shape and dampness. "I'll keep quiet next time, John. I won't try so hard. I'll try to let them come to me on their own."

"Honey," he said, closing his eyes. "I'm afraid. I feel like I've lost ground."

"Don't ask me not to come, John. Please."

"This is all so delicate," he said helplessly, "and maybe it's better—for now, just for now, just in this stage of it, honey—for me to go it alone."

"I can be delicate, John. Really, I can be delicate."

"Rita," he whispered, sliding his arms around me. "Honey. She isn't ours."

Need I say how these words entered me? She. Isn't. Ours. All those melting *s* sounds. I looked at his face. He was suffering.

"She isn't anybody's, John. Imagine feeling like that." I tightened my arms around his back. "I'm asking you, John. I'm asking you. Let me in."

"Rita. Honey, listen. There are all these people trying to work out such delicate—"

I put my fingers to his lips. "I'm asking you. Please."

He waited a long time. Perhaps he was remembering my hand on his heart that night in our snowed-in hotel, coaxing words from him. "All right," he said, and I collapsed against him, his weight and thickness feeling like a shield. He sheltered me down the stairs and ushered me into my car, quietly. He stayed there, his hand on my rolled-down window, until the enormous night felt tame enough for me to enter it and head for home.

• • •

My house looked to be in one piece, the plants grown another couple of inches. All the lights were out.

I found her in the yard at the back of the house, sitting at the entrance I never used, a set of stone steps under a door that led into the living room. "I locked myself out," she said.

"When?"

"Right after you left. I came out to get the paper and the door shut behind me."

"They don't deliver here anymore."

Her lips quivered. "I figured that *out,* Rita."

Her nightgown barely covered the pitiful knobs of her knees. Her bare feet looked muddy. Her hair, despite the new haircut, had gone stringy and unwashed, and she smelled as if she'd been living in the woods for a month.

"I had to shit in the bushes like a stray cat," she informed me. As if all this were my fault. "I had to hide back here like a criminal."

"Darla, for crying out loud, why didn't you ask somebody for help?"

"Who?" Her mouth slitted into a line. "What was I supposed to do?"

Borrow a phone, jimmy a window, I could think of a million things. Then I looked around. She had a point. I didn't have neighbors, not in the usual sense of the word. Her eyes were fixed on me, blank. She'd been out all night, two nights, in nothing but a couple of yards of thin cotton. No medication for two days.

"I tried to pray," she said. "But God can't hear me."

She said this very softly, but I heard it as a cry, something howlingly lost and human in my sister. Truly, she had lost her way, and for better or worse, she'd come to me to find it again.

I led her around the side, cupping her bony elbow, and tried the kitchen entrance. Which opened. Easily.

"It wasn't locked," I told her.

"Oh," she said, and tottered through the door.

Sheldon had a fit when he saw us; he danced back and forth on his perch, squawking furiously until I let him out. His water dish had tipped over and there was birdseed all over the kitchen floor.

I ran a bath for her and set out her medication and a bottle of my top-of-the-line shampoo. While I heated up some of her casserole, I could hear the sound of water as her body eased in and out of the tub. She used to bang on our bathroom door when we were in high school, blatting at me to hurry up, some guy was waiting for her down on the street, his horn making the first rude punctures in a hot summer night. Already my mother would be complaining, We don't know this boy and was he one of the River Street Joneses or one of the Silver Street Joneses and didn't anybody ever teach him to ring a doorbell? And Darla snarling back that she didn't give a rat's ass what street a person came from it's a person's heart that counts, and she believed it, befriended all the lost souls of Alton, which back then had a hefty share. She'd tear down the stairs and into some patched-up car with a dragging tailpipe making phosphorous sparks along the asphalt.

Back then Darla wouldn't wait for anything. She wouldn't wait for the urgencies of her own body, wouldn't wait for Gram to reveal her inner beauties, wouldn't wait for me to finish a sentence. She spent too much of her life in too short a time, then to make up for it slowed to a crawl at the House of Peace, and now that she was back in her former life she was being driven crazy trying to find that old speed, or that old zeal, whatever it was that made her put one foot in front of the other and move.

She ate quite a bit of the casserole, greedily, with a serving spoon. All at once she looked up, a whiff of papaya from her damp hair gusting across the table. "Do you pray?" she asked me.

"Sometimes," I said.

"How?"

"I just close my eyes and feel God's mercy," I said. That's about as close as I could come to describing it.

She was blinking at me, as if she'd just come out of a coma and I was the first object in her line of vision. Her face looked clean and solemn. "That sounds nice."

"Don't get me wrong," I said. "God doesn't know me from a chestnut tree. I'm just saying, I believe in mercy."

"Define mercy."

I thought about it. "Giveth and taketh," I said. "It all balances out somehow."

She finished her casserole, clanking the spoon down on the plate. "I was hungry," she said. "This is how I would've been if you hadn't come to get me. I'd have been out on a San Diego street someplace, looking for something to eat, a place to pee."

"What were you looking for out there with the . . . people? Was it God?"

She nodded.

"Did you find Him?"

"I thought I had." She shook her head. "Where is He, Rita?"

"Not in the palm of your hand. That much I know."

"Where, then?" Her eyes were big and watery, absolutely sincere. *Where, then?*

"He's not that man, Kenneth Boyd."

"Kenneth never said he was God."

"He said he had God's ear. He said God would smile on you if you gave yourself up to that place. What's the difference?"

"I wanted him to be God," Darla admitted. "I was lazy."

"You'll find your way back, Darla, I know you will."

"I should've gone to college."

"Me, too," I said. "Maybe I'd be teaching fourth grade, or testing nuclear missiles."

Then she smiled at me, a genuine expression of affection. It touched me more than it had a right to, and what I was thinking was how I used to wonder what it would be like to have a sister like this. "I'm going to do something for you someday, Rita," she said. "I'll pay you back."

"Get better. That's all."

"Okay," she said.

It was late. I walked her to her room and turned down her bed. On the bedspread was a pile of ladies' magazines that she'd swiped from my waiting room. Every night she read from those pages as if it were a series of manuals about breaking back into life after almost twenty years in a cave. I couldn't imagine what she thought the world had become in her absence. In February you got the carrot diet, in March the prune-and-grapefruit diet, in April they warned you that compulsive dieting shortens your life by five years. The articles not on diets were about how to find a man, how to keep a man, and how you don't need a man to complete you.

"Good night," she said.

I lingered at the door.

She stacked the magazines on her lap and sorted through them. When she realized I was still there, she said, "I forgot to ask how your visit went."

"It went fine. He's in love with her."

"I was right?"

"Yes," I said. "But he won't betray me. It's something he'll live with and never mention."

"You don't need a man to complete you," she said.

"Yes, I do. And I don't care who knows it. I wasn't meant to be alone."

"You've been alone all your life, Rita. You work alone. You have no friends except John, as far as I can see. If God intended something else, it seems to me you've done your best to thwart him."

"I have friends," I said. "Audrey and I have dinner once a month. We cut each other's hair."

"Who's Audrey?"

"Never mind."

Darla was flipping through the pages, but her eyes didn't light on anything. "If you had a heart attack at two A.M.," she asked, "who would you call?"

"9-1-1. Who do you think?"

"I wouldn't have had to call anybody," she said. "They were right there. If I so much as groaned in my sleep someone would be there, softly calling my name."

"Which wasn't your real name."

She closed a magazine with a soft flap. "I asked them to take me back."

"I know. I saw the phone bill." The lights from next door rinsed my sister's face in an eerie amber shadow. "What did they say?"

"They said no." She shook her head. "All I did was wonder. That's all I did. I wondered if maybe Kenneth wasn't a messenger.

Directly, I mean. I wondered if maybe God had plans for me that didn't square exactly with what Kenneth was saying."

"Question authority. That's what you used to say."

She smiled wanly. "The thing is, I want to go back. Even though I know he's not real, I want to go back anyway."

Until this moment I had believed forgiveness to be a special virtue, a beneficence God expected of good people. But it wasn't that at all. Forgiveness was an instinct, a desperate impulse to stay connected to the people you needed, no matter what their betrayals.

"Well," I said to Darla, "I'm awfully sorry."

"The shrink wants to put me into a group. I told him he could just forget it. Can you see me sitting around with a bunch of ex-Moonies?"

"Not really. But it might help."

She didn't say anything for a few minutes, and I thought she might have fallen asleep.

Then she asked, "What are they like, anyway? Those sisters in Portland?"

"The kind that go around donating kidneys to each other."

She laughed a little, then squared up the magazines and put them back on the nightstand. I moved back from the doorway.

"Rita?" she said. "Did you tell me you lost a baby?"

"Yes."

"Tell me again."

I had told this story exactly once, to John, on a clear, cold night when we first went to Portland. We stood on the balcony of the hotel, shivering. His eyes were damp and fixed in that way I loved, and he would have listened to it all. I told him I lost a baby, that it was very sad. But I didn't tell him about Mary, who turned out to be Tonya Kurgan. I didn't mention baptizing the baby clothes in Walker Creek. At the time I wanted so badly to be a healer, a person without wounds. I lost a baby, I told him. It was sad.

Darla's head was tipped up and cocked to the side, like Sheldon when he listens to his basketball tapes. "Tell me," she said again.

So I sat down on her bed. And told her everything.

19

Two weeks later, on a Friday evening, I got a call from a Martha Kreiger, who was in quite the pickle. I could barely hear her over the din of her bachelorette party. The gist was that her maid of honor had made reservations at Hair Tomorrow for the next morning, the wedding day, but when she called to confirm, the bitch at the desk—I'm quoting now—claimed never to have heard of them. So much for coffee in porcelain champagne flutes. I took pity on the poor girl, even though she made it crystal clear that I was her bottom-of-the-barrel last-gasp option. I said I'd take all three of them—Martha and her two attendants—provided they could come in very early the next day. Besides, I needed the extra cash to pay Darla's psychiatrist bills.

"What are they charging at Hair Tomorrow these days?" I asked the bride.

"You don't even want to know," she groaned.

"Yes, I do," I said, "because that's what I'll be charging you."

"You don't have a *reputation,*" she huffed, insulted.

"What I have, Martha, is *plans.* And it's going to cost you to make me rearrange them."

My plans, of course, involved a drive to Portland with John. Beth had asked him to come on Saturday instead of Friday, which already shortened his weekend, and now I had to ask him to shorten it still further. He promised to wait, agreeing to pick me up at noon. I took this as a sign that he still loved me.

Darla's medications had finally begun to kick in—although later she would claim just the opposite, that they weren't working, or working against rather than with her fragile psyche. All I know is that by the time I got downstairs on Saturday, she was brisking through the shop like a modern-day Mary Poppins, humming to herself as she tidied up.

My feeling at the time was that asking to hear my story, and then actually listening to it, had returned her to the world in a way she'd been resisting. She claimed later that my story supplied the fuel that propelled her actions, that she was running on empathy. I don't know. I'd like to think so—Darla had always been a tad short on empathy, and the fact that she could summon any measure of it, however misguided, was not entirely bad news. I intend to believe her explanation in full, eventually. With enough hindsight a person can believe anything.

At eight sharp the bridal party draggled in, looking old and hungover, including Martha, the bride, who was seven months pregnant. When I saw her, I realized I knew her vaguely from high school—she was either a couple of years younger or older than me, I wasn't sure. All three of them were from the before Alton, which, despite its voluminous virtues, wasn't perfect.

Generally speaking, in times of stress or trouble I like to schedule my dear ones, my regulars, on the same day, connecting them to one another. I like to think of chance meetings on the street, one dashing out from the dry cleaners just as another is pulling up to the curb. They exchange a glance, a knowing grin, the Alton two-fingered wave; in any case, there's a happy exchange that has its source nowhere but in me.

That morning I was surrounded not by dear ones but by strangers. The bridal party chattered away, their voices rising and falling around me, but I didn't say much myself. I was preparing delicate sound bites for later in the day—"What a delicately picturesque city Portland is"; "The children all seem so delicately well-adjusted"; "What's the secret to these delicate muffins?"—and mentally reviewing the contents of the overnight bag I had waiting near the door. Everything I packed was beige.

Martha, the bride, held court in the swivel, watching me like a house cat as I rolled her hair. She'd brought in a picture of Vivien Leigh in *Gone With the Wind.* I considered her well past the age for theme weddings, especially considering her present physical condition, but I was in no position to offer any opinions. "You know *me,*" she was saying to one of her cousins, "I like to look on the bright side, and I'm telling you guys, there's *plenty* of men out there."

"That's what all married women say," shouted her cousin Sally from underneath a dryer.

Despite the mountain of knowledge I have yet to acquire on the subject of human nature, I know one thing for sure: People who begin sentences with "You know *me*" don't know bingo about themselves.

"I'd like to snag one of those lawyers in the Silver Street

condos," the other cousin, Brenda something, sighed. She was in the waiting area leafing through ladies' magazines.

"Don't pick a lawyer," Martha said airily, as if all her cousin had to do was flip through the husband directory and choose. "Try a teacher. They've got patience to burn."

"Don't pick a shrink, either," Darla called over from the counter, where she was filling out reminder cards. "You start to show the least sign of getting your soul returned in one piece and they want to shunt you off to group therapy." She tsked, once, loudly. "Besides, you don't need a man to complete you."

No sooner were the words out of her mouth than a man walked in. It was Rodney, who looked as if he'd spent the night under a backhoe.

"I'm swamped, Rodney," I told him. "I've got to be out of here at the stroke of noon."

His hands fisted together, hard. "I need a reading."

"Rodney, there's no way."

"Can I schedule you for next week?" Darla asked, snapping the appointment book open.

He faltered over to me. "Help me," he said.

"You didn't get the job?"

"I got it," he said. "The cancer's back."

I took my hands off Martha Kreiger and set down my comb. "Come here."

I held him right there in the middle of everything and let him cry for a few minutes. A few minutes is a very long time when you're listening to the echo of a grown man's weeping. Everybody went quiet. Martha looked at him as if he were a thundercloud hovering over her wedding tent. "People grow from these things," she said, then drummed her fingers impatiently on her knees.

"That's true, Martha," I said, eyeing her over Rodney's shoulder. "And isn't that exactly what this man needs right now, another soul-filling personal-growth experience." Martha rose a bit from her chair, then thought better of it. With a head full of curlers and a wedding in three hours, she didn't have a whole lot of leverage.

"Now," I said. "Rodney. Listen to me. You don't need the cards to tell you what to do. You do what you always do."

"What do I always do?" His face looked long and streaked, his cheeks hollowed out, scraped clean. "Really, Rita, I forget."

"You go home to your wife and take your comfort there. You go for the treatments. You remember, at all times, that hope is your best bet." I squeezed his shoulders, looking him in the eye. "Hope is your best bet, Rodney. At all times."

He was nodding furiously, as if I were the font of all wisdom, when what I was doing was parroting back the exact words he'd said to me the first time he got cancer. "I will," he said. "I will." Then he gave me a squeeze, and staggered out of the shop toward the town square.

"Call his wife," I said to Darla. "They're in the book."

"What should I say?" She leapt to her feet, all business, and cracked open the phone book.

"Say her husband is wandering around East Main in the throes of grief and to come get him."

"Wow, tough break," said the cousin in the waiting area.

Martha shuddered. "Like the sign says, life is short. Play hard."

I wanted to slap her face, but instead I rolled the rest of her hair, jammed the pins in, stuck her under a dryer next to her cousin, and summoned the next victim.

"Life *is* short," Darla murmured, hanging up the phone. "You have to seize the day."

Nobody said much after that, which was fine with me. I'd heard enough pre-ceremony conversations to last me three lifetimes. Wouldn't you think the talk would be about love and devotion, the lilacs in the dooryard and the shape of his dear sweet hands? But it was never that, it was always would the cake get delivered on time, would the rain hold off, would her father's second wife show her rat-eyed face at the reception.

I was tired. I did their comb-outs and took their money. They left feeling like Southern belles and looking like extras in a high-school production of *Annie Get Your Gun*. It was not my best work. As they squeezed into Martha's Geo, Rodney's wife drove by with Rodney in the passenger seat, his head resting against the window.

I sat in the swivel, which was still warm from Martha's miserly butt, and rested my face in my hands. Darla edged over. "That poor man," she crooned. "That poor man."

Her voice sounded milky and sweet, and I flashed on a few nice times from way back, times when she was sleepy or heartbroken and would turn to me before thinking and ask, "What's wrong with me?" I'd tell her, "Nothing. You're great," the way I thought I was supposed to, and when she smiled in response, I'd realize I meant it.

"You have to seize the day," Darla said, but I wasn't sure whether she was addressing me or herself.

Then John arrived, uncharacteristically jittery, having already missed one-quarter of his allotted weekend. For me. "What's wrong?" he asked.

"Nothing."

Darla looked at me.

"Nothing," I repeated. "Let's go have our weekend."

He kissed my cheek, ran his hands across the small of my back. "Do I feel delicate?" I whispered. He smiled and picked up my bag. I was almost glad that I'd behaved badly, so he could forgive me for it.

"Now, Darla," I said. "Remember, the kitchen door doesn't lock automatically. You have to deliberately lock yourself out."

For a second she didn't answer. Then: "I want to come with you."

"Par— Pardon me?" John said.

"I'd like to come with you. I'll just toodle around town, do a little sight-seeing, while you two attend to your problems."

"Darla, we'll be there till tomorrow."

"They're not problems," John informed her.

"I'll stay in the hotel with you guys," Darla said. She smiled, quite fetchingly, I thought. "Don't worry, I'll get a separate room. If you'll lend me the money."

I heard a long, soft exhalation of air from John. I could feel his helpless stare.

"You're not packed, Darla," I said. "We have to leave right now. This very minute."

"I'll wear your clothes. That's all I've been doing anyway."

Suddenly—and this is the part that makes me realize how unbuckled my thoughts were, how badly Rodney's news had rattled me—I thought Darla's suggestion a magnificent idea. Just magnificent. I could be delicate to the point of invisible and not endear myself to that family; I could clothe myself in beige from head to foot and move that family not an inch. I was nobody, I had not so much as a pin drop of blood to connect me to a soul they knew; I could be married to John twenty years and budge their convictions not a whit. This much I had gathered after the giddy hopes of my first impression, which was, like all first impressions, not much more than a wish.

But what if I brought my sister? My sister whom I had taken in and nurtured back to the pink of health? Surely if there was anything they could understand, it was family obligation, sisterly love. They could admire me, at least. That was a start.

"Let me run up and get my toothbrush," Darla said, and I did not stop her.

"We won't even know she's there," I assured John. "She's been great all week, running errands for me, acting just like a regular person. I'm beginning to think she might even be employable."

John said nothing, simply stood there with my overnight bag the way I'd seen Mr. Rokowski do in many a department store, holding Mrs. Rokowski's big black old-lady purse while she sorted through a bin of lipsticks or white underpants. If there is a universal symbol of a good-natured marriage, it's a man holding his wife's purse. I thought John's possession of my overnight bag was a sign of everlasting comfort and joy.

"We'll drop her off downtown," I said. "I'll give her some money, we can meet later on at the hotel."

John closed his eyes. "Rita."

"She can do it," I said. "She can read a map. Here she comes."

Darla sailed through the door, and I did not stop her. She got into the car, and I did not stop her. She buckled her seat belt, and I did not stop her.

And John, because he had already squandered a morning's worth of Aileen and Beth, did not stop her.

We didn't talk much on the way up, but what conversation we had was normal. At one point Darla asked John to name his favorite musical composition. She mentioned how pleased she was over our forthcoming nuptials. She hoped Sheldon wouldn't be lonely without human companionship for two days, despite her having left the radio on for him.

John's fingers loosened on the wheel, his chin relaxed, he answered her questions by looking in the rearview mirror, reassuring himself.

A magnificent idea.

Then, when we got to Portland, she said, "I guess I'll stick with you guys."

John turned all the way around to look at her. "I thought you wanted to go shopping and whatnot."

"John, the road," I said, and he swiveled back.

"I changed my mind," Darla said. "I've heard so much about this little girl, this cute little Aileen person, I'd kind of like to meet her."

For a moment I let Darla's words drift down, take root. Then: "Okay," I said.

"I mean, she'll be kind of a relation to me, won't she? A niece-in-law or something?"

John kept driving, glancing at Darla in the mirror.

"She's family," I said to him quietly. "They'll understand that. They understand taking care of your own."

He slowed down, and I thought he was going to let Darla out, but then he speeded up again, bringing us off the highway and into Portland and up the hill. He pulled up directly in front of Balzano's Family Bakery. "Don't embarrass us, Darla," he said, as if that were the worst thing he could imagine her doing.

The bakery was busy for a Saturday afternoon. Some of the boys were gathered on the sidewalk with some friends. They seemed bigger than they had the last time I'd seen them, or maybe I simply mixed up which boy was which. They all had deep brown eyes and the carriage of well-loved sons. Callie was chatting up some customers just inside the door, her hands resting on Aileen's shoulders.

"Wow," Darla said.

That involuntary reaction is the kindest thing my sister ever did for me; her voice was all breath and smoke, making me realize I was not mistaken—that the family spread over each side of the bakery doors made a first impression that inspired yearning.

Whether because of John's warning or in spite of it, Darla was the picture of decorum. She held out a graceful hand, remarked how much she'd heard about all these beautiful children, how kind John and I were to give her a lift, since she had to be in Portland on extremely important business and her Mercedes was in the shop getting Simonized. John and I did not contradict her. His relief was palpable as a sigh.

Beth came out with a bakery bag that smelled of cinnamon. "How are you feeling?" she asked when Darla introduced herself.

"Oh, wonderful," Darla said. "On the mend. Absolutely."

"She's been ill," Beth said to her sisters, then gave me a look that reassured me she'd said nothing about Darla's former career as a pie-eyed apostle of Kenneth Boyd, Ph.D.

Beth. The keeper of secrets.

"Nothing serious, I hope," Susanna said without the slightest drop of sincerity.

Darla, who appeared to be reentering the real world by leaps and bounds before my very eyes, heard Susanna's I-couldn't-care-less. Her eyes blazed briefly before she replied, in a voice as bland and harmless as a field of wheat, "Not at all. But thanks for asking." Then she smiled so sweetly I wondered whether she held God's breath in her palms after all.

In the meantime Aileen had broken from her aunts to come over and stand next to John. She slipped her hand around his wrist but did not kiss him. Two weeks had made her shy, which reminded me how much care love requires, how nothing takes the place of physical bodies in contact.

She didn't kiss me, either. Or touch me. I smiled as hard as I could, and she grinned up at me, but I kept my hands to myself, trying to be delicate.

"It's my turn," she said. "I pick the beach."

"You pick the beach!" John said. This is how he always responded to her, repeating her words in a fever of enthusiasm, as if he'd never in this lifetime heard such well-formed, interesting phrasings. She laughed. "The beach," she repeated. "I'm going to start a rock collection."

"A rock collection!"

"Gray stones and white stones," she said. "No in-betweens."

"That's sounds like quite a challenge," I said.

She grinned. "And all the same size."

"All the same size," John said, chuckling. "Imagine."

The hint of a smile flared briefly on the twins' faces, and I saw what I had not before seen: The quality of John's love was simple, without disguise, taken up with nothing but this one child. His love made no noise. It took up little space. It threatened no one.

Although they despised the tide of sorrow his return had unleashed, although they despised his blood connection to the man who had wrecked their lives, they did not begrudge him this love.

John had dragged nothing but his heavy body to this place, while I, a mere friend of the intruder, had dragged a whole life up here with me, a muddy, weedy, squelchy mess that they could see and hear and feel. It was as if I'd hauled up from the bottom of the ocean with seaweed and eely creatures clinging to my shoes, leaving a thin wet trail to show where I had been living all this time. That they could see this—that *I* could see this, here, now—shamed me. How could loss, something so private, invisible, so *not there,* so *missing,* take on such a clamor that virtual strangers could hear me coming from a hundred miles away?

"Well, this all sounds just wonderful," Darla said. "I lived two miles from the Pacific Ocean for a million years and never so much as dipped my toe in the water."

This Aileen found fascinating. She and Darla got into the backseat of John's car while the rest of us milled awkwardly. Already the day was different: We would take our outing in John's car, not Beth's. Aileen sat in the back, not the front. Which left me to decide: Should I grab the back to be near Aileen, leaving Beth to sit in front with John like a wife? Or did I take my rightful spot, leaving Darla and Beth to take in the spark and scent of that child while I sat in front with my hands folded?

"Come on," Darla said from her open window. "We've got rocks to collect."

The twins eyed her cautiously, but in truth my sister looked liked her old self that day: a creamy oval face haloed by a sheen of honey-brown hair, like one of the girls in those old print ads for

Breck shampoo. Forty-year-old women used to show them to me back when I was in training, folded tear-outs from back copies of *Ladies' Home Journal* plucked from their mothers' attics. "These are *paintings*," I would tell them, comparing their wiry curls with the golden brush strokes. "You're a *person*." But Darla, on that day, did look like a painting, brushy and melting and slightly surreal.

They trusted her smile, her lovely manners, her physical beauty. She was nothing that day if not delicate.

"What time will you be back?" Callie asked Beth.

"By suppertime. Maybe some of us could go out to eat."

Callie shrugged. "We'll see."

Then Beth saved me the trouble of a decision by opening the back door and slipping in next to her niece.

"I don't remember the last time I had this much fun," Darla trilled from the back. She pawed John's shoulder. "Thanks, brother-in-law."

John sighed. "It's no trouble."

The beach we chose was an out-of-the-way spot in Scarborough at the end of a long access road with a small gravel lot close to the sand. John's was the only car, a big, grandfatherly presence under a flat blue sky. The day felt safe and open and full of possibility.

The place was all but deserted, the day being cool and breezy, too early for sunbathers, too late for the hardy types who claimed to love beaches only in winter. Beth passed out cinnamon rolls from her bakery bag. I felt like part of a regular family on an ordinary springtime picnic.

"None for me," John said. "I'm watching my weight."

Which was news to me. But there it was: his belt cinched

tighter, his winged cheekbones becoming barely discernible, like lost change under a rug. His eyes looked bigger.

We sat on the warmed sand, side by side, the five of us, gazing out at the green, petticoated water. Aileen got up first, patrolling the water's edge for rocks. Her body looked sleek, seal-like, of the sea. With a start, I realized she'd grown since I'd last seen her.

"Yum," Darla said, licking sugar off her fingers.

We spent an hour or so picking our way over the sand, stopping to wade, to examine shells and stones, to gaze out at the sea. For the first little while, Beth stayed close to Aileen, whom Darla was regaling with stories about California wildlife. According to Darla, she had borne witness to coyotes and condors, sea lions and sharks, hummingbirds with completely red heads. That she had managed this while hoeing cabbage and working two days a week in a copy shop and avoiding the Pacific Ocean was news to me. But she kept on talking, and, perhaps pleasantly numbed from the lull of Darla's voice, Beth lost her guard and drifted toward John, who was digging up a large, pure-black rock to lug into the trunk for Aileen, while Aileen and Darla and I drifted the other way, nearer the road, listening to the waves and the cackling gulls and Darla's enchanting voice.

I'm not sure exactly what happened next. I do remember being mesmerized by the sight of a full-masted sailboat far out on the horizon, its billowing whiteness resembling a cloud blowing over the water. And I remember moving my line of sight down the beach, to where John and Beth had their heads together, their arms crossed through each other's, lifting the black rock. I remember the soft, animated rise and fall of their voices, a rustle of laughter, a low grunt from John as he tugged. Beth's secret flared between them, a low, warm flame tempered by his forgiveness. They were oblivious, intent only on each other and their mutual task. My eyes filled, and I looked away.

Darla and Aileen were almost to the car then, each of them hauling a bag of rocks and a couple of sticks of driftwood. John and Beth were still bent toward the earth, pulling. I began to walk toward my sister, more curious than afraid, though tiny buzzers began to go off in various parts of my body. I heard a shout from John and Beth's direction, but they were a good distance down the beach and I couldn't tell which of them had called out. They didn't sound alarmed, merely curious. I didn't look back, couldn't bear to see them like that again.

Instead I fixed on my sister, who smiled past me, lifted the bag of rocks. She exaggerated her gestures, wiggling the bag high in the air and pointing to the car: *We're just putting the first load in. Don't mind us, go back to whatever you were doing.* She looked exactly the way she had on any weekday night when waving good-bye to my parents, who believed she was off to spend the night with her friend Karen Nichols and Karen's pillar-of-the-church parents. I used to watch her, awestruck: the blinding smile that could not quite mask the true intentions contained in the rest of her face. Whether Beth and John saw this, I don't know, because I was walking faster now, and then running, the deep, warm sand restricting my forward motion, tugging my feet earthward. By the time I caught up, Aileen had gotten into the backseat and Darla was starting the car that John, that trusting soul, had left unlocked, windows down, keys dangling in the ignition.

I flung open the back door, the engine roaring. "Darla, what are you doing?" I yelled. "What the hell are you doing?"

Behind me, running up the beach, shouting, was my second chance. He would have stuck by me forever by the grace of his gratitude and loyalty. I had only to reach over the seat, snatch the key. I could have grabbed the emergency brake, opened Darla's door instead of Aileen's. I could have pulled Darla's hair, twisted her wrist, yanked her out of there, saved the day. He would have married me. We would have been happy enough. This I know.

But I saw Aileen just then, perched in the backseat with a stick of driftwood laid across her lap. Eight years old and her shoulders set hard against the will of God. It struck me then, with the force of a blow, that I had all this time misjudged my dream.

Here was my crippled dog.

She looked up, this child with one impossible wish. A wish that had burdened her since the age of three.

"Get in!" Darla cried. "Get in!"

Time stopped. It was the kind of stop-time where your body moves in slow motion, of its own accord. Darla was shouting, Beth and John were running up the beach, shouting, the car engine was revving, but for the moment I existed outside all that noise, in this certain, quiet, slow-motion place where I thought: Well. You don't get to choose your obligations. Only whether or not to meet them.

I got in.

"We're going to get sodas," Aileen said, glancing uncertainly at Darla, who fiddled with the gear shift, ramming us into reverse and then shoving the stick forward again.

The car lurched ahead.

"Darla, stop!" I yelled.

"Hey," Aileen asked breathlessly, "am I being kidnapped?"

"Not at all," Darla sang out. "You're being rescued." The car lurched again, then roared forward.

"Darla!" I shouted. "Stop the car!"

But she took not the least notice. "Don't worry," she called out over the sound of the engine, the tires, the spitting gravel. "Buckle up, everybody."

That strange, still part of me took Aileen's hand. I felt each of her fingers as a sweet, separate pressure. At the same time another part of me—the part that didn't want to lose one more thing, ever—was shouting at Darla: "What are you doing? Darla, what do you think you're doing?"

In the side mirror I glimpsed Beth and John stumbling over the sand, their arms raised, their mouths open. Beth was closer now, her beautiful lips parted in a perfect O.

He would have married me. This I know.

"Buckle up, sweetheart," I said to Aileen, for the car was wending dangerously, skirting off the gravel lot and onto the access road and around the bend and toward the Black Point Road.

"Rita," Aileen said, fumbling with the belt. "My aunts are going to be really, really mad."

"I know."

"They won't let you come back."

I nodded.

"Uncle John will be mad, too."

"I know. It's all right."

She looked up, the picture of calm. I wonder sometimes if at that moment she saw all the way to the end of the day and decided to let it unfold. In any case, she didn't protest.

I squeezed her hand, which was warm and thin. "Don't be scared," I said.

She looked at me, bright-eyed. "I'm not scared."

"Here we go," I said.

Whether Darla turned the car around in five minutes or five hours, all I had left was to make the most of good-bye.

We had a good half hour's head start, as it turned out, though I didn't discover this till later. Beth and John waited fifteen minutes at the beach, thinking we'd played a terrible, bewildering joke, or, equally bewildering, gone back for something we'd forgotten, or—they went through a long list, their voices tightening as the minutes ticked down. Then they began to walk the length of the access road, which was more than half a mile, and they didn't find a phone until they'd walked another mile on the Black Point Road, trying house after house, each of which had long, winding driveways that ended in dooryards still buttoned up for winter. Finally they flagged down a motorist with a car phone, and there began the search.

This much I pieced together in the long weeks that followed: They gathered at the bakery, the tables dragged together, a control central of the sort you see in movies. They assumed we'd head south, back toward Massachusetts. John kept calling his apartment, my salon number, my house number. Over and over. They got out a road map to trace a likely route. The older boys got into their cars and set out after us. John kept telling them I was no kidnapper, that Darla was crazy, I must be kidnapped as well, but they wouldn't believe it, they wanted me to have planned the whole thing, the master criminal, the crazed woman desperate enough to steal a child.

If they put John into this scheme even for a moment, I don't know. If they did, he has forgotten it. Or erased it. According to him they worked together, as a family, spooning coffee into the filters, heating the oven to warm some biscuits, manning the phone, talking to the police detectives who clanked through the doors with their shiny shoes and their badges and guns and trench coats. Strategizing, questioning, looking for me and Darla and a kidnapped girl.

My guess is they all took a long look at John. I can see Beth beside him, saying to the police, Yes, he's trustworthy. Yes, we've known him quite some time now. No, he wouldn't be involved in something like this. No, he isn't involved with the perpetrators. John had to keep reminding everyone that one of the "perpetrators" was his betrothed. But Beth was in love with him already, willing to alter facts to fit her desires.

I, too, thought Darla would head south. Instead she steered us northward on the interstate, thinking she'd like to get a look at Canada, which, judging from Darla's average speed, would be about twenty-five hours away. If you didn't know that Darla had been out of the loop, so to speak, for nearly twenty years, you certainly would have been able to tell by her driving. After weaving between the driving lane and the shoulder for a mile or two, she settled for the middle of the passing lane at the speed of a tricycle.

"I'll drop you off in New Brunswick," she said, "and you can take it from there."

"For God's sake, Darla, what are you talking about?"

Her eyes met mine in the rearview. "You know."

"She means me," Aileen said. "You have to start looking for a hideout."

"You're perfectly safe, sweetheart," I said, still holding her hand. "Darla's going to bring you back safe and sound. Aren't you, Darla?"

"I've never been kidnapped before," Aileen said. Her mouth was partly open, her feet dangled calmly.

"This isn't a kidnapping," Darla said. "Jeez."

People were leaning on their horns, passing us on the right. I kept waiting for a siren, but none came. Aileen was looking at me, smiling. She was, in a word, thrilled. And who wouldn't be? A quick peek out of the cocoon, a glimpse of an alternate life. It struck me that somebody who'd spent the last five years in the middle of a human bed quilt might like to get a look at the rest of the world.

"Where are you taking us?" she asked Darla. She was speaking in a different voice, the voice of a heroine in one of her books, some Nancy Drew type who liked adventures. I liked that. The word *us.*

"I figure you two can spend some time with our peace-loving neighbors to the north," Darla said. Even as she spoke she lost conviction, her voice getting heavier, slower. "They've got free health care, all kinds of stuff. Once you get settled, you can send for John." Aileen and I both stared at her, astounded. I laughed out loud, or maybe it was a small cry. I don't know.

"I'm thinking out loud here," Darla snapped. "It's not like I planned this."

This much was a relief. "Darla—" I said.

"Look, I told you I'd do something for you and I'm doing it. Don't look a gift horse in the mouth." She sounded frightened now, her voice unhinging.

I could have said something then. *I don't want what you're trying to give me.* That's what I should have said. Turn around. Stop, now. But the truth is, I did want it. Aileen was cuddled beneath my arm, humming something to herself, fiddling with her collected rocks, separating light from dark. Gray in my lap, white in hers. She had set the driftwood on the floor, a slender, bleached stick that looked to weigh less than a sparrow.

My impulse was to start talking, to catch up like old friends. But eight years—almost nine, her birthday was days away—felt like a lot of years, and I didn't have that kind of time. So I helped Aileen sort her rocks, glad that she seemed to be enjoying my company. We remained mostly quiet. Time uncoiled in front of us, and we simply spent it.

Darla kept on driving, and I did not stop her.

"We'll have to change my name if I'm going to be kidnapped," Aileen said. "How about Esmerelda?"

"Too obvious," Darla said. "They'd spot you in a heartbeat."

I smiled down at Aileen, letting her know I realized this was a game, that what we were doing was pretending to be on the lam the way we had pretended to be prospective house buyers. "Maybe I could keep my first name," she said. "And think of a different last name."

"What about Aileen Wolf?" I suggested. "Aileen Andrews."

"Aileen Drew," she said. "Like Nancy Drew."

"Aileen Rockefeller. We could pretend you're rich."

"Or Reed," she said. "That was my real name once."

I cupped her chin. "Yes, I know." This was the nicest part. Just the two of us, away from the loving clamor that followed her every minute of her days.

"Aileen Reed," she said. "That was me." She looked solemn all of a sudden, as if she wanted something from me.

I nodded. "That was you."

"My father was a good man," she said.

"That's right."

"He did one bad thing."

"Yes."

"I can make him into anything I want."

I tightened my arm around her. "That's right."

"Then I make him into Uncle John," she said, and it sounded like words from a genie or a magician announcing the magic trick, the amazing illusion, the granted wish.

"Presto," I said. Then I saw the blue lights.

Darla pulled over in a crisscross of bleating horns. "Is it over?" Aileen asked, disappointed.

"Yes," I said, and kissed the top of her head.

"That was fun," she said, as if we'd been on a Ferris wheel ride. In a way we had, and I was grateful for it, that suspended time. We'd been on the road nearly two hours and had made it only to Richmond.

The trooper got out, asked for the license Darla did not have on her person, then wanted to know if the child in our custody was Aileen Doherty.

Darla wouldn't stop talking as the trooper got us out of the car and onto the shoulder of the highway. "We were putting rocks in the car," she explained, which was no explanation at all. "The key was in the ignition, just dangling there, and it came to me that I could do this one thing for my sister." I looked up. Her mouth was moving very fast, but suddenly I couldn't hear exactly what she was saying. Her silhouette throbbed in the sunlight; the blue pulse from the cruiser lent an eerie outline to her bent head, her arms folded tightly across her middle.

Finally she stopped. She faced the trooper with his big important hat and his hard cold boulder of a chest and began to weep, pointing toward me, crying, "She lost a baby! She lost a baby!"

After a few minutes another trooper pulled up and took over the questioning. Darla had to lean over a bit to spit out her words—or, I should say, my words. She was telling about the tiny pink shirt the policeman saved, about Layton's betrayal, about Tonya Kurgan's washboard hair.

In the meantime, the first trooper was trying to square this perfectly contented child with the kidnap victim that had come in over the radio. "You're telling me you know this lady?" he asked Aileen.

She looked a little afraid, but of him, not me. "They're kind of my aunts," she said.

He looked at me. "Through marriage," I added, without conviction. "In no time at all." By this time I could see the straight, inevitable line of her future, which by necessity eclipsed mine. If she had been able to spare me a loss, I believe she would have. But that child's one wish was to raise her parents from the dead, and I alone had been summoned to make that wish come true. After that, like the fairy godmother in the tales my grandmother used to tell, I had no further obligation but to disappear.

"Wait here," the trooper said, then he trudged back to the car, got on the radio, and conferred with the other trooper, who had an open pad on which he furiously scribbled the rapid-fire words of my sister, who was inconsolable.

In the end, they called it a domestic dispute. *Domestic* is a nice word; funny enough, I felt as if I'd finally landed where I'd intended to land all along—smack in the middle of that family. In such a way that they could not ignore me. Not that I would have chosen for myself the path that got me there.

When we arrived at the station, the police took the three of us—Darla, Aileen, and me—to separate rooms to get our statements. The room I ended up in had a broken light panel, which sent a jagged shadow over the otherwise sweet, walrusy face of the interrogating officer. He asked me some questions. He listened to my story, his mustache drooping in what I took for either sympathy or exhaustion.

When I got out, the corridor looked like a long strip of light with John standing at the far end of it. My King of Cups, his shoulders set low in despair. Behind him the family moved like a bouquet of let-go balloons, Susanna and Callie arguing with the police, the husbands and boys moving aimlessly through the lobby. Beth stood away from everyone, Aileen tucked close beside her. When John saw me, he began to move. He reminded me of a wild animal that had been sprung from a trap and didn't know it yet—a curious sort of capering, an expectation of pain in the way he wended down that corridor.

"Rita," he cried, his arms lifting. "Honey, why?" I think he was weeping, though I've tried to forget how his face looked that last time.

When he got to me, he clasped me by the shoulders, peering into my face. Beth and her family were clustered near the end of the corridor, watching us, and though he was distraught, and angry—of course he was angry—he had the guts to come to me, to claim me. If loyalty had a physical form, it would look exactly like John Reed.

I slipped from his grasp, as gently as I could, and stood a pace or two away.

"What were you thinking, Rita?" he pleaded. "Why didn't you stop her?" The anger on his face melted into something like fear, or confusion. All at once he resembled the man I'd met back in January, the lost soul who'd turned up at the wrong meeting.

By this time Beth was there, touching my sleeve. "How could you, Rita? We were frantic, how could you?"

"I lost my head," I told her. "I forgot myself."

Her eyes filled. "You have no idea what you've done."

Aileen stood next to her, her upturned face taking in, I believe, our full measure.

"I think I do," I said.

"How can we ever come back?" John said to me. He gave Beth a quick, anguished look. "Rita, we can't ever come back."

We, he said. Even then. This is the kind of man I loved.

"You," I whispered, slipping off my ring and handing it to him. "You come back. You have to."

He held the ring, which looked tiny and trifling between his thick fingers. He studied it for a few moments, not speaking.

My eyes met Beth's, briefly.

Then John handed back the ring, returning it not to my finger but instead folding it into my palm. His hands felt large and comforting. "This was a gift, Rita," he murmured. "It's yours to keep."

"I'm releasing you," I said. "You owe me nothing."

The twins were upon us now, furious, wanting Darla and me to spend our twilight years in a Turkish jail with nothing to eat but stone soup. They looked little pleased with John, too, as I recall it, though he contradicts me mightily on this one point. Not that it matters now. They forgave him eventually, for leaving the keys, for not locking up, for loving me.

Another officer—a sergeant or something, a tall, lean fellow with heavy eyebrows—strode in from another corridor. Darla appeared behind him, tear-streaked and shaky, but at the sight of all of us clotted into the corridor, she ducked into a ladies' room to hide.

"We've just talked to the D.A.," the officer informed us. "Everybody can go home."

Susanna made a little cry, her face blotched with rage. "I thought people went to jail for kidnapping," she said, her teeth clenched. "I thought there was such a thing as justice in this world."

"No ransom, no injury, no harmful intent," the sergeant said, ticking off the facts on his fingers. Quite patiently, I thought, under the circumstances. "The most we might charge her with—and I'm talking about the driver of the vehicle, not the passenger—is criminal restraint, which is a misdemeanor, not a felony. Frankly, the D.A. doesn't see much point. The child didn't seem to think her aunts were abducting her."

"Her *aunts?*" Callie squeaked. "Is that what she said?" She looked at Aileen, whose eyes opened wide and wild. Susanna instantly tacked to another subject. "They took a child without permission. You're telling me that's not a crime?"

The sergeant took on the mournful expression of a public servant stuck in the quagmire of human nature. "In this case, yes, that's what I'm telling you," he said. "Now, why don't you people go home, figure out a way to iron out your differences."

"We'll get a restraining order," Susanna said, her face inches from mine. "You're not coming near her again."

“I know. Don’t worry,” I said.

“You or that sister of yours.”

“Please. I know that,” I said. “Don’t worry.”

Callie was shaking her head at the officer, unbelieving. “Don’t people have to pay for anything anymore?”

“People pay,” Beth said softly. She turned to her family. “We’re through here. Go on. I’ll meet you at home.” She kept Aileen clasped loosely to her side.

The family waited in a blooming silence, their eyes darting, their chins lifting and lowering. But Beth did not yield, and eventually they drifted out in threes and fours, leaving her. The officer swept us all with a look of resignation, then strode off.

“Do you have to go home now, Rita?” Aileen asked.

I nodded. “I think that would be a good idea.”

Aileen took a little stutter-step, her neatly tied sneakers making the smallest noise. “Do you have to go home, too, Uncle John?” she asked, crooking one of her fingers around one of his.

I glanced at Beth, who was studying them, her mouth soft, on the verge of words.

“He’s staying,” I said, turning to John. “You have to stay.”

“Rita—”

“I’ll go get Darla.” I gestured up the hallway. “Somebody here will drive us to the bus station.”

He lowered his eyes. “I have, I have your things in the car.”

“Later,” I said. “We can do all this later.” I took his hands, felt an instant, desperate pressure, then let go. “You stay,” I said. “I mean it.”

Aileen caught me by the neck, pulled my face down, and kissed me. “Good-bye, Rita,” she said.

"Good-bye, sweetheart," I whispered. "It's been a pleasure. You have no idea." Then I slipped my ring into her pink palm and asked her to remember me.

They stepped through the glass doors into a white spring day that seemed to gather them as one body. Then they turned, and the light shifted. A slat of sunlight flared off her bright hair. This is the last I saw of her, that brief, bright flare as she turned eastward, heading home with her granted wish.

20

For a long time, this was my only story. That summer, Darla checked back into a hospital, where a new psychiatrist did, after all, put her in a group with ex-Moonies and Hare Krishnas and what-have-yous. She found herself a new church—a normal church where you sit in pews and listen to Bible readings. By winter she had improved enough to fly down with me to visit our parents in St. Pete—where she now resides, in her own apartment, finishing up the final units in a paralegal course.

John, too, moved that winter. It took him a long while to believe he was unleashed, that he owed me nothing, that I would not hold him to his promises. For a few weeks he called me often, stumbling through his ambivalent, heartbreaking apologies. Finally, though, he succumbed to loving Beth, gentling into the new shape his life had taken. The phone calls eased off, and then faded altogether.

They were married in the spring. I wasn't invited, but John

did call one last time, just to tell me, which allowed us a formal ending. I can't say I felt sad, only wistful, and a little proud, too, almost like a fairy godmother, imagining Aileen's enchantment—the blooming rapture she so deserved—as John and Beth walked down the aisle.

It was a few days later that I drove to Cambridge, planning to make an in-person cease-and-desist complaint against Danforth Outlet Centers, Incorporated, whose letters and calls had escalated in both frequency and length. They had hidden themselves a few blocks from Harvard Square, in a modest building fronted by a small, vacant plaza. This was the great empire I'd been shielding myself from all this time. This was the monolith that coveted my house and land. I was more than a little disappointed.

The plaza was bordered by a makeshift park where a few mothers trundled their babies around, careful not to step on all the dog droppings and tattered flotsam that littered the balding grass.

I heard no voice from above. I saw no sunbeam shooting from a cloud like the hand of God. I didn't have as much as a shiver of intuition. I just turned and looked toward that pitiful swatch of earth.

And there she was.

She was a little heavier, and older, of course, and tougher looking. But still pretty, in a hard-knocks kind of way. I knew her instantly: the washboard hair, the soulful profile. I walked toward her, feeling swimmy and off balance, as if I were walking on sponges. She was sitting on a bench, a baby in her lap, his hard shoes digging into her midsection. He had a pinkish face, no hair to speak of, and big eyes of a pale, whitewashed blue. Another child, also a boy, ran around nearby, in new sneakers and a bright-red windbreaker. He was carrying a plastic sword and hollering words I couldn't make out.

I stood in front of her, staring in a kind of wonder.

She looked up with those same green eyes. "You got a problem?" she asked me.

"I knew you a long time ago," I said. "You're Tonya Kurgan."

Her eyes swept over me, giving me a chill. "It's not Kurgan anymore. I got married."

"At the time you were calling yourself Mary."

I don't know whether she recognized me. In specific, I mean. She must have seen a lot of faces like mine. "What do you want?" she said. She sounded scared.

"Nothing." I edged a little nearer. "I just saw you over here. How are you?"

"Look," she said. "I paid my debt to society. The state's still docking my pay."

"I'm not asking you for anything."

"You have no idea what my life was like back then. Kyle!" she yelled. "Get over here!" The child paid her no attention whatsoever. He just kept charging at trees.

I sat down. "I used to think about you a lot," I said. "None too charitably, as you might imagine."

Then a miracle happened. Her face went all doughy, her soft mouth trembled, her green eyes glistened. "Hey," she said. "I'm really sorry." Two shocking tears dripped down her face.

"Don't cry," I said. "It's all right. It was a long time ago."

She blotted her face on the baby's shirt.

"How are you really?" I asked. "How's your life?"

"It's a bucketful of problems," she said, "same as it's always been." She looked directly at me. "How's yours?"

"I had kind of a rough winter," I said. "But it's good."

"Did you ever get a kid?" she asked.

"Not exactly," I said. "I did meet a nice little girl. I found her a family."

She looked at me, puzzled, then looked away. "You're not the first one I've run into, believe it or not," she said quietly. "Some mistakes follow you everywhere."

"I used to think that," I told her. "But not so much anymore."

We sat quietly for a moment.

"You can't keep hold of the future and the past at the same time, is what I mean," I said. "You let go of one or the other."

"Maybe," she said. "I suppose." She smiled a little.

I got up, but I didn't leave right away.

"Well," she said finally. "Take care."

"You, too," I said. "You take care."

She offered her hand and I shook it. Then I looked across at Danforth Outlet Centers, Incorporated, and decided it was time to make my peace with them, too.

It took quite a while—well over a year, in fact—to reach a final deal. With the amount we settled on, which was sizable, I bought the oldest house in Alton, a gray Victorian near the river, with a big front porch and room in back for a shop. A few neighborhood businesses remain: a tailor shop, an eat-in pizza place that I used to frequent back in high school, a couple of corner groceries, small-timers who have been holding out all these years just like me. Riverside, we call it, an original, tree-lined section of Alton that the town council, thanks to an information campaign I organized from my shop, decided to leave unmolested.

Mrs. Rokowski enjoyed the campaign, believing it was just the life boost the cards had been suggesting for years. Rodney and his wife came aboard, too, with their kids, mostly to take their minds off Rodney's cancer, which is in remission again. By the time we got the flyers printed, most of my regulars had joined us. On the night of the mailing, we kept the kids up thrillingly past their bedtimes. Little Amy Chang licked envelopes, her mother folded the flyers, Audrey brought pizza and cake and a tape deck. Sheldon groused and burbled all night, which enthralled the children. We ate and worked. We even danced a little. Everybody brought friends. We had a wonderful time.

It is possible, I know, that I tried too hard to shape the world to my desires. I believed I hadn't a moment to spare in fulfilling them. But life is long, if we're lucky. One story runs out, another begins, and there is nothing to do but marvel at the slow, glorious sweep of time.

My Only Story

MONICA WOOD

A Reader's Guide

A Conversation with Monica Wood

Amy MacDonald has been a friend of Monica Wood's for many years. She is the author of a dozen books for children, including Little Beaver and the Echo *and the forthcoming* No More Nasty. *Her nonfiction has appeared in* The New Yorker *and other magazines.*

AM: You were born in Mexico, Maine—a small mill town like Rita's—but went to college out of state, unlike, I'd guess, a majority of your classmates. Why did you come back to Maine?

MW: My mother died during my last year in college, so I came back to be with my sisters. I guess I wasn't ready to leave the nest. I did have plans to go back to Washington, D.C.—I was enrolled in a performing arts master's program—but on the night before my scheduled departure I realized I didn't want to go. I had my car packed to the seams, but something magical overtook me and I realized I did not belong anywhere else. I moved to Portland with a friend, and I've been in Portland ever since.

AM: How does living in Maine affect your writing?

MW: My subject is family, not place, but sometimes the two are hard to separate. The setting for *My Only Story* is a paper-mill town, and although the fictional Alton is in Massachusetts instead of Maine, it draws heavily from the town I grew up in. The book I'm working on now, a collection of linked stories, is also set in a mill town, this one smack dab in the middle of Maine. The arc of my career strikes me sometimes as ass-backward, as Rita might say. Most writers begin with autobiographical material and work their way out of it. With each subsequent book I seem to be working my way back home. I've found that I need about ten or fifteen years between an event and the good writing of it.

AM: One reviewer said *My Only Story* was a paean to avuncular love. I think it's even more than that. It's about sibling love as well, a theme you come back to repeatedly and write about better than any other author I know. Why is this an important theme for you?

MW: I'm very close to my siblings, especially because we're really all we have left. Our parents are gone, all our aunts and uncles, and even some of our cousins. I find sibling relationships endlessly fascinating. Your siblings are the ones who first show you who you're going to be in the world. They're the first people you fight with. Sibling love is ferocious, too. It's a relationship you can't escape: You can't divorce your siblings. They're the ones who knew you when, and sometimes that alone is enough to cover any slights or problems. When I meet somebody new I always ask, "Do you have any sisters or brothers?" And, "Are you close?" You get so many different answers. You get a sneak peek into their core.

AM: **Was there an "uncle figure" in your life, on whom you based the character of John?**

MW: I'm so glad you asked me that! I had a wonderful uncle, my mother's baby brother, a Catholic priest, whom we called Father Bob. He adored children and probably would have had some if he'd chosen a different vocation; my sibs and I were his lucky surrogates. In my town, chumming around with a priest was as close as a body could get to being royalty. In those days, toll takers would wave us through, movies turned out to be free—all by virtue of the Roman collar. But he was more than just a grand time—our dad died when we were little, so he took on the father role. To this day I'm committed to being a good aunt, having learned from a master. What better way to honor his memory?

AM: **Rita has so much loss in this story, yet she remains optimistic. How do you justify that optimism? What does she get from this journey? And do you share this optimism?**

MW: Rita gets what anybody gets, who gives. Optimism is a funny thing; it's something you're either born with or you're not. I was definitely born an optimist, and any losses I have suffered only strengthen my commitment to being happy. Pessimists, bless 'em all, take the opposite view: Loss, which is inevitable even in the luckiest life, serves only to prove their contention that life is a vale of tears. In other words, life's unhappy burdens harden the original mold, one way or the other.

I have been amply blessed—with a delightful husband, first-class siblings, a raft of nieces and nephews, and many lifelong friends. But I have also, like everyone, experienced loss. So I always end up chronicling my characters' relentless attempts to fill holes in their lives. The common human need to create, re-create, or supplement family infuses my work as it does my life. Like Rita's, my optimism springs from grief—strange as this sounds. I believe this is true of many people, and I hope they recognize their own resilience in Rita. As long as we remain living, we have a chance to rectify our losses. Most of Rita's words are hers, but when she says at the end of the book in a burst of hope, "Life is long, if we're lucky," those words are mine.

AM: People assume: Your second novel, it must have been easier than the first. Is that true?

MW: I think it was Annie Dillard who said that the only thing you learn from writing a novel is how to write *that* novel. That's so true! The one I'm working on is a big smudgy mess right now.

AM: That doesn't dismay you?

MW: Maybe that's the thing you learn, the only thing you learn, about writing novels—don't panic. Something will come out of it eventually. It might take years, so you just have to steel yourself.

AM: What was harder about this novel?

MW: I spent four years, at least, writing it from Beth's point of view, in the third person. Beth is such a good person, but she's so predictably good and conventional that she was just plain boring. I hate to say it about her but she was. She was too dull to carry the book. It took me four years to figure this out, unfortunately. Rita has many of the same qualities, but she is a looser cannon and more fun to be with. The only downside is that after I decided to let Rita take a shot at writing it, she took only ten months. I had fun for only ten months after four years of misery.

AM: When and how did you realize it was Rita's story?

MW: I think the moment was when Beth first opens the door to John and Rita, and Rita kind of clacks into the kitchen in her high heels—she's much ruder in the Beth version—she clacks in, puts her coat down, and makes herself at home. The door is open, it's freezing, and there's this literal breath of air coming into the novel. Rita didn't have many scenes in that first version, but every time she did, the writing felt electric to me. I sent the draft to my agent, who said she couldn't find the heart of the story. I put the thing away and cried for about a week. A month later I began hearing Rita's voice. I thought, All right, I'll let you take a crack at it. Once she started talking I couldn't shut her up. I missed her terribly when I was done. I felt as if my best friend had just moved away.

AM: **How did changing the point of view change the story?**

MW: I threw away the whole book and started all over again from scratch.

AM: **Were you tempted to give up on this novel?**

MW: Only for a month. I'm like a dog with a rag in its teeth. I will not quit. I have stories that I've sent out twenty-five times, and I'm thinking, "One more revision and then it will be all right." I never give up on any material.

AM: **But when you revise, you rewrite it utterly, don't you? No looking at old drafts, no tinkering.**

MW: I'm a ruthless reviser. Also there's no paper trail when I revise. No drafts. Nothing. It's just: Poof! Gone! I have a small writing space and I can't stand clutter so I throw everything away. I'm the only writer I know who didn't inherit a packrat gene.

AM: **I find that terrifying.**

MW: All my writer friends say that. It's funny. But don't you think it's a tremendous act of faith? It's like saying,

"There's more where that came from, baby!" There've been a couple of times when I thought, Damn, I wish I still had this scene or that line, it was so brilliant. But if those words suddenly reappeared I'd probably say, "Hunh. Never mind." So much for brilliance.

AM: Who was most responsible for forming you as a writer?

MW: My sister Anne, who was also my high school English teacher. When I was really little I would write her letters at college, and when she came home I would read my little stories to her. She scooched right down to listen, looking me right in the eyes. I remember the first time that it dawned on me that writing was a giving and a receiving: She was kind of nodding and listening, and this thing turned in me. I realized what writing actually was: It wasn't just writing some words and making up a story on paper, it was a communication process. I remember that so clearly. I was about five and a half, or six.

As a teacher, my sister was very old school, a real grammarian. Sentences had to make sense. They had to say exactly what you wanted them to say. She was a perfect teacher in that she would not suffer an inelegant sentence, but she also would never pass up an opportunity to give praise.

AM: What part of writing do you think can be taught, and what can't?

MW: Technique can certainly be taught, which is why I like to teach beginners. I feel like the all-powerful one: Two hours with me and their writing improves tenfold—only because they can now identify things like point of view and story structure, very easy, teachable things.

What can't be taught is how to be an empathetic human being. Empathy is a writer's best tool. Not necessarily observation, although that's useful. By empathy I mean the ability to imagine yourself as anyone—your first-grade teacher, a serial killer, a baby. You don't say, "How would I feel in this situation, what would I do?" No. You say, "What is it like to be *that* person in *that* situation?" There is a fine difference.

Now ask me if I have a cat.

AM: Monica, would you have any cats in your life?

MW: You know, Amy, it's funny you ask me that, because the writer Rita Mae Brown wisely insists that a person cannot become a writer without a cat.

AM: Then it's so lucky that you have one, and I have one, too. Why do you need a cat to be a writer?

MW: Because they will listen to your work without judging. Also, writing is lonely sometimes, so you need another being in your room. You wouldn't want a *human* being in your room, that would be wrong and bad for your work. But having another being in the room, especially with all that fur, it just kind of warms up the place, emotionally and physically. And cats double as lap robes during these long Maine winters.

AM: Your writing doesn't flinch from describing human failings and the crappy side of life, but it focuses on redemption, forgiveness, and second chances. Unlike much contemporary literature, it is neither edgy nor ironic. How does your fiction fit into the current literary scene?

MW: Fiction has tended to become more full-hearted in the last few years, especially in the short story: more filling and less "edge." Part of this trend is a backlash against the minimalist stories and novels of the eighties and early nineties, that kind of hip, edgier-than-thou urban stuff. I like reading edgy things about creepy people, but I prefer to read about people who have the capacity for forgiveness and redemption in their lives. I find them more interesting. They stay with me longer.

AM: You write about characters often overlooked by literature: ordinary people, not very glamorous, not very evil, not apt to take the world by storm, but who all bring a quiet dignity to the struggles of everyday life. Why?

MW: The short answer is, those are the people I like the best in my real life, so that's who ends up in my fiction. I think it is a lot harder to write about people like Rita, who are truly decent, than about extremely evil or deeply flawed people. Rita has her flaws, but at heart she's a good person, and I enjoyed the challenge of making her compelling.

Warning from the author: From this point on, we may discuss plot points, so if you are like me and like to read the author interview before delving into the book, please be aware that we might give away the story a little bit in the rest of our conversation.

AM: In *My Only Story*, you manage to portray very tender scenes between Rita and John without ever misleading the reader into thinking they are truly "in love." How did you do that?

MW: Well, they are both tender people. Tender and needy. It was that aspect of them that I concentrated on—and I love tender people, they're so clueless, such walking targets. So it was easy. There's no trick to it.

AM: John's not a typically heroic guy. Were you worried some readers might find him to be too passive, too "soft"?

MW: No! John has been so bludgeoned by life that I hoped readers would feel sympathy for him and see that he probably never was going to come out of this without somebody like Rita. I like John a lot. I completely forgive him for the choices he makes at the end. I think he's a decent person—they are all decent people—to whom something awful happened, and like the rest of them John is making his way the best he can.

AM: **You seem to have left a small door open for Layton. Does he have a future with Rita, or only a past?**

MW: I did kind of leave a little door, just a crack, didn't I? I guess Rita never really got over him. It's a chemical thing. Layton is at one end of the continuum and John is at the other: Layton is a cad with bucketloads of sex appeal, and John has all those nice husbandly qualities but no pizzazz. The next guy—and there will be one—will fall somewhere in the middle. He'll be *the* one.

AM: **I'm sure your readers will be very happy to hear that.**

MW: I have this fantasy about Rodney, the oil burner man: Something is going to happen to his wife, it will be really sad, and Rita's going to help him through. She'll end up with him and his kids.

AM: **You read Tarot cards for yourself and friends, as Rita does in *My Only Story*. Do you ever use the cards to help you with your writing?**

MW: I read Tarot cards for my fictional characters. I read Rita's cards many times, whenever I got stuck. There's nothing magical about the cards. They won't show you something you don't already know subconsciously, but occasionally they can save you some time. For example, I did Rita's cards at one point, and the Knight of Swords kept showing up, galloping on a horse at full speed and waving his sword. (Swords represent challenges or problems in life.) At the same time the card of childhood kept showing up. I finally put two and two together and thought, Darla has to come back into this story but in a really swooping way. And she did. I'd have come to that decision eventually, but it might have taken six months and a few dead ends, because I never intended to have Darla be a big part of the book. The cards have a way of jogging little spaces in the unconscious that have been asleep too long.

AM: Any other similarities to Rita?

MW: Haircuts. I can cut hair. I cut my own hair for years. I used to do it in high school, for my friends, and all through college. You didn't know that? I could cut your hair right now.

AM: That's okay, really. Thanks. Well, here's another similarity: Rita is obviously well read in the classics, such as *The Canterbury Tales* and *Little Beaver and the Echo*. I've forgotten now, who wrote that children's book?

MW: That sweet little story about a beaver actually was written by a marvelous children's author named Amy MacDonald who, when she's not writing, can be found drinking coffee with me at Pat's Meat Market on Stevens Avenue.

AM: I have to tell you, I fell out of my chair laughing when I read the reference to *Little Beaver and the Echo* in *My Only Story*, and I want to know, what can I do to repay you? I mean, aside from trying hard to make you look good in this interview?

MW: In your next book you can have a line that says "Fluffy the Bunny was nibbling on lettuce in Farmer John's garden when he heard a funny sound. Looking up, he saw acclaimed novelist Monica Wood typing away on her next bestseller."

AM: Consider it done: *Little Fluffy and the Collected Stories of Monica Wood*, coming to a bookstore near you.

Reading Group Questions and Topics for Discussion

1. "I'm not a hairdresser, John Reed. I'm a healer," Rita says in the first chapter. *Is* she a healer? Whom does she heal, and how?

2. Rita also says, "People don't turn into anybody but themselves, I've found." What does she mean, and is she right?

3. Does the book's epigraph, "We don't see things the way they are, we see them as we are," apply only to Rita, or to other characters as well? Do you think this epigraph applies to people in general?

4. Are the Balzanos really "doing the best they can," as John says? Is their hostility justified?

5. What did Rita see in Layton? Is John that much better a match for her?

6. The novel tackles the difficult choice between obligation and desire. How do the various characters—Rita, John, Beth—struggle with these opposing elements?

7. Rita describes her hometown as "being transmogrified from an expiring mill town into the outlet-store shopping capital of eastern Massachusetts." What is the significance of Rita's

quest to save "old Alton"? Why has the author set her story against the backdrop of this vanishing town?

8. In what ways does Mrs. Rokowski mitigate Rita's ongoing yearning for her grandmother?

9. Rita describes one of the cult members as looking "swamp-fed, a tad unformed, the type of person who might like to study slime." Where else does her penchant for speaking in images reveal her feelings?

10. Why is Rita so drawn to Beth? How are they alike despite their outward differences?

11. When Rita hears a "peaceful tolling" in the background at the House of Peace, she says she can "almost understand why [her] sister went there." Is Darla's spiritual search completely misguided?

12. What does Rita's willingness to take care of Darla reveal about their relationship?

13. Rita tells us her "only story." Do the other characters also have an "only story"? The Balzanos? Beth? John? Darla?

14. Do you agree with Rita's decision to sacrifice her own happiness for Aileen's?

15. Does Tonya Kurgan evoke your sympathy at the end of the book?

16. "I never intended to become this kind of person," Beth tells Rita after she reveals her secret. Would Beth be different if her life had not been touched by such loss? What kind of person has Rita become as a result of her own losses? Would she be different if she and Layton had lived happily ever after?